SAVAGE SEASONS

Winner of the French Voices Award
www.frenchbooknews.com

SAVAGE SEASONS

Kettly Mars

Translated by Jeanine Herman

Afterword by Madison Smartt Bell

UNIVERSITY OF NEBRASKA PRESS | LINCOLN AND LONDON

Saisons sauvages © Éditions
Mercure de France, 2010
English translation © 2015
by Jeanine Herman
Afterword to the English translation
© 2015 by Madison Smartt Bell
All rights reserved
Manufactured in the
United States of America

Cet ouvrage a bénéficié du
soutien des Programmes d'aide
à la publication de l'Institut
Français. This work, published
as part of a program of aid for
publication, received support
from the Institut Français.

This work, published as part of
a program providing publication
assistance, received financial
support from the French Ministry
of Foreign Affairs, the Cultural
Services of the French Embassy in
the United States, and FACE (French
American Cultural Exchange).

French Voices logo designed
by Serge Bloch.

Publication of this book was assisted
by a grant from the National
Endowment for the Arts. "A Great
Nation Deserves Great Art."

Library of Congress
Cataloging-in-Publication Data
Mars, Kettly.
[Saisons sauvages. English]
Savage seasons / Kettly Mars;
Translated by Jeanine Herman;
Afterword by Madison Smartt Bell.
pages   cm. — (Winner of
the French Voices Award)
ISBN 978-0-8032-7148-7
(paperback: alk. paper)
1. Herman, Jeanine,
translator. I. Title.
PQ3949.2.M33S3513 2015
843'.914—dc23
2014047484

Set in Fournier by M. Scheer.
Designed by N. Putens.

To Roland, traveler of eternity

SAVAGE SEASONS

How much longer do I have to wait? I've been here for almost two hours. I can't just get up and leave, since I've relinquished my own free will. The moment I set foot in this building, my time, my mood, my life have depended on the whims of the Secretary of State. There's no way I can give in to my growing need to get the hell out of this waiting room in the palace of the ministry when, after false starts and false hopes, I've finally obtained the favor of being received by His Excellency.

I'm anxious to get home. Shortly before leaving the house I came across a journal Daniel was keeping. It was nestled in the secret compartment of a hatbox placed at the top of a closet in his office. Perched on a chair, I was foraging through the closet shelves looking for a lost key, when the box fell to my feet, revealing its mystery. I held the journal in my hand for a moment, not understanding. It scared me a little, like an intruder in my heart. Instinctively I turned around to see if anyone was watching and hastily leafed through the pages covered in Daniel's crowded handwriting. He had only filled about twenty of them. His first notes were dated last October. Nine months, and I knew nothing about it.

It's hot in spite of the ceiling fan stirring the air. Almost all the ministry employees have left. The Secretary of State's secretary is leaving in turn. She gives me an indecipherable look as she covers her typewriter and tells me not to worry, I'll see the Secretary of State. Daniel has been in prison for exactly two months and one day. Two colleagues from the paper — Wenceslas Lamy and Hubert André, also members of the Union des communistes haïtiens[1] — were taken in the same day he was. The party's secretary-general, Michel-Ange Lefèvre, went into hiding. There will be no trial, no verdict or sentencing. After a period of torture and rotting in his jail cell Daniel will either be freed or executed. In case of the latter, I will know neither the day of his death nor the communal ditch into which his body will be thrown. Justice has no time for communists tangled up in their theories and pacifist struggles. They're annoying insects that the dictatorship must crush. The others, the *kamoken*, dissenters in favor of a putsch, are tracked down relentlessly, dismembered by the crowd or executed in the public square. He who lives by the sword . . . Sometimes their swollen cadavers remain prey for days, for flies and curious onlookers, fascinated and terrified. But at least they can be mourned. The hardest part is the uncertainty of death, the waiting, like a wound that won't heal and destroys life bit by bit. Certain relatives and friends think Daniel is wrong to provoke the government with his articles denouncing its violations of the constitution and its absolute disdain for citizens' rights. They also reproach him for propagating dangerous communist ideas. They may be right. But today I don't have time to think. I have to knock on every door, ring every bell, swallow my pride and fear and solicit his release. Beg that they free him, that they send him back to his two children. Incredibly, this miracle is sometimes possible. I will wait. Two hours, four hours, if necessary.

I haven't heard from Daniel. They tell me he's still alive. "They" is anyone with a bit of information, a sprig of hope. "They" is an acquaintance with a cousin in prison at

1. Haitian Communists Union (UCH)

2

Fort-Dimanche who was able to slip a note to the outside giving the names of a few survivors; that was a week ago already. "They" is the gardener at the prison, my cleaning woman's husband's cousin, who found out Daniel was being held in the right wing of the building in a cell where six men take turns sleeping on the only bed in the room. Each piece of information is paid for in cash or insomnia.

The Secretary of State shows me into his office himself. The chilliness of the room seizes me at the door. It must be ten degrees colder than in the waiting room. How can a person live in this glacial environment? The furniture is heavy and solemn. Wood everywhere, massive and somber. A careful order reigns. A neon lamp casts a glaring circle of light on a corner of the desk. The Secretary of State's palm is icy and dry, his handshake soulless. He is wearing a dark-blue suit, a white shirt, and a red tie. A banal outfit. A bit taller than average, his dark skin hides his age. Midforties, I'd say. Bulging eyes behind thick glasses, full lips, a strong nose whose nostrils look at you like another pair of vacant eyes. His woolly hair is graying at the temples. A face with no beauty that gives up no secrets. A slight paunch is visible under his jacket. I suddenly feel a pressing need to urinate, surely because of the cold. The secretary locked the door of the restroom in the waiting room as she left; I've been holding it for quite some time now.

"Have a seat, Mrs. Leroy."

"Thank you, Your Excellency."

A moment passes. I wait for the Secretary of State to speak to me. He doesn't seem to be in a hurry. He looks at me furtively and makes a strange face, as if he's seen a ghost, but he quickly regains his composure. I think I see the outline of a smile on his lips. Sitting down, the pressure against my bladder gets worse. I rearrange myself so that the weight of my body rests mainly on my thighs.

"I . . . was summoned by the president of the republic for an urgent matter . . ."

He speaks in the tone of someone talking about the weather. I suppose this information serves as an excuse for the four hours I've spent in the waiting room. But I'm no fool. This deliberate and calculated wait clearly defines the scenario. He has me at his mercy. His power can save or destroy me. I'm in the worst situation a citizen of this country can find herself in: up against the legitimate anger of the provoked absolute authority, at cross-purposes with the "revolution underway," in the camp of traitors to the cause. There is a door just behind the Secretary of State's chair. This is surely how he enters and exits the palace of the ministry without being seen by the droves waiting around all day outside his office. The door to my left must be the door to a restroom. The Secretary of State pulls a folder and a pen from one of the drawers of his desk. He observes me attentively without seeming to look at me. I play the same game.

"Hmmm . . . I've agreed to see you here, madam, due to the intercession of my friend, Dr. Xavier." The Secretary of State pauses for a moment. "An excellent internist, Dr. Xavier," he says, as if confiding in me. "He's a man I owe a great deal, a great deal . . . He saved my life. Ordinarily I don't see people for this sort of . . . grievance. But, as an exception . . . The first and last name of your . . . husband?"

His tone has changed. The hint of kindness in his voice startles me. My heart wants to force its way out of my chest.

"Daniel Leroy," I say in one breath.

"Age?"

"Thirty-nine."

"Profession?"

"Professor of philosophy, law . . . and history."

"And what else?" the Secretary of State asks, raising an eyebrow. His voice turns hard. For the first time since I've been in the room, he looks me in the eye.

I'm suspicious of the way the Secretary of State disconcertingly changes the topic of conversation and his tone like a runner, zigzagging. This is surely an interrogation technique that has become second nature. In fact, he knows everything about Daniel: his age, his relatives, his financial situation, his positions at the university, his newspaper articles criticizing the government, the color of his skin, the date of our wedding anniversary, the names of our children, everything. His job is to know everything about all the Daniels throwing wrenches into the mechanisms of power and to reduce them to silence.

"Journalist," I add in a feeble voice.

"Editor in chief of the journal of opposition, *Le Témoin*, and number two in the UCH," the Secretary of State adds, as if it were nothing.

There's a stabbing pain in my lower abdomen. My bladder can't take it anymore. But I don't dare ask the Secretary of State if I can use his private restroom. I don't dare remind him I have a body, a urinary tract, a vulva. Maybe he would hear the swishing stream of urine. I don't want him to imagine me in the next room, vulnerable and denuded. This function of my femininity would seem like a weakness at that instant, a threat to my own body. I should not have come to this meeting alone. My forehead is getting damp in spite of the air-conditioning. Dr. Xavier recommended I come by myself and keep my activities as secret as possible. Everything having to do with political prisoners must be handled with the utmost discretion.

"How long has it been since your husband . . . disappeared?"

"Two months and a day."

But I want to add what the Secretary of State already knows: that Daniel had not disappeared, that he had been taken away by three men as he was coming home one evening, that they'd piled into our car, which still hadn't been recovered. There were witnesses at the scene, but no investigation would be opened and no one would testify. The Secretary of State puts down his pen, leans back in his chair, and lets out a sigh. I've lost track of time. It must be dark out. The children are waiting for me. Since Daniel's arrest, they've undergone an apprenticeship of anxiety; they're growing up before their time. Only Dr. Xavier knows where I am at this hour. My pelvic muscles hurt because I'm contracting them so much, trying to keep in the liquid that is seeking a way out of my body.

"Do you know where your husband is now, madam?"

The Secretary of State's voice has become deep and gentle again.

"No . . . Your Excellency."

"You're lying, madam!" The Secretary of State smiles, and his nose flattens until it touches his upper lip. He shows me his long, even teeth, which are extremely white. A wolfish grin that lends a bit of beauty to this graceless face.

My heart is beating wildly. I feel like a child caught red-handed. What to do? I have to tell him the truth, since I have no other recourse.

"It's . . . it's just that I can't trust the rumors, Your Excellency."

"And what are the rumors, madam?"

"That Daniel . . . that my husband is in Fort-Dimanche."

"Fort-Dimanche . . . of course," the Secretary of State says, sighing. He makes a note. "You see, madam, rumors in our country are a double-edged sword, a merciless weapon. They free you and condemn you. They cost you money. They can bring you happiness, but never for long. They make you vulnerable. What is your address?" His tone is neutral again.

"Sixteen, Rue des Cigales . . ."

"Did you come in your car?"

"No . . . I came by taxi . . . We still don't know where my husband's car is . . ."

"All right, I see!" The Secretary of State cuts me off, annoyed.

He discreetly presses a button under the table in front of him, and a bell rings in the depths of the ministry. A few seconds later the door behind his chair opens, and a tall, thin kid with a ruddy complexion and strange dark circles under his eyes appears. He is in shirtsleeves and carries a gun in a leather holster attached to his right side. He approaches, looks at me guardedly, and stands silently beside of the Secretary of State.

"Jocelyn, take Mrs. Leroy home. Sixteen, Rue des Cigales."

"Yes, Your Excellency."

"Madam, don't trust rumors," the Secretary of State says by way of a good-bye.

"Thank you, Your Excellency."

I hesitate to get up. I suppose the audience is over; it lasted about ten minutes after a four-hour wait. The moment is awkward. The Secretary of State remains seated; he suddenly seems very tired. Jocelyn heads toward the exit, and I follow him, trying to walk as naturally as possible. The Secretary of State's eyes burn the nape of my neck, my scapulae, my buttocks, my calves. Outside a few passersby line Rue Saint-Honoré. Further ahead, on Rue de l'Enterrement, food merchants have already set up their stalls, illuminated by small kerosene lamps. The western façade of the National Palace, about fifty yards long, is brightly lit, and soldiers move from one post to another. Behind me the somber mass of Dessalines

Barracks stands out like a sphinx against a background of shadow. This building is full of prisoners; within these thick walls, men and woman suffer and die. I climb into a long, black car parked in front of the ministry after Jocelyn opens the back door for me. A figure emerges from out of nowhere and slides into the front seat, next to the driver. The trip from the palace of the ministry to my house lasts about twenty minutes. I'm tormented each time the car goes over a pothole. More than anything else, I'm afraid of losing control on the seat. Traffic is pretty sparse on Avenue John Brown. We finally arrive. Jocelyn gets out to open the door for me; the other passenger doesn't budge. I force a smile of thanks. The car takes off, raising a thick cloud of dust. I realize at that moment that the Secretary of State has promised me nothing, that he has not set up an appointment with me, that I still know nothing about Daniel's fate. As for his attitude toward me, I find it unsettling. My presence seemed to leave him indifferent, and yet at times I caught a wild glint in his eyes. It feels as though something is blocking my throat; I can't swallow. The pain in my lower abdomen extends to my legs, paralyzing me; I hinge forward slightly. Shall I squat and urinate on the dirt path of the sidewalk, the way traveling vegetable sellers do? No one is in sight. The house is silent. There's a blackout at the moment. Behind the living room curtains, the halo of a kerosene lamp flickers. All is calm; the warm evening breeze brings the heady scent of ylang-ylang. A storm is rumbling in the distance; perhaps it will rain. I close my eyes and breathe in deeply. It's just another evening in Port-au-Prince. Branches vibrate with stridulating crickets, like every evening in Port-au-Prince. Summer is letting out its warm vegetal breath. Daniel will come home in a moment, smelling of chalk and cigarettes. I can see Marie and Nicolas, their heads bent over their notebooks; Nicolas is pretending to work, but his attention is focused entirely on the cat at his feet. The end of the school year is approaching. I force myself to take a step forward and open the gate and, lacking the strength, feel the warm urine slide down my legs and fill my shoes.

More than an hour after her departure he still felt Nirvah Leroy's presence within the four walls of his office. The electricity she sparked finally faded, leaving him mentally exhausted. He couldn't focus on the documents lined up before him. He thought he had become immune to the battles of the flesh, master of his drives and indifferent to the young bodies offered to him on a daily basis, the price for his mercy or protection. He knew women of every shade and skin tone, who gave themselves to him freely simply to touch his power. He often visited the brothels on the south side of town, where the hostesses were light-skinned beauties with thick hair from the Dominican Republic, on the other side of the island. It was a crossroads, the site of every pleasure, an oasis south of the capital that was slowly losing its bucolic charm and becoming a haven for night owls, merchants, and hotel keepers; it was also a refuge for thousands of citizens from the backcountry, dropped off by trucks on the Champs-de-Mars to demonstrate their support for national sovereignty, unable to pay for the trip back. But this woman did not resemble any other. He was convinced of that just by looking at her. She was a woman any man would give anything for. Her scent of ripe mango still floated in the air. It made him salivate. She exuded strength and fragility, refinement and eroticism, serenity and vertigo. Behind her innocent eyes she hid a secret world of class, caste, whispers, discreet laughter. An elite, inaccessible world. A corrupt, hypocritical world. She held the key to journeys into forbidden territory under her skin. During the few minutes he'd spent in her presence the Secretary of State had reached the extremes of irritation and exaltation. She came to him because she was in despair, perhaps for the first time in her life. Because she finally understood that the tides had turned and supremacy had changed colors and teams. She came to plead with him shamelessly, forgetting that under other circumstances he would have been the object of her scorn, or worse, her indifference. She had waited for him for more than four hours, perhaps losing any hope of seeing him. Beneath her composed façade he sensed her flesh trembling, her soul gasping. She hid her fear poorly; she'd been suffering for weeks, not sleeping nights. Money must have been running out, since her husband's bank account at the Royal Bank of Canada had been frozen, his assets seized with the exception of his home. Daniel Leroy . . . the communist apprentice thought he could outsmart the ministry's intelligence services. He was double-crossing them, claiming to belong to the UCH, while devising vicious plans in the shadows, sowing confusion and revolt in the heads of peasants and young people, mining the foundations of revolution. He was even planning a coup d'état. They all want to be president. Hmmm . . . When you have such a beautiful wife, Leroy, it's extremely dangerous to dabble in politics. After many futile efforts, Mrs. Leroy had come to appeal to his power. His power. A drug he could no longer forego at this point. He looked for the measure of it in the eyes of the detainees he interrogated, in the eyes of the bleeding, sweating prisoners who begged him to stop torturing them. He kept a collection of handkerchiefs stained with the blood of young virgins he deflowered as he raped. Today he was one of the most powerful and feared men in the country, and this had just been confirmed with utmost certainty by the presence of the desperate woman seated before him, placing her fate in his hands. A woman who symbolized a divided nation, a country that had gotten off to a bad start, with well-being and privilege for an insolent minority and a legacy of contempt for the majority of men and women for far too long. Today he could do anything; he controlled money, corrupted, bought consciences, persecuted, and gave sentences and acquittals in a cobbled-together country where laws changed every day. The Secretary of State could not believe he was now the architect of this visitor's fate, a visitor from a world whose doors had always been closed to him. She embodied what he hated most, what he wanted to see disappear from the earth, everything that had impeded generations of men and women like him from reaching the fullness of their humanity. She also represented what he desired most in the world, what he was ready to die for. Her velvety skin, her straight nose, her long lashes shading large, wet eyes, her red, almost violet mouth, her straight black hair pulled back in a bun, which he imagined loose around her bare shoulders, touching her breasts, her nipples the same fatal lilac of her lips. He could have slapped her, stripped her, publicly humiliated her for all the times those of her kind had ignored his existence, denied his intelligence. He could have bitten her until he drew blood for the subtle, arrogant contempt, the private clubs, the inaccessible jobs, the oligarchy. He could have caressed her all night long, bathing her in his tears, asking for forgiveness for so much hate. He could have taken her brutally, without a word, drunk off her protests, savoring the confusion in her eyes at the moment of climax. He did not stand to say good-bye because at that moment his besieged body would have shown Nirvah Leroy all that his lips did not say. Because he had the erection of a man of twenty, when blood knows no deficiency.

October 3, 1962 — I'm confiding my anxiety to the pages of this journal, an anxiety that grows watching the dark clouds that have covered the sky of my country in an ominous veil since Dr. François Duvalier came to supreme power five years ago. A country doctor, a humble practitioner, modest and self-effacing. An ethnologist and engaged ideologue familiar with the Haitian soul and mindset and all the blended social strata. A man from whom most citizens expected clear-sightedness and progressive vision — until he revealed himself to be a master of the art of deception. A deranged person possessed by acute megalomania, which his enemies have been striving to exacerbate in an attempt to overthrow his power. To bear fruit, every struggle against this burgeoning dictatorship requires time and the appropriate techniques. Frontal assaults only result in sacrificing lives uselessly and justifying a limitless cruelty. Underground work must be done first, in the provinces as well as the cities. Pockets of dissent must be created all over the land in the most clandestine way. A task I have undertaken and have been coordinating for about three years now. Very few people know this, even within my own network. Our only chance of success lies in the impermeability of our cells. Even my wife has no idea of my true plans. The propaganda and spontaneous armed struggle advocated by the opposition of the right will get them nowhere; it will only intensify the repression. If Cuba brought Fidel Castro to power three years ago and overthrew Batista's corrupt regime, it was because this revolution was

*primarily the fruit of a coming to consciousness of the island's
best and brightest followed by armed struggle that went on
for over five years. A challenge that only communism could*
*take up in the history of this century. Here, the failed attempt
of Pasquet, Perpignan, and Dominique to invade in July of
1958 gave Duvalier the chance to make the existence of the*
cagoulards, *who were terrorizing the population, official,
creating the corps of Volontaires de la sécurité nationale.*[2] *The*
macoutes.

*October 5, 1962 — By expressing the fear that is gradually
paralyzing every citizen of my country, by giving it a face, a
story in these pages, maybe I can rise above it, demystify it,
and then find the courage to continue the struggle. The Haitian
left is defending itself against Duvalier's multiple assaults.
Many communists have fallen and will continue to fall because
they thought and still think they can use the weapons of speech
and law against madness. Certain Haitian Marxists have
allowed themselves to become enchanted by Duvalier's siren
song and today are the spearheads of his power, in the cabinet
of the secretaries of state, in the university where young people
newly converted to Duvalierism crack down on their defiant
fellow students with hateful ardor. Others find balance in
ambiguity and escape. But there is a left that is still standing:
intellectuals, youths, unionists, Haitians in the backcountry
who refuse the absurdity and madness of a dictatorship that
has been mortgaging our future for decades. Today the time
has come to take up arms in our combat. We will lift ourselves
up from within. The few attempts at overthrow that have come
from elsewhere have failed pitifully. The Dominican military
has too much connection and affinity with the Haitian military*

2. National Security Volunteers (VSN)

to be seriously complicit with Haitian rebels. The CIA makes light of our young, exiled countrymen and sends them to be massacred, giving them false guarantees. The agency respects an unspoken pact with Duvalier. Communists in exchange for rebels. When will we understand that the impetus has to come from within our own ranks and not from white Americans manipulating us like pawns in the Caribbean basin, which they control for their own interests? Monroe has decided America's course for over a century. As long as we're killing each other, controlling us is easier. If Duvalier managed to get himself reelected last year for a new six-year term, even before the end of his first term, nothing will stop him in his despotic folly. No one wanted to believe it; no one knew how to prevent it. We counted on the Americans, on the good Lord, on the president's poor health to foil his plans. Pathetic! Between the theoretical, wait-and-see attitude and peaceful struggle of the left and the furious attacks of the right, we've left plenty of room for the dictatorship. Time is of the essence. His next ambition will be presidency for life. My comrades think my predictions are apocalyptic, that I'm a bird of ill omen. But I'm convinced Duvalier will follow this logic through to the end. He's crossing every hurdle in systematic fashion. He should be arrested.

Seventy-two steps. I've kept my childhood habit of counting the steps I climb. At the landing, I stop for a moment to catch my breath. I didn't come across anyone on the way. Bizarre. The stairway leads to an office. I go in. At fairly even intervals on the red and yellow tiled floor, there are small piles of soft, grayish matter that resemble fresh chicken droppings. I have to watch out not to soil my shoes. Still no one in sight. I have the strange impression, though, of people breathing nearby. After a few moments of hesitation I approach one of the desks and rise to my tiptoes to look behind it. A woman with tousled hair emerges from beneath the table and asks me what brought me to the ministry. She opens and closes her arms, like wings, in a sweeping gesture. I think I see an egg under her chair. From the office next door comes the sound of thin sheets of paper being crumpled. An egg rolls to my feet. I state the reason for my visit. I have come to attend the trial of the union leader of the guinea fowl hunters of the metropolitan area. The secretary tells me to take three lefts and continue to the door at the end of the hallway. Daniel is waiting for me there. Something intrigues me about the tousled-haired woman's demeanor, perhaps the carriage of her head, the way her neck tilts forward, or the way she abruptly changes the direction of her gaze, which makes her double chin jiggle. Why has Daniel invited me here at night? The dimly lit building looks more like a dance hall than an administrative building. As instructed, I turn left three times and walk along the hallway, but as I gradually make my way toward the door it seems to be receding. Still, I can hear the sound of countless voices at the end of the hall, a muffled commotion. Finally, I place my hand on the doorknob. A small sign affixed to the middle of the door bears an inscription in tiny writing: *Death to the Heroes*. A man cracks the door open, as though he sensed my presence.

"What are you looking for, ma'am?"

"I'm here to attend the trial of the union leader of the guinea fowl hunters of the metropolitan area."

"You've knocked on the wrong door . . . The trial room is three corridors to the right, next to the yellow amphitheater."

"But they just told me . . ."

"You're mistaken, ma'am," he says with some annoyance. "See for yourself," he adds, pushing the door wide open.

Two men and two women, naked and lying on a bed, are spreading bird droppings all over their bodies. It's everywhere, in thick layers on the floor and walls. I recognize one of the men: the Secretary of State. He's getting ready to take his secretary doggie-style when his knees slip on a pile of shit; he falls on top of the others, who burst out laughing. The Secretary of State notices my presence and cries to the gatekeeper:

"Bring her to me! Bring her to me quickly so I can cover her in droppings!"

I run away as quickly as my legs will allow. The putrid smell follows me everywhere. I remember the new instructions and take three corridors to the right. I should find the yellow amphitheater. Oh, there it is! I'm saved! I knock vehemently on the door nearby, which bears the inscription: ICI-22. The door yields to my hand. I take just one step, my foot slips — there's bird shit at the threshold of the room — and this time I land in the Secretary of State's bed with the three others. No way to hide.

"Cover her in droppings right away! That's an order!"
The Secretary of State, standing, displays a glorious erection.

In two minutes, I'm naked and covered in bird shit from head to toe. How exquisite! What bliss! Under my skin a gentle electricity makes every sense more acute. A silky tinkling delights my ears. The unguent slathered on my skin releases a musky aphrodisiac perfume, a blend of jasmine and vetiver. I feel like a cat in heat. I don't know which of the two men is sodomizing me violently, maybe both of them. Ejaculating, he shouts a single word— *TAKWÈT!!!*—and simultaneously sets off a dazzling orgasm in me. I tremble for a good five minutes. I don't want to leave, my relaxed body is sinking into a pleasant lethargy, but I make a superhuman effort to rouse myself from my torpor. Daniel is waiting for me. The others are asleep, so I take off. As I move quickly down a corridor, a woman waves me toward her. Without thinking I slip into an opening that seems to call out to me.

The swirl of voices assaults me at the threshold of the room. A shrill, irritating cacophony punctuated by the words *there she is, there she is*, an incessant refrain. I finally see Daniel. He is standing on a bench in front of a judge seated behind an elevated pulpit. He is balancing an egg on his head while reading one of Antonio Gramsci's *Prison Notebooks*. The jury members are seated to his left, the lawyers, prosecutors, and other members of the legal team to his right. Onlookers occupy seats on either side of the main aisle. The judge at the pulpit bears a striking resemblance to the receptionist. The same tilt of the head, the same furtive, darting eyes that make her voluminous double chin quiver. From time to time she spreads her arms, and the sleeves of her black gown stir the air around her. As I enter she forcefully slams her wooden gavel against her pulpit.

"Order in the court! *Takwèt, takwèt* . . . Order in the court! The trial is almost over!"

The noise subsides for a moment; all eyes turn toward me. The judge speaks again.

"Has the jury reached a decision? I remind you that we are judging Mr. Daniel . . . uh . . . Daniel . . . *takwèt* . . . *takwèt* . . . well, we are judging the dissident here present . . . *takwèt* . . . for the crime of high treason, the offense of the unauthorized hunting of the guinea fowl of the republic, and the abusive consumption of guinea fowl eggs. *Takwèt* . . . *takwèt*."

"Yes, your Honor! The jury has reached a decision."

I have the impression I know the woman. She's holding a cigarette between her teeth. I observe her more closely and am astonished to recognize Arlette, Daniel's older sister. She is strangely made up for the occasion: a thick layer of white foundation and blood-red lipstick that extends to her cheeks. Her nose is beak-like, I'd never noticed that before. A little clown's hat sits on her head like a pyramid, a crest. In the end she looks oddly like a guinea fowl.

"Well then, what say you? . . . *takwèt* . . . *takwèt*," the judge says.

"We confirm the crime of high treason for Daniel . . . uh . . . Daniel . . . um . . . well, the person known as Daniel, for conspiracy and genocide of the guinea fowl of the republic. We request that he be given capital punishment. And since he has placed countless guinea fowl eggs at the feet of this female, we ask that she also be given the death penalty!" Arlette suddenly turns and points at me. "We ask that she suffer the same fate as he . . . death by slicing open a vein with a butcher's knife!"

Transfixed with fear, I can't move. The grotesquery of the situation makes me gasp. Daniel looks at me, holds out a hand from a distance. A harrowing cry escapes from his chest.

"Nooooo!" And he throws the egg he was balancing on his head in the direction of his sister with all his might. He misses her by a little, and the egg cracks on the chest of a juror.

A great clamor rises from the crowd. "The butcher! The butcher!" Everyone calls for the executioner.

"Get the butcher . . . *takwèt* . . . *takwèt* . . . the butcher!"

The judge is on the verge of hysteria. She's not keeping it together. She pounds her gavel on her pulpit over and over. The door of the room opens noisily and instead of the butcher it's the Secretary of State bounding in, armed with an automatic rifle. He's wearing his blue jacket, white shirt, and red tie. I notice that he's naked from the waist down, his skinny legs covered in black feathers with white spots. The Secretary of State starts shooting in the room. Panic swirls through the court. Feathers float through the air, blood splatters. The occupants of the room, the judge, the jurors, the lawyers, all rise in a single winged motion and fly out the window with a deafening noise . . . *tawkèt* . . . *tawkèt* . . . the grating sound of a rusty mechanism. A few slaughtered birds lie on the floor. I look for Daniel. He has disappeared, carried away by the guinea fowl. The Secretary of State approaches me, his gaze triumphant. With the automatic rifle strapped across his shoulder, he takes me in his arms and we waltz through the room; from time to time we trip on the motionless bodies and his weapon hits me in the ribs.

I dislodge Nicolas's knee from my side, where it is stuck. My God, what a terrible dream! I turn on the bedside lamp. Three-twenty in the morning. Marie's arm hangs over the mattress and down to the floor. The three of us can barely fit in the bed, but our shared warmth is the best remedy against the anxiety of our nights. As long as our skin is touching, the specters of darkness are kept at a distance. Marie and Nicolas have come to sleep in my bed every night since Daniel has been away from us. I think of Daniel's journal. I've slipped it under the mattress. It draws me like a magnet. It has Daniel's scent in its pages, his sweat, his sleeplessness, and when I flip through it there is a pulsing in my sex like a beating heart.

"I've knocked on every door, Roger. Since Daniel's been in prison not a day has gone by that I haven't tried some path, set up a meeting. The university rector . . ."

"Bah! That guy! He won't lift a finger . . . The revolution has eaten his balls. The senior state officials are all scared shitless. Everyone's clinging to their jobs, trying not to make waves. Deep down I can't blame them, given the brutal, senseless prosecution at the least sign of protest over the government's actions. In fact, since Duvalier came to power, the notion of the government is replacing the notion of the state. So Duvalier, as head of the government, is also the state."

"I saw the bishop of Port-au-Prince . . . I'm counting on him to . . ."

Roger interrupts me, sighing. "You don't get it, Nirvah. That bishop has no more power than a newborn baby. The church is in the same trouble as all the other sectors of the country. Duvalier is declaring himself vested with full powers by tutelary forces . . . by the devil . . . That madman said he would shake the country to its foundations. I for one am taking him seriously. There are plenty of *macoutes* in priests' clothing. The dictatorship has been controlling the church under the pretext of indigenizing it. The sacrosanct Christian no longer inspires any respect or fear. Members of the clergy who resist are imprisoned or defrocked. Some have to pretend to compromise with power to bring aid to the persecuted." Roger sighs once again. "Who else have you seen?" he asks me.

"The president of the Senate, Mr. Boniface, the former judge at the Court of Appeals, you remember, father's friend . . .

But nothing . . . nothing. I haven't gotten any further. I'm coming up against walls, silence. It's as if everyone were fleeing me, as if I were suffering from some repellent, contagious disease . . . And yesterday I saw the Secretary of State . . ."

I think of my visit of the day before. I'd like it to be a distant event, detached from my present and relegated to the sphere of bad memories, like last night's horrible dream. Yet I sense this meeting will have consequences; the Secretary of State has entered my life, though he shouldn't have. By speaking to this man, I've elicited reactions whose impact on my future and the future of my loved ones I have absolutely no way of predicting. I have to stay optimistic and pray that God has mercy on me.

"Yes . . ." Roger seems extremely preoccupied. "I understand. But the Secretary of State . . . That pig. I wouldn't take a glass of water from him if I were dying of thirst! Do you know he sometimes does the torturing himself? Apparently, he had air-conditioning installed in one of the interrogation rooms so he could do his dirty work there. Do you know he ordered the massacre of dozens of innocent people after the kidnapping attempt on Jean-Claude and Ti Simone Duvalier?"

We all know what's been happening since 1957, that wretched year. Month after month we saw the tentacles of dictatorship tighten around people's lives, but it was always other people's lives. We only fully grasp the horror when we're snatched up in the jaws of the absurd madness of power. Until then they're rumors, whispers, a hell far away from our everyday lives, which we prefer to forget or deny. But when we are forced to touch the reality, the ground gives way beneath our feet.

"Yes . . . I heard about that. But what should I do, Roger? He's my last chance. Dr. Xavier assures me he's already freed political prisoners . . . He's all-powerful."

"Hmmm . . . but at what price? There's always a price to pay with that sort of man. Have you thought about that? I'm afraid for you, Nirvah. I shudder to think of that guy breathing the same air as you. I don't like knowing you're indebted to that person."

"I'm afraid, too. But don't worry . . . I can take care of myself. The silence around Daniel is making me crazy, Roger, fit to be tied. I can't sleep. I haven't heard anything reliable about him since his arrest, which was two months ago now."

"Hmmm . . . Yes . . . I understand. Michel's brother-in-law is an officer in the navy. He promised to intervene for me, but I don't have much hope. The military is not in the president's good graces these days. They threw my friend the colonel, Jean-Édouard Malbrun, in jail the day before yesterday. He spoke to me last month about his troubles, he was scared. Two days ago Captain Max Oriol and Colonel René Jeanty were court-martialed for high treason; they'll be shot tomorrow at dawn. François Duvalier suffers from conspiracy paranoia, which is costing the lives of the best men in the country. It's a catastrophe! How can he be stopped?"

"How is Myrna? How are the kids?" I ask him, to lighten the weight of our words.

"She's fine . . . She's worried about you, too . . . The kids are fine as well. On Saturday we're celebrating Carole's birthday. I'll expect Marie and Nicolas around three o'clock . . ."

"Oh, that's right! My goddaughter's going to be . . . thirteen already! Of course we'll be there."

"Do you have money?" Roger asks me point-blank but with some awkwardness.

Tears come to my eyes. I recognize my brother here, his sensitivity, his thoughtfulness. His business is not doing very well. I turn my head away.

"Yes . . . I still have some. But if Daniel doesn't come back soon . . . They shut down the paper before they ransacked it . . . our employees are unemployed."

"Let me know . . . don't hesitate . . . I'll help as I can . . ."

"Roger . . . I . . . accidentally found . . . a diary Daniel had been keeping for several months; he wrote in it until the day before his . . . I never know what to call Daniel's absence."

"Oh, yeah?" Roger says, his eyes wide. "Did you read it?"

"No . . . I mean . . . just a few pages. I only found it yesterday."

"What does he talk about?"

"About Duvalier . . . and the dark clouds he's brought with him." Roger looks so tense I don't dare admit that Daniel has instigated an armed coup d'état to overthrow Duvalier.

"What?! Burn it, Nirvah! Destroy it immediately!" Roger's voice, in spite of its low tone, manages to convey a sense of panic that troubles me; his fear is growing rapidly. "Don't keep anything in this house that can be held against you or your kids. Do you understand, Nirvah?"

"Yes," I reply, at once convinced and desperate.

Roger and I whisper as a reflex, an instinct for self-preservation. Certain words here have the power to roil the blood and cause alarm. And yet there is no one in the room. My children have left for school, Yva is cooking in the kitchen, and the boy in the courtyard is spraying the leaves of the trees in front of the house with a garden hose. The scent of wet earth rises like a prayer. I close my eyes and am suffused with this moment, this smell, as stubborn as childhood. When I was a little girl I dreamt of being able to stop time by pressing a button, of being able to make a peppermint lollipop or an ice cream cone last forever. Dust from the street consumes everything—the leaves of trees, the stones in walls, the wooden furniture. It infiltrates everything—our socks, our sheets, our private lives—it persecutes us, spies on us like the ears we don't see that betray us. Every day, two or three times, we have to hose down the street in front of our gate, bathe it, for a bit of respite. The neighbors do the same. Daniel waited at the Ministry of Public Works several times and even had all the residents sign a petition requesting that the authorities pave our street, one of the last in this neighborhood still waiting for a layer of asphalt. Daniel and his delusions. I knew that approach would go nowhere, but I said nothing so he wouldn't call me a defeatist. We no longer spoke of the dust because the topic always led to a fight. Daniel and his big words. In spite of all his diplomas and erudition, he never managed to understand the subterranean workings that make our country run. This street will be paved for a reason that has nothing to do with the residents' well-being or their rights as citizens. When a government official, a big shot, or their mistress moves in, we might have the good fortune of seeing work begin.

Roger has left to open his shop in town. I remain seated, palms facing outward, with the sense of having to do something for Daniel. I don't have the courage to burn the journal, but I feel reluctant to return to it—as if by reading it I were holding a dangerous weapon I could hurt myself with. I promise myself that I will destroy it as soon as I've finished reading it. No one is safe from a police raid, especially me. I will only read it at night when no one in the house is up.

In the course of a day if I'm not active for five minutes, I feel guilty. Who can I talk to about my despair? How can I get Daniel out of this mess? Across the fence to my right, there

is a great burst of laughter. A thick laugh that rolls, rumbles, swells to erupt from between two enormous breasts. A laugh that is unabashed, unapologetic. A laugh that always takes me by surprise. The laugh of my neighbor, Solange. For about six months she's been living in a little house on the large property next door. It's an old shack that belonged to a bachelor who lived there until his death last year. Yva, my cook, told me once, rolling her mysterious eyes, that Solange is a prostitute and a voodoo priestess, that Solange invites *macoutes* into her house, that Solange is dangerous. I am going to see Solange this afternoon.

Solange is one of the last people on Rue des Cigales to have seen Daniel alive. I trembled when she told me that. She lives here, next door to me, and I had no idea that for two months we've shared this emotion. All of a sudden this woman is no longer a stranger. She's welcomed me, her bourgeois neighbor, without ceremony or inhibition. As for me, once at her house, I fell to pieces. In the end instead of pouring out my heart to her, I listened to her tell me about her life for almost an hour.

"I knew you'd come to see me, Neighbor. We have things to say to each other, but I didn't dare knock on your door. I'm not that well liked in the neighborhood . . . hmmm . . . It's true I don't fit the neighbors' criteria at all . . . But today things have changed. The country belongs to everyone."

I pretend not to get the reference.

"They practically took your husband before my eyes," she tells me. "Night had just fallen. He had come home at the usual time; I was smoking a cigarette on this very stoop, like today. Three men were waiting for him for a while on the street corner, under Mrs. Pierresaint's genipap tree. I can smell *macoutes* a mile away, believe me." Solange chuckles. She raises an arm and scratches the hollow of her armpit with the red-painted nails of her free hand. It makes a grating *crap crap* sound. Solange is wearing ornate rings with fake stones on every finger. "Of course I had no way of knowing they were coming for your husband, and had I known, what could I have done?" She stops her scratching and sniffs her fingertips.

"They slipped into the car before he turned the corner to go to your house. The one with a gun ordered him to turn the car around. He glanced back at the house and left with them. That was it. What do they have against your husband?"

"He wrote . . . things against the government . . ."

"Thank God I can't read or write!" Solange let out that laugh that makes her enormous breasts wobble. "What good did it do him to know so much? You shouldn't read too many books; it's upsetting to people."

I say nothing in the face of this blissful ignorance, but I don't have the strength to leave yet. I observe the woman as I would a bird with a human head on a low branch of a tree in my garden. Solange is a *jolie laide*. The prominent arches of her thick brows frame two large, light chestnut eyes, a rather rare feature in a woman with such dark skin. Her frizzy hair, flattened with a hot iron, hangs low and pointed on her forehead — a mystical sign here in Haiti. She was born under a lucky star. She breathes in great masses of air through her flared nostrils. Her smile is ear to ear. She is big-boned, and the small of her back is practically at a right angle to her enormous ass, which speaks every language of love. A real thoroughbred, as we say here of tall, buxom women. Her upper teeth are separated in the middle by a very wide gap, which is surprising when you see her smile for the first time. Watching her speak, I could not take my eyes away from that small filet of gum descending halfway down the space between her first two incisors. She lives in her house with Krémòl, her slightly deranged younger brother, and Ginette, a little *restavek*, around ten.

"I'm from the South, from Saint-Louis. I came to Port-au-Prince with my mother when I was still a little girl — she was running away from my father's beatings. I've been living off my body since my earliest childhood. I've always refused to be a maid in some Lady's house, or to wash Mister's underwear, or to bring them coffee in bed. I'm a . . . hooker and a priestess. Did they tell you, Neighbor?"

Solange looks at me behind her cigarette smoke. She provokes me, pushes me into a corner. She wants to know if I'm worthy of her friendship.

"No," I lie, not knowing why.

She's not fooled. This woman unnerves me. She must be around thirty, but it seems like she's already lived several lives. Her gestures, expressions, and words seem older than she is.

"Yes . . . it's true," she says, letting smoke out her nose. My clients are *macoutes*, for the most part. You know why?"

This obsession with asking questions . . . she doesn't even wait for an answer. What am I doing here in the company of a woman who frequents *macoutes*? I hate *macoutes*. They took Daniel away. Solange is talking, talking. The timbre of her voice, a warm and sensual throaty voice, is strangely comforting to me. I forget my life for a moment. Solange answers her own question.

"Because Déméplè claimed me. He made me become a priestess. The *macoutes* knew I was a priestess; they came to buy amulets, magic charms. Now I've set up my own business. I don't slave away in cafés anymore. The five-gourde tricks are over. Today I give consultations for fifty gourdes or nothing. I only have sex for my own pleasure or when Déméplè demands it so that a treatment will work."

Solange's laugh fills the tall trees of the courtyard. The sun seems stronger when she laughs. I lift my head.

"Déméplè?" I can't help but ask. As far as I know, that Creole word refers to an individual with an unpredictable nature and a nasty character. It's not a proper name.

"Yes . . . Déméplè . . . my spirit, that's his name all right . . .

He comes and goes in my head as he pleases. An unpredictable spirit, shadowy . . . a Nago. He claimed me. One fine day I fell sick, sick as a dog. I couldn't work anymore or feed myself. A great weakness had settled in my bones. I started to waste away, my breasts sagged, my ass melted away. No tonic had any effect, the doctors at the hospital lost interest in me. I lost my clientele. A sick hooker is a dead hooker, Neighbor. I made pilgrimage after pilgrimage, said novena after novena, I climbed the hill to the grotto of the Miraculous Virgin of Désermites on my knees. Good neighbors took me in because I lost consciousness along the way. And then Déméplè appeared to me in a dream. He had a priest's rattle in his right hand and his penis in his left. A massive, massive penis, Neighbor. A member the likes of which I'd never seen in my entire career as a prostitute. Déméplè is hung like a donkey. He ordered me to kneel before him, to place my forehead on his massiveness and my right hand on the rattle, and to say the "Our Father" seven times. I was scared—not of his penis, that's my job—but of the rattle. I vaguely understood that he wanted me to take the rattle, to be initiated in my sleep. He suggested I serve the spirits. I refused to do it. Become a priestess, me? I knew nothing, or almost nothing, about that stuff. I had other ambitions in life. But I didn't understand yet that it was this or death."

I couldn't believe my ears. I couldn't get over the fact that I was sitting on Solange's stoop as she smoked cigarette after cigarette and told me this ridiculous story. But she had seen Daniel taken away at dusk by armed men. She kept an image of Daniel alive in her memory. I stayed to listen to her.

"Déméplè pursued me relentlessly . . . he came back regularly in my sleep, like a curse, a pest, a persecution. I became obsessed. And then, bam, he disappeared from my dreams, he stopped all his demands. I was relieved, but I was feeling worse and worse. Then one night, sensing my last hour arrive, I spoke to Déméplè. I solemnly promised that if he came back I would obey him, I would take the rattle, and the penis, I would be his servant. And he gave me back my life. I became a priestess in my sleep. And since then my business has thrived. You don't believe me, Neighbor. But it's the honest truth."

October 7, 1962 — I'm well aware this notebook may mean
my sentencing without appeal. I won't record any information
that might put my comrades in danger. If it falls into enemy
hands it will mean my plans have failed. As for me, I'm ready
to die for the causes of liberty, dignity, and progress, while still
possessing an incredible urge to live. But living as we do today
is not worth the trouble. In retrospect I understand the fire that
burned early on in my friend Jacques Stephen Alexis. A fire
conveyed, fortunately, to future generations in the pages of his
novels. He loved his country with passion and pride, a pride
that sometimes made him arrogant. He was often reproached for
his arrogance. Just before returning to Haiti for good, I met him
in Paris at a few meetings for youth in the French Communist
Party. Small in size, he found a way to fill an entire space with
his presence. When he moved, his feet didn't seem to touch the
ground. I'll never forget his ardor and sincerity, even though I
never understood how he got mired in that petty dispute with
René Dépestre in 1958. The debate raged on in the columns of
the Nouvelliste *for over a month and did a lot of damage to the*
left. In the course of that cabal around the so-called legitimacy
of Alexis or Dépestre to direct the new Haitian branch of
the Society of African Culture, bitter and persistent political
resentments came out of the shadows. Where was the capacity
for transcendence in these two leaders of conscience? Did they
realize they were only putting Duvalier in the spotlight as he
went about his plans for national destruction? But perhaps

*that's easier to say . . . Jacques's atrocious death last year
devastated me.*

October 9, 1962 — Nirvah, my beloved wife, knows nothing
*about my underground activities. She finds my militancy
absurd. I sometimes see a look of astonishment in her eyes
mixed with ironic condescension. My refusal of the status quo
upsets her. Nirvah grew up in poverty. Her father's financial
failure and suicide left the family in disarray. She knew a
sort of hidden misery; she lived on pretense, identifying with
a class she had nothing in common with aside from external
attributes. Of mixed race, she had little to recommend her
aside from her beauty. In response she pretended to dislike
the traditional bourgeois society that had rejected her. And
that's what I liked about her immediately. She didn't have
the arrogance and hardness conferred by money. I was madly
in love with her. But I soon realized that Nirvah had married
me at seventeen to protect herself from need and to find her
place in a society she wanted to be part of while at the same
time disdaining it. Nirvah is a hybrid being, bourgeois when
she wants to be, of the people when she feels like it. A mixture
that can be delightful. I don't doubt her love for me, but what I
took for revolt and empathy for the Haitian reality was in fact
just a mask covering her existential malaise. Nirvah did not
find herself in my struggle and my ambitions. Hurt at first, I
learned to love her for what she was, an extremely intelligent
woman with a practical, down-to-earth, realistic intelligence.
She is raising our children with a certain severity that she
inherited from her childhood. A carnal woman. She came to
the marriage a virgin, and in spite of the sensual pleasures
she discovered with me, I sense an unappeased curiosity in her
flesh, the intuition of more sublime amazements. I'd give so
much to reach these heights with her, which she seems to long*

*for unknowingly. Marie and Nicolas save us every day by
rebuilding a place of love for us.*

36   *Debating with my comrades, devising plans and secret
codes, setting up networks and cells, sharing our exaltation
and dreams is fine. But to whom can I confide my doubts and
insomnias? Nirvah is a survivor; she knows how to protect
herself from fear by denying the existence of what makes her
afraid. All of that takes place in her unconscious. And perhaps
it's best that way; her calm body of water, a harbor, saves me.
With her I can laugh and be the husband and father my family
needs. With other people I always have to measure my words
and opinions. Michel-Ange Lefèvre, my friend and secretary-
general of the UCH, knows nothing of my work with comrades
from the interior. I keep him in the dark to guarantee a credible
cover. Still, there's an exception to the rule: Dominique, with
whom I sometimes find a harmony of language, a community
of thought. Even if she is viscerally anticommunist and does
not wish to be implicated in my secret activities in any way, she
advises me and sometimes gets me to look at Haitian problems
from unexpected angles. I've long since stopped thinking of her
as a woman who might be desirable because Dominique is . . .
Dominique.*

*October 17, 1962 — Commemoration of the 156th
anniversary of the death of Emperor Jacques I. The founding
crime of the Haitian nation. The original parricide. A date
to erase from our annals. A day of mourning. This crime
and its context should be studied objectively in schools and
universities and not celebrated. There are so many things to
do here; everything has to be reconstructed. Minds, first of all.
Our salvation remains education, always and forever. The
government put on a great show of demagoguery in Pont-
Rouge this morning. Duvalier never misses a chance to make*

an impression. Voodoo priest Cyprien Bonaparte celebrated
a religious service on the site of the Pont-Rouge monument
during which he invoked the spirit of Dessalines in front the
entire government, diplomatic corps, and various assembled
military, clerical, and civilian personalities. Three asòtò *drums*
accompanied his invocations into the ether. Then Dessalines,
speaking in the voice of the priest in a trance, predicted a
tumultuous but enduring presidency for François Duvalier.
He reminded everyone that his assassination was fomented
in 1806 by black and mixed-race generals alike who were
unsatisfied with his agrarian policies and the distribution of
viable homes after the massacre of the French colonists. It was
a recommendation to trust no one. The emperor finally left in
a sulfurous breath while enjoining the president-doctor to be as
cunning as a guinea fowl, as cruel as a jackal, and as elusive as
a shadow.

October 25, 1962 — Since Duvalier's rise to power, the
conscious Haitian citizen, by which I mean the sensible person
able to reflect, step back, and analyze, is becoming suspicious.
Something new and bad is happening here. Retrograde, savage
forces or spirits are occupying spaces of power. In response we're
returning to a stage of primitive flight.

I read Daniel's words locked in his office, with the sense of
committing a sin, a grave indiscretion, even though these
words talk about our life, the great sorrows attached to our
small joys, and the expectation of a future we will each paint
in different colors. The Nirvah I read of in Daniel's words
does not resemble me, or very little. I married him out of
love, and I'm not insensitive to the misery of my country.
But can I be reproached for wanting to live in peace, raise my
children, and enjoy life's simple pleasures? Marie and Nicolas

are already asleep in my bed; I will not reveal the existence of this journal to them. The principle of silence can be applied

between spouses, parents and children, masters and servants, employers and employees, and at the lowest echelons of society. It's a way to protect one from the other. My mind comes back to this journal again and again, but I'm afraid of these confidences that were not meant for me.

October 29, 1962 — State violence is omnipresent, shifting and multiform. It relies on the armed militia, which knows only one principle: terror. A terror without precedent in our political culture, established with the genesis of Duvalier's presidency. Yvonne Hakime Rimpel paid for this new violence with her body — a broken woman hiding away in silence to protect her life and that of her loved ones. Everyone who sticks his head out gets decapitated. A sworn Déjoist during the 1957 elections, this woman was not afraid of words and in her newspaper, L'Escale, *went so far as to rail against Antonio Thompson for his obvious manipulations of the elections in favor of the country doctor. Mrs. Hakime Rimpel's error was to underestimate the infernal being that existed beneath Duvalier's fragile, nice-guy mask. After subjecting her to unnamable abuses the President's henchmen put a bullet through her head and left her for dead. How she survived no one knows, but they say the* macoute *leader who was supposed to finish her off took pity on her and pretended to blow her brains out, when in fact he shot over her head. Hakime Rimpel paid because she accepted neither the dictatorship nor its abuses and decried it with the means at her disposal. It's been reported that children and the elderly are being tortured. When I think of Nirvah and the children I shiver. I have to find a way to get them out of the country for a while.*

Night was falling. He was waiting for me in my house, in my living room, sitting in an armchair next to a table dominated by an empty vase and a picture of Daniel and me surrounded by the children. It was Friday, eight days after my visit to the ministry. I was both hoping and dreading that I would see him again. I would have preferred never crossing paths with him for the rest of my life, but I also knew he was the only tenuous link between Daniel and myself. I was returning from visiting Daniel's mother, my spirits at an all-time low. If he doesn't come back that old woman will die. Daniel's sisters and brother were also visiting their mother. They get along like cats and dogs, they love and hate each other with equal passion. Each of them suggested a course of action without believing in it very much. I noticed a certain resentment toward Daniel, which made me feel uncomfortable. But I understood — whether they admitted it or not, the fact that he was in prison had profoundly disrupted the routine of their lives. We had become a blacklisted family. Of course I said nothing to this distraught family about Daniel's notebook or plans. That afternoon we looked at recent events: the curfew from ten at night to four in the morning; the censorship of the press, only allowed to release government communiqués; the tracts that were circulating; the enormous tax increases. What about Daniel in all of this political muck? What was to become of the forgotten men and women in the government's death traps? Well . . . We do what we can . . . There's nothing

to be done but wait and hope. Some have come back. Like
so-and-so . . . and so-and-so . . . but what about those who
haven't come back? Who is to blame? Bad luck, misfortune?
On the way home, in Pont-Morin, I went into the church of
Saint-Louis-Roi-de-France, my head as heavy as an Artibonite
Valley watermelon. No prayer came to me, but for a moment
I expected Daniel to emerge from the church walls, the altar,
or the chapel of rest.

I suspected his presence when I saw two men standing in
front of the house. I also recognized the big, black American
car. It's crazy how hard my heart was beating, hard enough to
hurt. The car was parked on the other side of the street, Jocelyn
at the wheel with his smoky eyes. Who let him in? Probably Auguste, my courtyard boy. Why did he let a stranger
into my house? While my kids were there? My orders are
very clear: no one is to enter this house without my express
permission. Nirvah, dear . . . could Auguste honestly have
prevented the Secretary of State from making himself at home?
This *macoute* Secretary of State surrounded by an army of
shadows? I went in through the back door. In the pantry
the children were watching cartoons on TV. Betty Boop lost
in a forest, in a clingy dress and high heels, running franti-
cally, about to be devoured, the monstrous head of Louis
Armstrong with two enormous eyeballs in a corner of the
screen, singing the blues. What cruelties don't we feed our
children on television? Without turning his eyes away from
the images, Nicolas announced that a man was waiting for me
in the living room. Marie widened her eyes. "Who is that?"
I reassure them with a wave of my hand. Everything is fine.
They quickly turn back to the small screen. Today Auguste
picked a basket full of mangos from the garden. Entering the
pantry, the overpowering smell of ripe fruit intoxicated me. I

felt like I was in a dream state with the sweet, heavy scent of ripe mangos in the warm kitchen and the cold scent of death lurking in my front room.

"Good evening, Your Excellency . . . What a surprise! You should've let me know . . ." I approach, hold out my hand.

"Mrs. Leroy," he replies, standing. "Excuse me for this intrusion into your home. Your children told me you would be back soon. Charming kids . . . I wanted to wait to give you the news myself. Your husband is doing well. I spoke to him a few days ago."

The Secretary of State addresses me but his eyes never leave my neck, the hollow of my throat. He seems fascinated by this point.

"Sit down, Your Excellency. He's doing well, you say?"

I feel thrown off balance, as if a very heavy weight has suddenly been lifted off my head.

"Hmmm . . . Rather well. I gave orders so that he would no longer be . . . mistreated." The Secretary of State's voice reveals no emotion. He is now sweeping the room with his eyes.

Did I understand correctly? Is the Secretary of State talking to me about mistreatment, orders he gave so that Daniel would not be tortured? Why does this news surprise me? I know that prisoners undergo torture, that most do not survive. But to hear it with this coldness, this detachment, makes me aware of the reality, my reality. What does the Secretary of State know about Daniel's true activities? Until the discovery of the journal the other day, I've always thought that his activity was limited to his opinions in his weekly paper and to public activities within the context of his party. If the powers that be thought it acceptable to arrest him even though he has been tolerated up until now, I have to conclude he was betrayed.

"Thank you," I reply.

The Secretary of State adds nothing else. He is warm; beads of sweat form on his forehead. His eyes are even more globular than I remember. He's breathing heavily. I turn on the ceiling fan.

"Sorry . . . it's really hot in this room."

"No, it's fine . . ." But I can tell he's relieved. "Have you lived on this street for a long time?" he asks me.

"Yes . . . since our marriage. We were among the first residents."

"Your children . . . are already pretty big. You got married young." He looks at me, trying to guess my age.

"Yes, I was seventeen."

"How old are your children?"

"Marie, the older one, is turning fifteen. Nicolas is eleven."

"Hmmmm . . ."

After these brief words the Secretary of State settles into a comfortable silence, satisfied. His gaze now rests on my feet, naked in their sandals, as if my whole life were contained there. There is dust on my toes. I should have washed them before coming into the living room.

"They're so white . . ."

"Excuse me?"

"Your feet . . ."

I can barely understand the words being whispered by the Secretary of State, who is attentively observing my feet. Did he say something about the whiteness of my feet? Why my feet?

"I don't . . ."

"Never mind," he says, reluctantly detaching his gaze from the lower half of my body.

The sounds of the television come to us from the pantry. The sugary scent of ripe mangos drifts over to us. Life goes on with its everyday noises and smells. My children are waiting for their father's return, and I find myself with the Secretary of State in a bubble of silence, a floating bubble that sucks me up in its passing.

I'm dying to speak to him, though. I'd like to ask him for more information about Daniel, about his detention, his health, his food, his dreams. I'd like to ask when he'll be freed. But in the face of the Secretary of State's silence those questions seem incongruous, almost indecent. His presence under my roof should be a measure of Daniel's safety.

"Do you know if . . . when Daniel will be released from prison, Your Excellency?"

I can't hold back the words. I live for the day Daniel walks through our door again. Otherwise everything will remain suspended: the dust, our laughter, the sun, and the will to live. This challenge is beyond my strength. The Secretary of State emerges from his blissful state. He looks at me like a parent both moved and exasperated by a child's innocence. A fleeting expression. The words he says next are almost contemptuous.

"He won't be out anytime soon, ma'am, I won't lie to you. He has questions to answer . . . many questions. Your husband had schoolchildren distributing tracts . . . he was sowing the seeds of communism among the youngest . . . among the farmers . . . he pollutes their brains with Marxist ideas . . . he's sabotaging the future of the country . . . But the worst thing, the most unforgivable thing, is that he thought he could play both sides and use his party as a screen in order to conduct his criminal activities freely. Were you not aware of this, ma'am?"

I do not answer this question, which seems like a trap. I think of the notebook hidden under my mattress. My heart beats wildly. Did Daniel confess under duress? Did he denounce his comrades? I think he would rather die than betray his colleagues. I pretend I know nothing. I continue to ask questions and am stunned by my own audacity.

"Hmmm . . . But what are his chances, Your Excellency? Will he be given a trial?"

"That doesn't depend on me, ma'am. My power has its limits. I can only assure you of favorable treatment. For now. There are high authorities who resent him . . . very much. The processing and handling of his case will take time, a lot of time," he answers me, looking back at my feet.

I try to think quickly. Things are a little clearer now at least. Daniel is alive and, thanks to the Secretary of State, he will be spared corporal punishment. For the time being. I hope. A car passes in the street, and a few seconds later the dust raised by its tires comes imperceptibly through the living room windows at the front of the house. The Secretary of State sneezes twice. I smile, embarrassed.

"Oh, that dust . . . I'm always fighting it, but it always gets the better of me."

The furniture, the dried flowers in their pots, the mirrors are covered in dust. Dusting the rooms at the front of the house is like carrying water in a sieve.

"I see," says the Secretary of State somberly, pulling a handkerchief from the inside pocket of his jacket. He seems sick all of a sudden.

"Can I offer you something to drink, Excellency?" I ask him, back to playing hostess.

"No, thanks. I'm leaving. Thank you for having me . . . Do you need anything, ma'am?"

"Do I need anything?" I repeat mechanically, looking at the Secretary of State. It takes me a second to understand he is offering me something, but what? Money, no doubt.

"No . . . thank you. You're already doing so much for me and my family."

He's started to sweat again in spite of the fan. He gets up without saying another word, without a good-bye, without my knowing if he'll get in touch again.

I accompany the visitor to the gate. I still have so many things to say to him. I'd like to write Daniel a note and ask the Secretary of State to have it delivered. I'd like to obtain special permission to visit Fort-Dimanche—one of those authorizations they give out sparingly to people with relations in high places. But I don't dare. Not yet. I watch him get into his car. He gets into the front, next to his driver, while the two bodyguards settle into the backseat. He will be back.

The Secretary of State had decided to surprise her at home, Daniel Leroy's home. He would drop into her world unannounced, like a rain shower at midday under a blazing sun. She would surely be thrown off by this abrupt approach; she would no doubt expect him to call her into his office. Did she think, since coming to the ministry, that her visit had been in vain and he wouldn't get in touch with her? Did she have any idea of the tornado she had set off under his skin? For a week he chomped at the bit, calculating the best time to see her again without revealing his impatience. For a week the Secretary of State had invaded this woman's virtual world via his obsessive imagination, and that evening he would invade her daily life, the four walls that protected her. He had entered the house with a sort of profane fervor. An exalted sense of total power that stayed with him for the length of his visit. He controlled the situation perfectly. He had penetrated the private life of the dissident known as Daniel Leroy, and the fate of his wife, children, domestics, and cat all depended on his appetites. The days ahead looked gratifying on so many levels. No barrier would prevent him from attaining this woman, becoming master of her mysteries.

Her children were beautiful, as he expected. Middle-class, mixed-race kids growing up in a cocoon that had just cracked open. They'd looked at him with a certain suspicion but without much interest. The teenager bore a striking resemblance to her mother except that she was already a head taller. A wonderful, blossoming young woman. The boy with his thick eyeglasses seemed the intellectual heir of the household; he would probably be a bookworm, a devourer of books and ideas like his father. The Secretary of State thought of his wife and two daughters, who were occupied with social climbing, aware of the new and abundant privileges he was bringing them. For a while now their personal relationship had boiled down to the administration of their material comfort. He had contempt for his wife, whose outward pious modesty concealed a voracious appetite for earthly goods. For a long time now they no longer opened any worlds to him and were just mouths, always thirsty for more luxury and comfort. He loved the atmosphere in Daniel Leroy's house, the light softened by the curtains covering every window, the patina of the mosaic floor, and the floating scent of ripe mango that rose from the depths of summer.

Hostile shadows inhabiting the space had tried to push him away; he was worried briefly by a pressure against his chest. Had his old illness resurfaced at this crucial moment to humiliate him before this woman's eyes? Nothing had happened, fortunately. He was used to fighting pain, resisting its attacks. He'd jostled the specter of Daniel Leroy walking the hallways of the house, trying to get rid of him. His victory was confirmed on visible and invisible planes. But the front room where she received him was so hot! A true foretaste of hell, which he both endured and enjoyed. To possess her he would gladly step through the gates of hell. But how could they live covered in all that dust? A neat and tidy little house, exquisitely furnished, lost in a lunar landscape. Rue des Cigales had something unreal about it with all that gray, powdery matter stuck to trees, foliage, façades of homes, even transmission towers and electrical wires. What a mediocre bourgeois Daniel

Leroy made! To let his family live under these conditions, to let a woman like Nirvah endure this environment . . . If he had really wanted to he could have found a way to bribe some authority at the Ministry of Public Works to get his street paved. In the end you can always find satisfaction; it just takes good contacts and affability. Leroy was an intellectual, a fighter of intellectual duels, a scribbler of subversive articles who was unworried about his family's well-being. A man of mixed race with no ambition, basically. The worst. They think their hands are pure. True mulattos try to build on their fortune. Since he had been at this job the Secretary of State had had to engage in marginal dealings with moneyed, mixed-race bourgeois who were concerned with increasing their assets; *they* were able to recognize authority, handled concessions well, did not recoil at the prospect of compromising their principles to arrive at their goals. Whereas the so-called intellectuals who thought of themselves as incorruptible, like Daniel Leroy, seemed pathetic to him. They did not inspire his respect. They inspired his contempt.

Her feet. He had Nirvah Leroy's feet engraved in his memory — the delicacy of her heels and ankles, the light shading along her calves. The dust that sullied her toes had touched him to his depths; he could have licked them with devotion. She had square, unpolished toenails, indecently naked feet. He'd sunk into their universe and had trouble not touching them. And then there was everything about her, that beauty mark at the base of her neck, right next to the jugular that pulsed and reminded him of this creature's other private impulses, this creature he wanted to possess like a thing, an object of great luxury, an inaccessible moon. He would pay whatever price was necessary; everything would be done for her well-being. He would also put the necessary force into it. He would be a brute, a cynic, because she would only yield through force, and he could only come through force. He would lie to her shamelessly about her husband's situation, about her husband rotting in Fort-Dimanche, so that she would need him completely, desperately.

"What's happening on Rue des Cigales? What's all this mess?"

Arlette releases a thick cloud of smoke and whips her ponytail around. She's just arrived at my house, and she's already oozing venom. Arlette is a woman whose proximity is toxic and exhausting. You can tell she hasn't been sleeping. Insomnia is making her cranky and leaving circles under her eyes. A week after her brother's arrest she was laid off at the office of the Ministry of Foreign Affairs where she'd had a job for several years as deputy director of protocol. Without notice or explanation. The army major whose mistress she is has been placed on a list of military personnel soon to fall from grace. Maggy told me this in confidence, but to avoid any unpleasant exchanges I pretend not to know. Arlette has never liked me. She thinks Daniel deserves better than me.

"It's obvious the street's going to be paved," Sylvie responds, annoyed. "They're building sidewalks."

The two sisters are at the antipodes of good manners. Sylvie is a gentle, sensible woman with all the tact Arlette lacks.

"I don't know how you've managed to live on this lousy street for so many years. We'll finally stop having allergy attacks when we come to visit you."

"I'm so glad, Arlette," I reply.

"You've still got manners," Sylvie remarks.

"I say what I think, Sylvie. You know that, you're my big sister. Tell me," Arlette says, turning to me. "Who's having the road paved?"

"The Ministry of Public Works . . ."

I know my sister-in-law won't be satisfied with that explanation.

"That much I understand, my dear. I want to know what bigwig just moved to your street. Daniel spent so much time fighting to live in a better environment . . . wasting his time writing letters to Secretary of State So-and-So, getting petitions signed in the neighborhood . . . How ironic that this should be happening now that he's in prison. As if they waited for him to be thrown in jail to cover this fucking street in asphalt! So who is it, Nirvah?"

"Daniel will have a paved street upon his return," Sylvie says philosophically. But the sigh that punctuates this sentence betrays her doubt and anxiety.

"Daniel's return, hmm . . . That's another story, Sylvie." Arlette leans over to stub out her cigarette in the ashtray. The nail of her right index finger, stained with nicotine, shines like amber. "Nirvah, you still haven't told me whom they're paving the road for?"

"I don't know, Arlette. I'm not exactly sure, but there don't seem to be any new residents in the neighborhood. Maybe someone important bought the two empty lots by the intersection. But whatever prompted the construction, I'm not going to complain about it, believe me. That dust was driving me crazy."

"Even if they're doing it for a *macoute* head, one of those big black pigs in black sunglasses? It doesn't bother you having a v s n for a neighbor? You don't care, Nirvah?"

Arlette's smile is as vicious as her words. I look around to make sure Auguste isn't listening. Does she know the Secretary of State visited me? Did the news reach the Leroy family that quickly? No . . . no, probably not. I think Arlette is just being herself.

"There are *macoutes* of all skin tones, Arlette. Light skinned, honey colored, light brown, dark brown, black, very black . . . Power has no color or size."

"Well, well! You know them that well? My compliments, my dear. I unfortunately do not have the privilege of knowing many *macoutes*. I don't see how Daniel is still in prison when his wife has these connections . . ."

Arlette is mocking, and I feel like slapping her. I don't know what to think. Did she get wind of my visit to the Secretary of State or of his visit here? I'm scared, but I won't allow myself to be dismantled by my sister-in-law.

"Arlette! There are times when you should learn how to keep your big mouth shut!" Sylvie, infuriated, beats me to it. "You have no respect for Daniel's home, his wife and children . . . You only think about yourself and your own problems. You . . . you . . . you are venomous!"

"Let her say what she wants, Sylvie. If it makes her feel better. Arlette is the way she is. She's mad at the whole world, at women, *macoutes*, Daniel . . ."

I can't restrain myself from lashing out. I can breathe now. The effect is immediate.

"Okay, that's enough! I won't allow you to tell me what I think about Daniel, Nirvah. I'm his sister, do you understand? His sister! You'll never be anything but his wife; he can leave you whenever he wants, he can get a new wife whenever he likes . . . You're not his blood. After all these years I still don't see what Daniel found interesting about you . . . aside from being light skinned. You refuse to work — *Madame* is a housewife! A man who went to graduate school in France, who's rubbed elbows with great men! You're nothing but a pretty piece of ass, without a brain and without a cent. Basically, you've brought Daniel nothing but bad luck! Come on, Sylvie, I'll take you home." Arlette stands, rummages angrily through her bag for the keys to her car, and motions with them for Sylvie to follow. They leave. Sylvie doesn't have a car. She looks at me apologetically, kisses me quickly, and follows her sister.

I know who's having the road paved. I knew right away, though at first I didn't want to believe it. The enormity of the thing threw me for a moment. But I don't dare translate the significance of the act, which is not something to be done lightly, into specific ideas. Secretary of State Raoul Vincent does not do anything lightly. My health and well-being cannot interest him simply out of brotherly love. I'm starting to understand the meaning and depth of the word *power* in my country. Power in the service of urges, instincts, and lust. My impending future is gathering like black storm clouds. He has not come back to my house in over a month. Maybe he's on vacation? Generally a secretary of state does not stay away for that long. So I've had no reliable news about Daniel. Time passes, and hope like a golden thread stretches out endlessly, precious and so fragile. I asked Dr. Xavier to go see him, to speak to him without mentioning my name, just to get some news about Daniel. When I saw him again the doctor didn't have much to tell me. The Secretary of State did not receive him.

Marie and Nicolas have successfully completed the school year, though Nicolas, for the first time in his life as a student, just barely passed. What more could I ask of him in a situation like this? They're going to Paillant to spend almost three months of vacation with my mother. Their neighborhood friends come over less often. It will do them good to leave the house, to forget about waiting, not to jump every time the gate of the house opens. I have the impression they're the ones protecting me. They're less demanding, more helpful. They squabble less often, but the questions in their eyes are unbearable. I know they're also worried about the money we need to live on. Marie asked the other night if Daniel and I had savings. The energy I spend trying to make life normal for them is wearing me out.

November 1, 1962—All Saints' Day. High mass at the cathedral attended by the First Lady of the republic, Mama Simone, a woman with an inscrutable face. The sphinx of the National Palace. Apparently her family descends from Indians of the pre-Columbian era who lived in Yaguana, in the chieftainship of Xaragua, today the Léôgane region. Her light skin, flat features, and slightly almond-shaped eyes would seem to suggest that. When this nurse married a modest country doctor in the Church of Saint-Pierre de Pétionville in 1939, she surely had no idea she was linking her fate to that of a man who would take the country down a sinister path. Mama Simone can be generous with the poor. Beggars, the disabled, the homeless, all the humanity living in the mud of Croix-des-Bossales and La Saline flooded toward the church for the occasion. Even the Cité de l'Exposition, that dream space that President Estimé bestowed upon the capital for its hundred and fiftieth anniversary, loses its luster and is covered in mud after every rain. The mass was celebrated by two priests who still sympathize with the government. The church made the mistake of believing François Duvalier could not stay in power. Some priests have lashed out from their pulpits, been provocative. That was all the doctor-president needed to condemn the clergy, both Haitian and foreign. He intimidates them, persecutes them, throws them out of the country still in their cassocks. He dreams of his indigenous clergy and threatens, through an ambassador, to make voodoo the official religion of Haiti.

But the concordat ties his hands. The Vatican won't budge.
Meanwhile Catholics and voodooists have been waging a latent
war, while the Protestant movement is furtively infiltrating the
backcountry. Religious fanaticism has to be fought in Haiti like
any scourge. Between a debilitating messianism and the hoax
of populism, people are caught in a trap. Now the future is at
stake; the masses must be helped out of ignorance and poverty
or our children and grandchildren will pay the price. Nirvah,
who knows I'm a staunch atheist, would be very surprised to
know I'm actively collaborating with priest friends to aid in
the reception and cover of young activists. They're returning
one by one from Eastern Europe, from Moscow, to convey their
knowledge of guerilla warfare, subversion, and destabilization
to youths from the interior. These clergymen have astonished
me and earned my respect, proving their ability to conduct
clandestine activities with citizens who do not profess their faith.

November 5, 1962 — Dominique is my friend and
confidante. An erudite, exacting, and reactionary petit
bourgeois. There's nothing more exasperating than a woman
who knows she's smart. Dominique suffers from an irritating
lack of modesty, but the cold eye she can cast on things, her
analyses and deductions, command my respect. We often spend
hours discussing the reality of the country and the Haitian left,
the history of which she knows well. We have never made love.
There have been moments over the years that could have been
taken for a call of the flesh. But knowledge of this unexplored
potential pleasure between us has reinforced our complicity.
Dominique compensates for her haughty reserve with fierce
intelligence. Nirvah on the other hand can give herself over
to love with all that is deepest and most secret within her. But
I like Dominique very much. She warned me about Michel-
Ange Lefèvre. "He's sold out," she told me peremptorily. I

had a hard time believing it; the man has been thrown into Duvalier's jails twice. The UCH *is the ideal screen for my activity. Aside from my obvious occupations, I was able to put together micronetworks of provincial youths and instill in them the knowledge and methods of the simplified principles of communism. The future belongs to the young. It's true that Michel-Ange has been questioning me somewhat persistently of late about my extra-*UCH *activities.*

November 11, 1962 — If he's not arrested, Duvalier will establish a tyranny over Haiti as ferocious and long as Rafael Trujillo's. Both men use the same principles to terrorize: the army and the secret police. Trujillo, unlike Duvalier, maintained a strict policy of alignment with the United States, whose methods sometimes produce leaders. An American secretary of state apparently said of him: "He may be a son of a bitch, but he's our *son of a bitch." They still crushed their son of a bitch last May, after thirty years of absolute power. Getting rid of him was more in their interest than keeping him as head of the Dominican Republic. The doctor-president must have been taken aback when he heard about his colleague's assassination. More wary, he's playing a little game of* marronnage[3] *with Americans and Haitians alike. He pursues communists relentlessly and the Americans leave him alone; they pretend not to hear the cries that rise from the island. In the context of the Cold War, the Americans couldn't ask for anything more. Still, to create confusion Duvalier is planning a Marxist wing in his government, the president's left.*

November 17, 1962 — I had a long talk with Michel-Ange about the next editorial. I have to react, inform national and international public opinion. That is also a tactic of my

3. Runaway, escape

struggle, to shout loud and clear, scream even, to retain my status as innocuous opponent-journalist-intellectual. In the eyes of some, we pass for a salon Communist Party, a Communist *Party for polite society, a club of eccentrics. I am in some ways proof that there is still so-called freedom of expression in Haiti. The Kennedy administration does not always use carrots in its relations with Duvalier. From time to time it brandishes a stick, and the dictator has to curb his bloody impulses. Nevertheless this policy of apparent intolerance and actual compromise troubles me deeply. We have distributed a few tracts attempting for the nth time to awaken slumbering minds. The general apathy is heavy and demoralizing. Duvalierist propaganda is an affront to the mind. Dozens of men and women from every social class of the republic disappear every week. Last week Duvalier went to Fort-Dimanche; upon his request several prisoners were pulled from their cells, tied to posts, and shot without further ado. Some were his friends. Before their execution the president wanted to have a little conversation with them. Michel-Ange thought the tone of my article too vehement. He recommended prudence.*

December 3, 1962 — Marie's birthday. The apple of my eye. She's fourteen today. I'm so proud of her; she's so beautiful, so intelligent. Sometimes Nirvah resents my relationship with Marie. Can she fault me for loving my daughter and telling her so at every opportunity? I love Nicolas just as much; there's a sort of male bonding between us that gets more intense as he gets older. But a daughter gives her father another sort of love. She's already a little woman who has her father at her beck and call. Marie is jealous of Dominique's presence in my life, whereas Nirvah makes the best of it. Dominique . . . her name reflects her personality. Neither male nor female. A strange, loyal, supremely proud person. We grew up together and our parents

planned our engagement when we were still in the cradle. It
was logical that I marry Dominique. Everything predestined it.
Similar paths, study in France — sociology and anthropology
for her, law and economy for me. Dominique did not object to
the loves of my youth; she knew I would come back to her. I
deviated from the path laid out for me. I didn't want a middle-
class life planned out twenty years ahead of time, when mine
is a country where people deny what they once believed because
of hunger or ignorance. Dominique, disenchanted, married a
French music professor whom she divorced eight months later.
Now here we are, the pair of us, living in Haiti. She thinks of
Marie, her godchild, as the little girl she never had.

December 7, 1962 — Nirvah has gone to Paillant to be at
her sick mother's bedside. In her absence Marie and Nicolas are
more open, freer to be themselves. In the house we're like three
accomplices. We find laughter in everyday tasks and ways to
communicate beyond words. Nirvah may worry too much about
our children's good education. She doesn't take enough time to
love them, to love them without rhyme or reason.

Possessing Nirvah had become the Secretary of State's obsession. He wanted to go back to the house on Rue des Cigales to feel the same emotion that brought a tingling to his limbs. Something he could not understand had shaken him. It had nothing to do with the vague thrill of horror and pleasure that shot through him at the cries of the tortured or the somber joy he found in possessing the unknown bodies he violated on a frequent basis. A new dimension had opened for him, a harbor of purity where he found true peace. He already longed for this woman and her two beautiful children. Yet he knew the Leroy family could cost him his power, his might, and his money. The folly that was taking root in him would make him vulnerable; it would finally put the crack in his shell his enemies had been seeking. He was well acquainted with bitter rivals who had already made heads roll. Friends who had fallen from grace before him knew more serious fates. Some were on the payroll at the Grand Conseil Technique, an administrative entity where old troublemakers were warehoused who should have been glad to be getting humane, if somewhat humiliating, treatment. Others lived in exile. Some experienced the worst: imprisonment. He would not last long locked away in the jails of the dictatorship, of that the Secretary of State was sure.

Raoul Vincent was one of the few secretaries of state in the government who could ask the president of the republic to pardon a political prisoner directly. A supreme privilege. His rare interventions in this regard had earned him eternal gratitude along with enmity and resentment. Power was divided into clans that waged terrible, relentless war against each other, where anything went. Even the presidential family was not exempt, split into two camps that took refuge under the chief of state's or the First Lady's wing. The blood of reprisal had still not completely dried in the streets of Port-au-Prince after the attempt to kidnap the dictator's children, and though the revolution had triumphed again, it left gaps of flesh, bone, and blood in the ranks of its sons, a heap of the dead, the echo of torture, the chill of violence, and untold, ruminating hatreds.

The light-skinned secretary of state, Maxime Douville, had been sitting on the secretaries of state council for six months. A few weeks earlier, on the day of the aborted kidnapping, his maternal uncle, a retired army general, had been pulled from the veranda of his house in the Tête-de-l'Eau neighborhood in Pétionville and unceremoniously shot in the road, under the pretext that the plot must have come from men with military training. At least ten retired officers lost their lives this way. Douville, however, remained a steadfast member of the government, sacrificing his pain and his convictions to Duvalierism. His status as a mulatto gave him a particular advantage in the ministerial cabinet. He and a few others of his skin tone who occupied important positions in the government or parliament were living proof that the watchword of power was loyalty. Skin color and social condition didn't matter — whoever defended the interests of the revolution with the greatest determination, the most ingenious corruption, or the cruelest annihilation of the enemy was propelled into the circle of the faithful, generously spoiled by power. Loyalty required that you accept everything for the good of the cause, even the assassination of close relatives. Maxime Douville fostered a hatred as pure as a diamond for Raoul

Vincent. A vision of power was one thing, Secretary of State Raoul Vincent quite another. A haughty and vicious black man whom so many of the president's collaborators distrusted. A somber, unpredictable, superstitious, unfathomable being who still retained Papa Doc's trust. He was among the earliest supporters, the hardliners, the untouchables. Raoul Vincent had resisted several waves of firings of former Duvalier partisans. He was familiar with the antechambers of power. But his time would come: he would end up falling, committing a fatal error. Maxime Douville was convinced of this, since he was determined to find the element that would be at the origin of this fall. He belonged to the new wave of men of power, the intrepid ones who injected Duvalierism with new blood. Marriage into the First Lady of the republic's family had had given him entrée to the maze of palace intrigue, and he found himself at the head of the Ministry of Finance and Economic Affairs. He fattened the bank accounts of members of the presidential family, invested their fortunes, served as their front man. He shamelessly extorted money from shopkeepers in town and along the seaside for bogus developments, played around with taxes, accorded favors and counterfavors to please his masters. The First Lady of the republic swore by his vision. His position grew stronger every day, since the revolution needed to be protected against the uncertainties of the future. The clique in power had not forgotten about Papa Doc's fragility. A heart attack less than two years after taking power had almost taken his life.

Raoul Vincent knew he couldn't get Daniel Leroy out of prison. More than the *kamoken*, who were caught up in their thirst for conquest and power and were captured without much difficulty, Leroy was a true enemy of the Duvalierist revolution. An eminently intelligent, well-educated, charismatic man who could work in the shadows and take his time. If communism had a chance of triumphing in Haiti as it had in Cuba, with weapons on the ground, Daniel Leroy was the man to make it happen, provided he was given enough time. There were also too many personal things between him and this man. To free a light-skinned opponent would be a chance for his adversaries to take him down. He already loved the dissident's wife. He wanted to protect her, spoil her, control her life, know the perfume of her mouth, take pleasure in her body. Daniel stood between him and his happiness. There was no room for both of them in Nirvah's life. Daniel might as well stay where he was. The Secretary of State had a clear conscience because Daniel was the author of his own demise. The prisoner had to know of the almost inevitable consequences of his activities. He got himself caught without realizing it. He got a taste of his own medicine. Now Raoul Vincent would play it safe, watch himself, and untangle the nets around his feet so as to continue enjoying his power and know the taste of Nirvah Leroy's lips.

There was a knock at the gate. I was reading in bed by the light of the gas lamp when I heard the repeated knocking of metal on metal. The gray canvas notebook burned in my hands like fire. I quickly put it back under the mattress. Reading Daniel's journal destabilizes me. I'm afraid of the words to come; I can never predict my next discovery. And yet I'm dying to know more. Sometimes I skip pages to be done with them, to get rid of this object that both attracts and terrifies me as quickly as possible. Other times I reread certain passages until I know them by heart. In those moments I feel as though I'm stopping time, saving an hour, a night, from the jaws of the beast that has come to devour our lives.

I sent Auguste to see what it was. He came back to tell me the Secretary of State was asking for me, that he was waiting in his car, in the street. The Secretary of State came back one month and ten days after his first visit, around eight o'clock at night, after a violent downpour that caused a blackout in part of Port-au-Prince. For a couple of minutes I stood in the middle of my room, my head empty, unable to connect my thoughts to each other. I could stop this ambiguous, unsafe relationship once and for all. But could I really? From time to time the government went after relatives of imprisoned opponents and persecuted them; the Secretary of State might be protection against that. I also knew I shouldn't be having him over. But . . . Daniel. The repression of the regime had been ratcheted up a notch in the past several weeks.

Schoolchildren, students were disappearing every day. The rumor has become more and more insistent. The doctor-president, Papa Doc, with his sickly air, will get himself elected president for life next year. He's clearing the terrain with automatic weapons. Daniel was right then. The propaganda is at its height. The *macoutes* punish the slightest notion of protest, the slightest suspect phrase, with blood. It's insane. Two parliament members had the courage or folly to oppose the plan; they were physically eliminated. Nobody is rising up to condemn this odious act. Repression against the clergy is hardening; sometimes priests are taken from their homes and driven straight to the airport. Hmmm . . . I never thought Daniel would be collaborating with church people, he who believes in neither God nor the devil and often accused them publicly of being antennas for foreign governments. Daniel has been playing both sides all along. In the end, did I really know this man who slept in my bed for fifteen years? "Communist" is the password that explains everything, justifies everything. We've already become zombies. In order to live a seemingly normal life you mustn't have an opinion, you mustn't rebel against anything arbitrary, against the terrorism of the state. You mustn't even try to figure out what's going on. It's a *macoute* peace, a savage peace. The current situation is condemning people who are already imprisoned. They are forgotten; there are other dissidents to control, other *kamoken* to track down in the hills in the depths of the country.

The Secretary of State's handshake is ice cold; he's been waiting in the confines of his air-conditioned car. He didn't want to sit on the veranda even though it's much nicer there than in the living room, the warmest room in the house. I think he wants to avoid any indiscretion, or he's thinking of his safety. He may be right, but his car outside will surely not go unnoticed. And anyway I should be the one worrying about indiscretion and gossip. I'm the woman, the one who brings scandal. Rue des Cigales has been graced with a new skin since the day before yesterday. There are only a few piles of gravel and a roller compressor to take away. The rain, like a blessing, washed the genipap trees, the mango trees, the bougainvillea, and the clumps of flowers dying under the dust. The leaves exhale a perfume, green and new like childhood. The façades of our houses take blissful breaths. The Secretary of State, settled in the living room, is like a familiar who has come to visit the neighborhood. We chat for a moment about this and that. Not a word about his long absence. No commentary on my part regarding the work on the street. So little and at the same time so many things are already creating a strange complicity between us. The thick heat sticks to our skin; the rain has saturated the air.

"I came by to ask you, ma'am, to stop asking questions about your husband's situation."

I think I've misheard him. I forget the ridiculous, stilted protocol of our exchanges.

"What? What?"

"Yes . . . I'm asking you to stop trying to find out about Daniel Leroy. You're compromising yourself and the people you ask questions of. It might also be . . . irritating certain people. And it won't change anything as far as the detainee's situation."

I have trouble containing my anger.

"Mr. Secretary of State, my husband, the father of my children, has been imprisoned for almost four months now; I haven't heard a word from him, not a line, and I shouldn't knock on every door to find out what's happened? To try to find out if he's alive? Because it might be irritating people? What sort of monsters are running this country?"

The Secretary of State is sweating profusely, he's sweltering, but he has not removed the blue jacket he wears over his white shirt and his red tie. From time to time he closes his eyes and tries to take in some air. I do not offer to take his jacket. I cannot relieve him with the ceiling fan — there is no electricity at the moment. The wick of the kerosene lamp on a corner table in the living room is malfunctioning and every so often coughs up tiny sparks. He should leave if the heat is bothering him so much.

"I have no opinion to share with you about the political motivations of the government, ma'am," he says finally. "But I will reiterate my advice. Stop what you're doing. Do not inconvenience people with your questions. Reports have been sent out regarding your activity. Think of your children."

"Then whom may I address?" I throw out the question like a slap.

"Me, only me . . ." he says with a vague smile that increases my vexation.

"So tell me why Daniel's car was seen in the streets of Port-au-Prince driven by a notorious *macoute*?"

"Because, ma'am, that is part of the normal course of things . . . That car is considered the spoils of war, legitimate compensation for the devotion of a partisan faithful to the cause of the revolution . . . Do you know how to drive, ma'am?"

I do not respond to the Secretary of State's question. Surely he must know that I drive. I'm choking with rage but I have to swallow it. I'm trapped in my own home. The Secretary of State's enormous eyes in the half-light, his thick lips, nostrils, and nose hairs that seem to breathe me in, his dark, sweaty skin, his breath in my living room. My God! . . . If Arlette could see us. No, I must, I will wake myself up from this bad dream. I put shoes on to receive him; he will not revel in the bareness of my feet tonight. What does he want from me? Does he really intend to help me? Where is this leading? This man is compromising my reputation by visiting me. He knows it. All of Rue des Cigales must know by now. The circles he's tracing around me are getting narrower and narrower. He's given me no news of Daniel.

"Do you have any news about my husband? I . . . I'd like to write him a note. Could you . . . ?"

"No . . . I can't give him anything on your behalf, or give you anything on his behalf. He's been placed in isolation. I only know that your husband is still alive. Are your children enjoying the country, ma'am?"

An alarm goes off in my stomach. He knows Marie and Nicolas have gone to Paillant to stay with my mother. His harmless question is just a reminder of his omnipresence in my life, of his power over our lives. I'm suddenly afraid; he knows I'm alone in the house, at his mercy. The Secretary of State starts to leave; I take a breath. He stands and so do I. But he doesn't move toward the door, he faces me, his right hand is raised to say good-bye, but he places it on the nape of my neck instead; I feel his fingers slide over my scalp. My entire body contracts in complete refusal of this man's touch, his sweat, his scent. He brings his face close to mine. I try to move back. His grasp of my neck is firm, I already feel his breath on my cheek. A grimace suddenly contorts his mouth; he closes his eyes, then suddenly falls to my feet. Lightning striking the house could not have been more shocking.

I watch stupidly as the Secretary of State convulses on the living room floor like a chicken, its neck just cut by Yva. In falling, his left leg folded under his buttocks. His head is stuck between the armchair and the table beside it. Under the open panel of his jacket a large gun appears, the presence of which I did not suspect. His body is shaken by increasingly violent spasms, while foam rises to his mouth, slides to the corners of his lips. My heart is about to stop beating, I'm about to have a stroke, a coronary, I'm dying of fear. I should react. Call for help. But I don't want the Secretary of State's men in my house or Auguste's or Yva's curiosity around me. I try to free his stuck leg. The Secretary of State's veiled pupils look at me without seeing me. With each movement of his body the barrel of his gun hits the ground, *cop cop cop*. And what if the gun goes off? Water, I should splash him with water; I saw that done as a child for my cousin Alberte, who suffered from epilepsy. I run to the pantry and bring back a large carafe of cold water, which I pour liberally over the Secretary of State's face and chest. There is a spasm more violent than the others, and then he gradually calms down.

Leaving, he was still confused. All of this lasted no more than twenty minutes. Unreal. I lent him one of Daniel's undershirts to replace his soaked shirt because he was shivering with cold. The Secretary of State avoided my gaze, and I turned my head while he changed. We did not exchange a word until he left.

She had to be protected. Surely she carried invisible protection, or a talisman, otherwise he didn't understand why he got an electric shock when he touched her. A crossing of energies had knocked him down. An experience that must have had its source in something mystical. No one could make him believe he had simply succumbed to heatstroke. He had never felt anything like it in his entire life. Contact with Nirvah Leroy's skin had opened the world of the dead to him, as well as the world of the living. The whole time he was in the house a heaviness in his body tried to bog down his thoughts, control his will. He waged a silent battle against these forces compressing his skull. He could not say if these forces came from the woman herself or from the lingering presence of Daniel Leroy, assaulting him one last time. But whether it was he or she, something put up ferocious resistance to his presence. The combat was mortal — he thought his heart was going to give out at any second. But his need for Nirvah, even beyond his instinct for survival, kept him in the house. He'd agreed to confront death in order to possess her. What spirit did she serve? Bossou, the terrible spirit with the flash of lightning? Marinette, the violent, powerful wife of Ti Jean Petro? More likely, Baron Samedi . . . or the Guédés, spirits of the dead and fearsome guardians of cemeteries, since he had fallen into that state of limbo. Many of those very evolved Christian, light-skinned intellectuals also frequented voodoo priests and priestesses. The Secretary of State was in a position to know because these priests and priestesses were precious adjuncts to the intelligence service. As soon as an individual or group of any social or political provenance called upon their services to obtain potions, powers, or protection for an undertaking, even a nonspecific one, this information was reported to the authorities. The agents at the Ministry of Defense and Public Safety were very interested in these people and, in the case of suspicious, subversive activity, swooped down on them before they knew what was happening. The Secretary of State also knew that staying too long in the sticky heat of this living room would make him sick even though he regularly took his medication. But his so-called epilepsy went beyond the doctors' understanding; he knew this was not a matter of medical science alone. It was a matter of birth, a legacy of power that sometimes turned against him. He knew it had been more than a year since he'd offered a sacrificial ceremony to Sogbo. He had to go back to Chardonnières, his hometown, to his own people, the source of his power. The enormity of his political responsibilities kept him away from his mystical duties. He had become vulnerable. The combination of all these factors had translated into failure. The Secretary of State was seething with rage and bitterness against himself, against Nirvah Leroy. She must be laughing at him. Now she knew his weakness, she could delude herself into thinking she could dominate him. He swore to himself to be harder on her, to set things straight.

And yet she had splashed him with water. Had she not done this he would not have come back from his visit to the shadow world. And this water that had brought him back to life sealed a pact of life and death between him and this woman. Was she aware of the consequences of her act? Bringing back his vital breath through the offering of water over his body, she had sought him out and found him. Like the first time, when she came to ask for his help at his office at the ministry. There was no longer any doubt in his mind. The signs were clear. Something was forming between them, something bizarre and terribly exciting. He became more and more obsessed with it. His feelings toward Nirvah Leroy terrified him. His sense of gratitude terrified him. For Papa Doc, supreme leader of the republic of free black men, all gratitude was cowardice. He repeated it to whoever would listen. Gratitude was just weakness because we resent the person who relieves us of a misery we should not have had in the first place and for which this good neighbor must surely be partially responsible. Anyway, why would they help if not to be relieved of some nagging sense of guilt? The Duvalierist principle of survival is to bite the hand that feeds you, to eat the whole arm if you have to. Was it cowardly to be moved at the thought that he owed his life to Nirvah Leroy? Yes, since being grateful to her meant feeling sorry for himself, a state that debilitated him. He decided to offer her a piece of jewelry, a small thing of great value that women like. A jewel to embellish her beauty, gold to rest on the warmth and perfume of her skin, precious stones to bring out the sparkle of her eyes and to stud her dreams with stars.

*December 12, 1962 — The government is making a big
to-do about all of its achievements, particularly paving the
large street that has been renamed Boulevard Jean-Jacques
Dessalines. As if these investments constituted a personal favor
from the chief of state to his people. When I know, as many
others do, that these projects have been financed by state bonds
that the industrialist Kurt Bloomfeld was forced to buy under
pressure. Duvalierville, same scenario. The erection of this
modern city with no economic or strategic usefulness was a
pretext for outrageous enrichment. "Voluntary contribution"
is the new catchphrase of the president's zealous advisors.
Merchants and businesspeople are being held for ransom. The
alternative is pretty simple: for Haitian shopkeepers, threats to
pillage their stores; for foreigners, expulsion and confiscation
of goods. And on top of it they have to write open letters to the
doctor-president in the press, thanking and congratulating
him for his devotion to the Haitian people. The famous letters
of allegiance. Some are eager to write them in order to be left
alone. Too bad for their consciences that the dictatorship is
devouring everything through phagocytosis. Others run away,
claim to feel the opposite of what they feel, dance with the devil
not to get eaten. In the end they all want to live. We all want to
live.*

*Every father or mother of a Haitian family maintains a
special relationship with his or her* macoute, *a protector no
meaner than any other, provided his power is not questioned.*

*How do the intellectuals manage to deal with their consciences?
Who will know in ten years or twenty that in our hearts we
were consumed by powerless rage? Unbeknownst to us we are
developing a threshold of tolerance that adapts to the stages of
our descent into hell. Hell is becoming familiar. We're learning
how to manage. We try to banish it by praying, doing penance.
We are pathetic. Is ending this nightmare even possible? Many
have fallen in the struggle, but we have to be smarter, more
perseverant, have more faith than they do. My compatriots
are leaving the country in droves; do they have more courage?
Go or stay? What is the worst or best choice? How can you
not leave when that's the only way to escape certain death? I
won't go because my conscience will go everywhere with me.
Duvalierist doctrine and ideology are rotten to the core, nothing
but vulgar opportunism. The ideas cannot endure because they
cannot find healthy soil in which to take root. Duvalier and his
accursed souls foster confusion about the true face of this fascist
power, whose goal is power for itself and by itself.*

*December 18, 1962 — Nirvah is firmly convinced Dominique
and I were lovers. I went to see Dominique last Thursday.
I needed to speak to her. I'm always a bit somber around
Christmas. It might be time to end this grotesque tradition.
Celebrating Christmas here is scandalous. Fortunately Marie
and Nicolas have not believed in this farce for a while. The
center of town and the seaside shine with a thousand lights,
shop windows brim with tantalizing items, crowded streets
attract mobs of feverish buyers. But beneath this surface
euphoria great destitute masses still bear the weight of their
misery. It hurts more to be penniless at Christmas.*

*Blood must flow for the darkness to go away. Guilty blood
as well as innocent blood. Even if my determination flags at
times, I do not doubt my will and courage. Dominique knows*

how to listen to me and sometimes even manages to calm me down. Gets me back on my feet. I wonder in the end if she's not a lesbian or just plain frigid. Since her divorce I haven't known her to have lovers. Unless she's been able to hide certain corners of her life from me. Who knows, maybe she's having fleeting affairs with students in the ethnology department at the university. She lives off private income and teaches for pleasure. Dominique lives alone in a big family house that she inherited and could be living the most unbridled life without anyone knowing. And it would be her absolute right. That day, I sensed an unusual reserve in her. She offered me a martini with ice cubes and a slice of lemon, the way I like it, and then she let me make the conversation. She was somewhere else. She said nothing but looked at me much more intensely than usual. Her eyes were shining with a secret fire, perhaps caused by fatigue or lack of sleep. Or desire? Dominique seemed to want to read into my soul, and it made me a little uncomfortable. Night was falling, and I decided to go back home. I took the same complaints with me. She accompanied me to the gate without saying a word. I was troubled. I left with a feeling of frustration. If she had made the slightest gesture, even one, I would have spent all the frustration ravaging me in her body.

Toward the end of last year I noticed Daniel needed more and more time alone, sometimes staying in his office to work until morning. His trips outside Port-au-Prince became increasingly frequent and were under the pretext of giving free history classes at schools in the provinces. I thought for a moment he was having an affair. I clearly had no idea. His trips had to do with his revolutionary activities and his preparations for an uprising against Duvalier's dictatorship, while I was attributing them to some fling outside the capital. Wouldn't it have been better if it had been a matter of T and A? The consequences certainly would have been less dramatic. And why did Daniel think I wouldn't be interested in his political life? Does he think I'm that shallow? He never wanted to understand or accept my points of view on what's happening here. I know another side of life, I grew up in hardship, keeping up appearances just to survive and find my place in this society. The whole country lives off appearances. I couldn't afford the luxury of dreaming. I don't know what will help us do away with the mindset of the once-colonized, which still shackles us, but communism doesn't seem to be the solution to me. In the end it would've been better if I'd never found Daniel's notebook. There are things you're better off not knowing. I swing between wanting to set the journal on fire and wanting to consume it. For the past few days it has been stealing the little sleep I have left. I'm in much more danger than I thought. Now

I know why Dominique left two days after Daniel's arrest, when she wasn't supposed to leave for two months. The house without Daniel must have seemed as empty as her life. When she suggested I leave the country with the children, I found her reaction excessive. Daniel had just written a few articles in the paper; his imprisonment was just meant to intimidate him. But there had been much more to it than that. Why didn't she tell me anything? Didn't she know I was unaware of Daniel's plans? And what about me? What will become of me? Am I supposed to agree to the Secretary of State's advances?

December 20, 1962 — I asked Dominique: "Do you think I'm right to want to use force to uproot evil?" I was having my doubts again. I'd said so often to young comrades that the revolution could not happen with just a handful of intellectuals and journalists. The revolution had to be the work of the people, who would find its light in labor unions, political parties, farming organizations. Those were the weapons of peaceful struggle in a world with the right to speech, the speech that differentiates us from animals. Haiti's problem is not and has never been one man, one chief of state, however outrageous a dictator he might be. And yet I was ready to dismiss my convictions, to eradicate evil with evil. I remember Dominique replied: "Are you scared?" She asked again: "Are you scared of failing or succeeding, Daniel?" I said, "Dominique, I'm afraid of blood. Duvalier holds on to power through blood. His power is bloody." After a minute of reflection Dominique added, "You can't cure someone of a fever if his wrists are slit." I looked at her. A jolt of tenderness slipped under my skin. She's more suited to be a leader than I am. Her powers of clear-sightedness never cease to amaze me. She knows how to turn doubt into energy. Dominique, a true bourgeoise *whose sociology thesis dealt with the movements that led to the genesis of a Haitian left, always reminded me of what a militant on the left in our country should be. Beyond polemics and lecture halls, she reminded me that to reach the masses, who could change everything, I had tools like Creole, voodoo, the scent of the earth, the phases of the moon, caterpillars destroying ears of corn, bugs biting the soles of farmers' feet, rainy seasons. She reminded me of the legacy of leftist theoreticians like Christian Beaulieu, who since the 1930s had advocated the education of the rural masses through Creole. I thought of my university years. The discussions with my comrades, students like me, in Paris. The world was changing, the people of the former colonies were waking up. In a way we belonged to this change, but chains still shackled our minds. I found my dream for Haiti again, and a strength transformed by the purity of my love for this country. Years had passed, and my dream was bleeding away. The world was not changing because there were several worlds. Too many worlds.*

Dominique told me today of her decision to leave the country in a few months. She'd sent job applications to a few universities in Canada and was awaiting their replies, which would surely be positive given her qualifications and Quebec's policy of aggressive immigration in recent years. I didn't know what to feel or think. Why hadn't she told me about this major life decision? I now understood the reason for her strange behavior the last time we saw each other. I couldn't discourage her plans, it would just be selfish of me. I had a family to support me; Dominique had no one. Perhaps it was better this way. I am going to miss Dominique. But I will use this feeling of loss to harden myself even more, to rid myself of any sentimentality. I have to sever all ties. Nirvah and the children will leave in the coming year at the end of the first trimester, as soon as the clandestine shipment of weapons has been sent . . .

Maggy contemplates the finery, removes the earrings from their case, and holds them up in front of her eyes.

"Shit! These are beautiful! I have to say, these are fucking amazing! He sent these to you, here?"

"Yes, through Jocelyn . . . his driver."

We don't speak for a moment. Maggy and I feel like Alice on the path to a terrifying wonderland. The Secretary of State had Rue des Cigales paved so that the dust wouldn't bother him when he visited me. I figured that out. But I can pretend to be oblivious, that the government has simply finished a long-awaited project. In fact he and I did not exchange a word on the subject the last time he was here. This episode has come to form the first element in a series of unspoken things building up between us. But today these jewels upset the fragile balance of the innocence maintained until now. They speak to me directly, call out to me, they seek my neck, my earlobes, my wrist, taking up residence there like the tentacles of some fearsome beast. Now a man is speaking to a woman in the language of lust and possession. The Secretary of State is filtering out everything that separates us; he's forgotten about Daniel, he's overlooking my children, politics, enemies, mulattos. He is putting his stamp on Mrs. Leroy's file and taking it over. Jewelry of such splendor given to a woman one wants to possess marks a decisive step in her conquest or, should I say, capture? The Secretary of State knows the value of money. He does not spend it lightly; money buys the impossible, dreams, deep pleasure. These jewels also bear the promise of other treasures, a certain largesse that presages a reassuring material comfort for me. The Secretary of State wants to play the game according to the rules of the art. Every mistress has her price, her standard of living. I am a luxury object. He flatters me by telling me this with these onerous baubles. These jewels burn with a cold fire, the brilliance of the diamonds wed to the blue mystery of the sapphires. The earrings, necklace, bracelet, and ring seem to occupy the entire bed, a new source of light absorbing the light of morning. Is it too late to turn back? Can I erase these past few weeks of my life in one fell swoop? Everything that comes from this man carries an unsettling charge of authority.

Maggy is caught up in the magic being released by these jewels, I can see it. I felt the same thing opening the package, which was wrapped in ordinary paper. The Secretary of State is a master of discretion. Maggy has had lunch with me every Sunday since Daniel's departure. I wanted her to come over to show her these things. The story I told her made her gasp, the Secretary of State crumpling to my feet while trying to cross the threshold of my lips. She would've thought it was a joke had there not been these jewels, their light flooding her eyes. They confirm to her, more than any other proof, the ludicrous story of a prince that no kiss can release from his spell of ugliness. A fairytale with no final wave of a magic wand. The frog will remain a frog, the precious stones and gold will not make the horrors of my reality magically disappear.

Maggy is a beautiful black woman, a woman with class. She is my best friend, to the dismay of my sister-in-law, who does not understand our friendship. More than once she has reproached me for the people I associate with. This is how Arlette evaluates my level of refinement, my background, by these little details. To her I'm just a vulgar little *mulâtresse* without class or dowry who has bewitched her brother. Without his communist ideas Daniel would never have been interested in the likes of me. I don't know bourgeois etiquette, the rules of living well, and the hypocrisy of the upper crust. I am part of the fallen class that experienced a reversal of fortune, bad political speculations, or, worse, misalliances. The kind of bourgeois class that has only a name; a certain amount of pride; a great, dilapidated villa at times; and women in search of marriages that will restore their economic stability, if not their prestige. There is no shortage of good matches in the black middle class aspiring to this supreme level of success, marriage to a light-skinned woman, even a poor one. In short I have all the flaws of the people, except for my color. I know who I am; I know my value, even if I don't drink cocktails with the bourgeoisie in private clubs. Maggy always smells good. Her fall, a tuft of fake hair, never leaves the top of her head and bounces with every movement. Her very long nails are generally the same deep red as her lips. Maggy will not remain a widow for long, even though she was devastated last year by Henri's death. She is not the sort of woman who can live without a man. She works hard all day handling hot irons and hair straighteners in her beauty salon. At night she needs the rude tenderness of a man in her bed, his hardness resting nicely against her ass.

"So?" I ask her.

"Hmmm . . ."

She picks up the little white card that has come with the package. Just two words are written there, in tiny letters: *with gratitude*. No date, no signature, no trace. The gift of a shadowy man, an unknown and powerful person who has graced me with his favor.

"But why does he feel gratitude toward you?" Maggy asks.

"I suppose it's because I doused him with water the other night, while he was dying on my floor . . . but it's also a pretext. So?" I repeat.

"Well . . . you know my fascination with jewelry, Nirvah . . . I would give anything to own amazing jewelry like this, but all this is scaring me a little . . . what does he really want?"

"We're big girls, Maggy. You know what he wants. He wants rights over me, and this," I say, pointing to my pelvis.

"And what about Daniel?"

"Actually, that's the problem. I would gladly plug my nose and drink the Secretary of State's medicine, but there's no guarantee Daniel will profit from it."

"And if Daniel ever gets out," Maggy says pensively, "he'll surely know that you've . . . had the Secretary of State . . . over. Is Daniel the sort of man who would accept that sort of . . . compromise? Wouldn't he be mad at you?"

Daniel will have to learn how to compromise. Sleeping or not sleeping with Raoul Vincent isn't an innocent choice for me. It's a matter of great urgency, and I have to decide whether it's advisable or not for my survival and that of the children.

"I'm going to send his present back," I say to Maggy, in response to her question.

She quickly shoots me a look, then gazes again at the sparkling stones.

"Yes . . . maybe you're right," she sighs. "This situation is starting to get out of hand. The Secretary of State thinks anything goes. He shows up at your house without being invited and stakes a claim over you. He paves your street. At least we think so. But this jewelry, this is a little much. A good man would know that you don't give these sorts of presents to a married woman."

"Maggy, my dear, let's leave principles aside. I'm in a pretty exceptional shithouse, don't you agree? I understand Secretary of State Raoul Vincent is trying to buy my favors. And I also see that he's willing to pay dearly to get them. The question is whether to go against his logic or not and to weigh the consequences in both cases. For now, the idea of fucking that guy is unbearable to me. But I've asked him to save Daniel, and in a way I knew I was knocking on the devil's door . . ."

My friend widens her eyes; she's never seen this pragmatic side of me. I have to grow up fast, Maggy. With every passing day Daniel drifts further away from me, from the children. With every passing day a little bit more of what we've built so far is destroyed, and it was already pretty fragile. I have very few weapons left to fight with. I just have my skin, my body, my sex. But I can always wash them later. Like earthenware, they'll be even lovelier.

The need for Daniel is consuming my life. I can't stand being alone anymore. My body feels like it's missing something essential, like water or salt. Anxiety and fear have killed the impulses of my flesh, even though for the first few days of Daniel's disappearance I was tormented by constant desire for him. I couldn't sleep at night. Now I eat when I'm not hungry. I no longer feel the need to be beautiful. Daniel will have to reacquaint himself with my body, reawaken my skin and sex with his hands and mouth. But how will he come back to me, in what state? I'm mad at him, but I know I won't hold a grudge for long. He knew how to make me love life. Our moments of deep harmony were worth the days we woke up like two strangers washed up together on a desert island. With him everything was more intense, truer. His enthusiasm put a sort of depth in the simplest things, and our complicit laughter lightened the darkest days. But I've never been able to understand the anger seething within him, his refusal to leave well enough alone, to live simply with his wife and children without trying to fight absolute evil with pitiful weapons. While watching others fall or be devoured. Why are you doing that to us, to me and the children? If you come back, Daniel, I will stifle you, hide you, tie you up if I have to, to silence the words that are tearing us apart. The dust is gone from Rue des Cigales, but it remains on my face, in the back of my throat, in the hollows of my body. I feel gray, desiccated. Anxiety never leaves me; time is just waiting, nothing but waiting. I deny myself any respite; I don't respond to friends' invitations to go out, to get some air. They want to take me to the beach in Arcachon or Montrouis or for walks in Kenscoff, places where life is good. I want to give my sorrow my full attention as long as Daniel has not returned, as long as he's suffering and in despair.

I think of the Secretary of State. The Secretary of State convulsing on my floor. How incongruous. How can I look him in the eye again? An executioner in the throes of an epileptic fit. An executioner who can't tolerate the heat here in Haiti. How ironic! Every time I think of him I'm overcome with disgust. Will he hold it against me that I know his weakness? He scares me, he makes me sick. But he's my only lifeline. Will he come back to my house? Of course he'll come back. I'm not big enough to resist him, control him, fend off his advances. I have something he needs, I am something he covets. The power dynamic is in his favor; he's all-powerful. But if there's just a chance, I have to take it. For Daniel, for Marie and Nicolas. I haven't returned the jewelry; in case of hardship I can always trade it in for fast cash at a pawnshop.

Solange's laugh has risen in the air, rolling like a storm to fade away in little uneven spasms, and I want to be near her. With Solange I don't have to act, I don't have to pretend to be strong, I don't even have to speak, and I think I could cry without shame. With her I don't feel the need to understand. I don't have any more questions. With Solange I know there is life, and life has to be lived.

"Hmmm . . . Rue des Cigales has been revived, Neighbor. Are you happy about it?"

I don't answer her. Her question is just the intro to the rest of her thoughts. From behind her ear she pulls half a chicken feather with a few fibers left at its tip. She places it in her mouth to wet it with saliva, slips it into the tube of her right ear, and, holding the tool between her thumb and index finger, gyrates it quickly, taking great pleasure in it. For a good minute I hear the song of the feather gathering earwax. Same thing with the left ear. Satisfied, Solange emits a few clucks from her throat that make her sound like a turkey. The chicken feather is returned to its place.

"Women's *foufounes* are like earthenware," she goes on. "Once washed, they become new again. We keep no trace, no mark, on our bodies. Do you understand?"

I am struck by Solange's analogy, because I made the same one moments ago. I understand her allusion but do not nod in agreement. I tour the property with my eyes. My gaze lingers on the oak trees, the mahogany trees, the enormous yellow mombin tree and its tiny yellow fruit. They seem to have blossomed the night before during the heavy rain, their leaves free of dust, shining in the sun. On my first visit I didn't notice all the fowl pecking around in the weeds — roosters, chickens, and their chicks. At the end of the property a family of guinea fowl has formed a separate group, squawking with metallic cries. The sight of their white faces with tints of blue, their red wattles and bare necks, makes me shiver. In spite of their beautiful gray coats dotted with beads of white, I find these short-legged birds repulsively ugly. The *macoutes* wear this terrible animal as a logo on their uniforms. Like them, they are shady and elusive. They say that in colonial times wild guinea fowl represented slaves running away, the *marrons*. But what master are we fleeing a century and a half later? When will our nation stop running away? I wonder if Solange keeps them out of solidarity with the regime or if she sometimes prepares them with *sauce créole*.

"The last time you were here the dust was burning our

eyes. Today everything is clean and fresh. Miracles are not for dogs but for living Christians . . . Isn't that true, Neighbor?"

Solange reels off her sibylline sentences, looking at me through the smoke of the cigarette she's just lit. She's watching my reactions. Does she know? Of course she knows about the Secretary of State's visits, about the paving of the road, too. She's an instinctive woman. She must think I'm sleeping with him. I'm not afraid of her opinion. I just want her to know that at this point in my life I don't know what boundaries I will cross to see my husband alive again.

"He's not my lover, Solange. Not yet. I need more than asphalt . . ."

Solange's laughter reaches the edges of the clouds.

"You're stronger than you seem, Neighbor. The owners on Rue des Cigales are all happy — the rents will surely go up — but they're already calling you all sorts of names. Who has offered their help?"

So they knew. They were condemning me. I didn't think my misfortune would take so many forms, pursue me with so many thorns. Now I have to deal with the opinions of the good people of the street, and pretty soon the town. Solange understands my quiet surprise.

"I knew him . . . back in the day," she adds. "When he was still nobody. Watch out, Neighbor . . . He . . . the Secretary of State is a man . . . with particular pleasures."

"What does that mean, Solange?"

I feel an alarm go off in my head.

"He likes men as much as women. I'm sure you had no idea."

My blood leaves my body and returns to throb behind my forehead. My descent into hell is only beginning.

"Yes, I had no idea . . ."

"I don't know if he's changed since . . . maybe he has . . . but, you know, people like that don't change . . ."

Solange moves on to other topics of conversation. She tells me about her night with Déméplè, about the client who irritated the spirit with his outsized ambitions, about the dance at the Palladium where the Webert Sicot Ensemble played and during which *macoutes* exchanged gunfire and killed a young girl. Meanwhile I'm in a black hole, holding out my hands, feeling for the walls of my fear.

A man with a wiry body, bushy brows, and triangular sideburns comes through the little wooden gate that leads to Solange's house. He looks suspicious and doesn't seem to appreciate me speaking with the priestess. He is wearing very dark sunglasses and a gun at his side.

"Well, I better get going, Neighbor . . . I have a job to do . . . One of these days I'll have to prepare a bath of leaves for you. I'll do it when Déméplè is in my head."

I look at her, surprised. She winks as she goes.

"Yes, a bath to get rid of bad luck, the jinx . . . the bad air. For you, it will be free . . ."

Maggy dragged me to the Paramount Theater. She finally convinced me to go with her. She made me think I was doing her a favor, instead of the other way around. It was Sunday. I put on lipstick, a little white silk-cotton dress that was chic in an understated way, and the earrings from the Secretary of State. I was seized by a desire to wear the earrings, a sudden impulse. I put my hair in a high chignon to show them off. I told myself the sparkle of the gems would rouse me from the gloom I was mired in. Or was it that I wanted to get used to this other side of myself already, this woman who would open her house and her body to Secretary of State Raoul Vincent? Maggy cast a quick look of surprise at the glittering jewels on either side of my face and made no comment. I was grateful to her for that. The electricity of the jewelry penetrated my skin like a virus. On the street I felt like another woman, expecting every person I came across to see the Secretary of State's desire imprinted on my face — a feeling that troubled me deeply. Maggy and I chose the five o'clock screening so that we wouldn't get back too late. They were showing *Elevator to the Gallows*, a movie that had already been out for a few years. The story was intense. An almost perfect crime starts to unravel, taking a terrible turn. Well-paced, oppressive suspense. I love Jeanne Moreau. I wandered through the streets of Paris with her as she waited for news from her lover. I felt her anguish, her doubt, as seconds, minutes, hours passed, and he didn't show up for their appointment. Like her I looked at shop windows without really seeing them, my eyes seeking only one face, my ears listening for only one voice, to begin living fully again.

Maggy didn't like the movie, because it was black and white and too cerebral. She prefers comedies or epic adventures like *Gone with the Wind*. Maggy was my brother Roger's girlfriend when they were in high school. Our friendship has stood the test of time. She knows all of Port-au-Prince, especially who is sleeping with whom, thanks to the gossips who come to her beauty shop. Her husband died last year of a strange disease; they say he was slowly poisoned by an associate. But in Haiti literally no one dies a natural death. If not for the jealousy or meanness of other people, we would all live forever. Maggy is working hard to raise her daughter. She understands my situation. She knows the Secretary of State's wife because she comes into the salon regularly to get her hair dyed. She's always swathed in gold jewelry but very pious, Maggy says. She gives frequent donations to the poor. For the first time since I've known her I can tell Maggy's upset about my situation. She's scared for me.

When we come out of the theater it is no longer daytime but not yet night. I love these long days in the middle of the year that never seem to end. The air is sweet. I'm surprised to see so many people in front of the Paramount: happy women in their low-cut dresses on the arms of freshly shaven companions; young people on their first date; unruly children; sellers of sweets; taxis, their red ribbons hanging from rearview mirrors. The movie theater was fragrant with a mixture of strong perfume and peppermint candy. I find it strange that life continues to go on, the theater's neon signs casting yellow and green light on the surroundings and people who have come to unwind. While Daniel is rotting in Fort-Dimanche.

Maggy suggests getting a drink at the Rex Café, but I want to go home.

Standing on the sidewalk, we wait for a taxi. The breeze lifts Maggy's flared skirt as two young boys pass by. They whistle. We burst out laughing. I feel the weight of a gaze on my face, I look for it and find it, it stops my laughter in midair. Daniel's brother, Raymond, and his wife, Marlène, stand before me, observing me, their eyes full of reproach. I pretend not to see them. A taxi stops; my friend and I jump into it.

January 10, 1963 — Dominique has been coming over less often, and I haven't gone back to her place. I'm already anticipating going underground completely. The tension and lack of action are slowly killing me. This year, 1963, will be the year of the great Duvalierist offensive toward supreme power, presidency for life. In spite of the coolness of the Americans, who have reduced their aid to the country by more than half. You just have to look at Duvalier's appointments in the last ministerial cabinet to see it. Hard-line ideologues, propaganda experts like Maurice-Robert Badette in Education, Jean-André Colbert in Social Affairs, and Simon Porsenna in Information and Coordination. Raoul Vincent in Public Safety; in other words, head of the secret police. Trade agreements have been signed with Czechoslovakia and Poland. They're telling Uncle Sam to go to hell.

January 13, 1963 — I didn't want to believe it when I read the letter in Le Nouvelliste. *Yvonne Hakime Rimpel publicly refuted an article published in an issue of* Paris Match *a week earlier. She denied being raped and beaten by government henchmen. She denied that her passport was used as blackmail to ensure her silence. She denied that her daughter was summoned to military headquarters and threatened by one of the same soldiers who visited her that infamous night in January 1958. Yvonne Hakime Rimpel denied everything. There was no outcry on the right or the left or anywhere at all. The corruption of minds is total. The French journalist who uncovered this woman's story didn't know the damage he would do to her. This poor woman, years later and in solitude, is still undergoing the government's persecution. I'm going to write an essay in response, in solidarity with this woman, this evening.*

February 21, 1963 — My request for an exit visa for Nirvah and the children still hasn't been approved. It probably won't be. As long as my loved ones are here I'm bound hand and foot. The border will be the last resort if I don't get these visas before the end of April.

March 3, 1963 — My informant is positive. Michel-Ange Lefèvre is working for the government. He's attached to the secret service that Raoul Vincent directs. The news did not surprise me; I noticed warning signs in the man for some time. He's played his role well. Now I have to find out exactly what he knows. I passed the information on through all the satellites. We're putting everything on the back burner. Stopping all activity. I'll await the consequences, which won't take long. Otherwise my life goes on as a professor and the editor of the paper of opposition. My days are fragile and yet my strength and conviction are being reaffirmed with the prospect of the danger threatening me.

April 8, 1963 — It's been over a month since I've recorded a word in this journal, laid low by a viral hepatitis that almost killed me. Dr. Xavier treated me with competence and devotion. This man, a close family friend, has taken the place of my father, who was his best friend. I'm doing much better now, though I'm still a bit weak. Marie, my little nurse, slips past her mother at times to come to my bedside, despite doctor's orders that I remain quarantined in my room. Nirvah is tired; she needs a good vacation. I'm mad at myself for neglecting my family life. All I want is for them to be far away from here in complete safety.

April 11, 1963 — Another failed coup d'état by the military. Three conspirators managed to find asylum in an embassy. A fourth member of the military, apparently not implicated in the plot, was killed by a zealous colleague. I must admit all this trouble suits me, drawing the government's attention to other areas of threat. My contact in the army is still at his post. The consulates and embassies are overflowing with citizens who are voluntarily going under cover without even being threatened. This is a time when being the distant relative or friend of X or Y is not a good thing. The Duvalier government's relations with the Kennedy administration are at their worst. There are persistent rumors of Duvalier's overthrow by the Americans.

April 17, 1963 — Shock. I really wasn't expecting this. The chief of staff of the Secretary of State of Information and Coordination came to my office yesterday morning to offer me the job of editor in chief of the daily paper Le Palmiste, *the government's official organ. They're not wasting any time. A strange trap. What role did Michel-Ange play in this? I still don't know if my network has been discovered. Is this an attempt at a takeover, pure and simple, as Duvalier does so well? Since I claim to belong to this bogus communist party and have been able to express myself so long with complete impunity, time for payback is coming. The doctor-president controls a personal left that he would like to see me join. A populist left wing of the left that was corrupted by the class and power struggles of 1946. A reactionary left that has become the proletarian right, prisoner to a deadly ideology of color. Does Duvalier really think I'll let myself be reeled in by his populist, antibourgeois discourse? No, I don't think so. There is something else going on. There is something more to this. I have to think quickly, consult my base. I have to speak to Dominique.*

April 23, 1963 — The chief of staff gave me eight days to think about it and reply to his offer. In a strange coincidence the deadline is April 25, in two days. My comrades are sure something is being planned against us. The next few days will tell us what other decisions to make. Dominique thinks I should either accept the position or leave the country before the deadline. Go into voluntary exile like the others, in a matter of hours. François Duvalier's government can no longer legally exist starting April 25 of this year. Despite the charade of reelection by last year's deputies, on constitutional and legal levels his six-year term will expire on that day. My next editorial will remind the Haitian people and the world of this and will also be my answer to the government's proposal.

The generator was already installed and purring quietly when I came back from the dentist. The sun, blazing the way it can during the rainy season, was haloed by particles of water that stuck to my skin the whole way home. The giant machine seemed alive, with blood, nerves, and teeth. In the shed a technician was putting the finishing touches on it. Inside the house I came across two workmen in blue coveralls standing on stepladders, measuring the height of the walls. All of a sudden I understood. The van in front of the house should have tipped me off. Four air conditioners, still in their packages, waited in the shade of the almond tree in front of the outbuildings. That's why he wasn't coming by. The Secretary of State was preparing his pleasure, making sure the heat wouldn't send him tumbling to the floor, flat on his back before my eyes. I saw this coming, but the forms that this slow assault was taking threw me. The trap was closing in on me, I panicked. My jaw was seized by throbbing pain because the anesthesia was fading away. Auguste looked at me, an intelligent gleam in his eyes. Yva watched my reactions while going about her business. The rage of powerlessness rose up in me like a wave. I started to shout, "Fucking shit! Fucking bullshit!" I hurled insults at whoever was there. Nothing could contain me. My anger was choking me, I had to let it out or I would fall to the floor, gnashing my teeth. I was mad at Auguste for letting these strangers in my house, for my sleepless nights, the Secretary of State, Daniel. Auguste was jinxing me; he was the one who let the Secretary of State in the first time, like a worm in the fruit of my life. Who knows the real reason for his presence here? Was he a spy among us? A disguised *macoute*? I never liked his shifty look. My God, help me! I'm no longer in control of my life. People decide for me. And all these so-called workmen, who were they really? How could they invade my home, my privacy, without my permission? And what will the children think when they return from Paillant? Papa is in prison and we're sleeping in cool air. Papa is being eaten by vermin but we no longer have blackouts. Who's going to pay for the fuel? For the upkeep of all these machines? How do I explain to Daniel, when he comes back, these transformations beyond our means? What is the Secretary of State up to? First Rue des Cigales, then the jewelry, and now the generator and air conditioners in my home. He hasn't even given me the option to refuse. He's invading my space, determining my needs. The paved street is one thing; it belongs to everyone. I have no particular right to this public good. It profits the whole community. The jewelry . . . might represent the homage of an admirer and a so-called gesture of gratitude. But this is going too far: he's meddling in my life, my home, my refuge, my sanctuary. The Secretary of State is weaving his web around me like an evil spider. Does he know Daniel isn't coming back? That's it: Daniel is dead; otherwise he wouldn't be shamelessly taking over his house. I need to cry but the tears won't flow. For weeks I've felt tears poisoning my body, devouring my throat, refusing me the grace of relief. I have to believe that Daniel is alive and that I can keep him alive by accepting this man.

After I violently sent Auguste packing I calmed down. I didn't think of the consequences of my actions; he was a tumor I had to remove. It was a question of survival. I was surely committing a breach by firing a father of nine, but my aggravation would not listen to reason. The workmen observed

me with a circumspect air while continuing to work. My fit of hysteria probably startled them. I asked the one who seemed to be in charge the name of the person who commissioned these services. Of course he knew. "Secretary of State Vincent," he replied, consulting his order form nonetheless, and wondering what sort of game I was playing. Obviously my opinion didn't matter to him; he could not *not* install these machines. I can't find a way out, either in my head or around me.

Arlette came to scout things out. After our last altercation I didn't think she would come over again so soon. She turned up out of the blue one late afternoon with Nicole and Ghislaine, her best friends. She probably couldn't convince Sylvie to come on this reconnaissance mission. What did she know? Had she finally gotten wind of Raoul Vincent's visits here? As soon as she entered the house she looked for possible changes, something new to confirm the rumors surely circulating in town by now. The neon-green generator did not escape her, though she pretended not to see the giant contraption resting in the shed. Arlette was not particularly interested in my fate. Well, she was a little, since it was linked to Daniel's. But above all she wanted to find other reasons to resent me, to justify her distrust of me.

For a while we spoke of the heat. Here in Port-au-Prince these months of sweltering heat always seem hotter than the year before. How do we survive them? By spending the hardest weeks in the country or the mountains. Then we spoke of fashion trends, princess dresses that made you look slimmer, and the wearing of pants, which was becoming more and more common for women. There was also Vitiello's, a shoe store on Rue du Centre that had the new Italian styles. You had to see the leather sandals and patent-leather stilettos. All the rage. Yva served us fresh orange juice. But there were other words on the way, sharp, impatient words waiting for the right moment to snake in between us.

"I know who had the road paved, Nirvah . . . A friend at the Ministry of Public Works confirmed it. This person asked or, should I say, ordered Secretary of State Philibert to have it done."

Finally, here we are. A frontal attack. Arlette doesn't beat around the bush. She takes a long drag on her cigarette and releases the smoke, tilting her head back. Nicole is nervously rolling her thumb and forefinger over the beads of her necklace. Ghislaine is crossing and uncrossing her legs, smoothing her chignon. When I invited them to sit on the patio just now, I promised myself I would not let myself get annoyed or get caught up in their games. I would be a welcoming and patient hostess. And I would lie without shame, reserve, or remorse. Starting today I would learn to say the opposite of what I thought, to build a screen around my life behind which I would protect myself from odd ducks like Arlette.

"You're decidedly well informed, Arlette. I still don't know whom I'm indebted to for this early Christmas present and you already do. Hmmm . . . Does this mean that all this time you've had the resources and contacts to have Rue des Cigales paved? And you did nothing? In any case, all the residents of Rue des Cigales will be eternally grateful to this . . . this person . . ."

"Don't you want to know who it is?" Arlette pretends not to get my innuendos and observes me with great attention.

"I know you're dying to tell me, Arlette. Who is it?"

"Secretary of State Raoul Vincent. Do you know him?"

"Oh!" Nicole says with a start, as if hearing the name of Beelzebub. What a bad actress.

I answer Arlette calmly: "I know him by name . . . like everyone else."

"He's the head of Duvalier's secret police, in other words

one of the most powerful men right now. Don't you find it strange that he had Rue des Cigales paved while Daniel was in prison?"

I pretend to consider the question. "That might seem strange, yes . . . but why do you want to connect the two facts? Secretary of State . . . Vincent . . . surely has personal reasons for being interested in this street."

"Like . . . a new mistress?" Ghislaine blurts out with gentle treachery.

"Why not?" I respond coolly, looking at each of them in turn. "Sex can be useful when you know how to use it . . ."

The Secretary of State turns on the air conditioner in the living room himself. He checks the installation, tracks the electric cable winding from the appliance to the socket with his eyes, and nods his head in satisfaction. For three days this box has been suspended from the wall, and I have not touched it or the ones in the bedrooms. To handle the levers that start these machines would be a betrayal of my pride; still, I appreciate his concern for the comfort of all members of the family. The Secretary of State sits down and closes his eyes, taking pleasure in the gentle hum of this machine lowering the room's temperature. So much so that he seems to forget about my presence in the room. His breathing becomes slower, more even. He does not allude to his ailment of the last visit; it's as if nothing happened. If he thinks I'm going to ask about his health, he can forget it. The living room's cool air portends a new phase in my relationship with this man. I spent the week dreading his next visit and hoping for it at once. There was no doubt he would come back to this house; I just wondered what his next victory would be. Today is Saturday. For the first time I'm seeing the Secretary of State in shirtsleeves and linen pants. He's even more awkward without the camouflage of his jacket. A small gun has been slipped into his belt. The lack of proportion between his upper body and lower body is ridiculous. His stomach tugs at the buttons of his shirt; his knees touch — he's knock-kneed.

"What if you and I became friends, Mrs. Leroy?"

The Secretary of State speaks to me with his eyes closed; he seems reborn with the growing cold. I'm irritated that he's speaking to me as if I weren't in the room, as if his words were a pure formality. These words provoke a low-grade panic in my stomach. They're leading me inexorably to the point of no return. What sort of friendship is he proposing? Doesn't he have the courage to call things by their names? I refuse to play little games of love and chance with him. He has to tell me clearly what's in the back of his mind. I will not accept a relationship whose conditions are not clearly expressed. I owe myself at least that much. This man should tell me that he wants to possess me, in my house, which is Daniel's, while my husband, imprisoned at Fort-Dimanche, is at his mercy. It should be clear between us that I am submitting to his desire, that I am accepting the profanation of my home, knowing that this is the price to pay to save Daniel. I will not give him the gift of the illusion of conquest. He won't have to force me; that would be a waste of time, I can't fight him off. But he won't have my consent.

"Aren't we already friends, Your Excellency?" The bold tone of my reply pulls the Secretary of State from his apathy. I go on right away. "Otherwise, how would you explain . . . some of the changes in the area? How would you explain this . . . outrageously lavish present? Are you this generous with all the wives of imprisoned opponents?"

"A temperamental woman," he says, smiling. He observes me with his eyelids half-closed. "You're mistaken, ma'am. For the moment you are the only wife of a dissident to enjoy . . . the privilege . . . of my generosity."

"You must see that I'm flattered, Your Excellency."

The Secretary of State ignores my irony.

"Call me Raoul, ma'am."

"If you wish . . . Raoul."

The Secretary of State gets up and moves slowly toward
the corner table where our record player sits. He chooses an
LP from the record collection and places it on the turntable.
Then he clicks the mechanical arm, and the needle lowers onto
the vinyl with a faint swish. Chopin. The waltzes, Daniel's
favorite. I would like to run away, but the four walls of this
room are suddenly a prison.

"I like temperamental women, Nirvah. You don't have to
mince words with them. I'll tell you right away, I want you.
I wanted you the moment you walked into my office at the
ministry. I couldn't believe my luck. Your husband is an idiot
to get himself locked up in Fort-Dimanche, with a wife like
you. An idiot tilting at windmills. He has ideas . . . hmmm . . .
poor fool."

The Secretary of State reflects for a moment, and when he
goes on his voice has the hardness of metal.

"François Duvalier will be named president for life in a few
months. Nineteen sixty-four will be the year of total victory.
Legal experts in parliament are working to modify the country's constitution to that end, and too bad for the malcontents.
He'll be overwhelmingly approved by referendum . . . a formality . . . and nobody's hackles will be raised in this country,
I'm sorry to say, ma'am. The communists who have infiltrated
don't measure up. Look . . . the UCH, this Haitian Communists
Union your husband belongs to . . . it's a setup, the control lab
of the opposition, it's theater. Its secretary-general, Michel-
Ange Lefèvre, is our man; we've rehabilitated him. That
communist party was fashioned out of whole cloth. Beautiful
work. It receives regular allocations from my ministry. Daniel
Leroy and others along with him—young people, still teenag-
ers—followed their convictions to the point of sacrifice for

nothing. They played a dangerous, illusory game. The naïve ones got royally screwed. You are now one of the few people to know this, and I would be grateful if you could keep this information secret, because it places your life in danger. Your dear husband thought he was making fools of us. He thought he could hide behind the UCH to plot against the government, arm the youth, and start an uprising in the backcountry. His plan was clever, I'll admit. He did fool us for a long time. But his plan could not come to pass. We control every source of potential agitation: schools, universities, churches, unions. Our agents are present at cockfights, in stadiums, in brothels. Every day more men and women of every social class enter the ranks of the VSN to infiltrate homes, bedrooms, clinics, and on and on. They work night and day. Like a flock of guinea fowl they travel across the territory in every direction, locating any unusual rumblings, any suspicious movements from afar. It would be wrong to underestimate their efficiency. Like those squat birds that still move so quickly, they're the true sentinels of the revolution. Resistance will be swept away as easily as a wisp of straw. We aren't afraid of anything, not even the Americans. Duvalier threw out that United States ambassador who had the gall to offer him a million dollars to flee the country with his family. He only had twenty-four hours to get out. The impertinence! John Kennedy sent his destroyers to drop anchor in our waters, a tactic others before him have used throughout our history. But it takes more than that to intimidate the sons of Dessalines. A woman like you, ma'am, drives men mad, mad to possess you. I like seeing your veins under your transparent skin. I imagine your soft hair tangled in the heat of love. Your lips were made to curl around a man's pleasure; your eyes leave traces of fire on my skin. Your hands hurt me. The curve of your body makes me ache. You're a woman I'd never dare dream of, a woman who doesn't look twice at a man like me. And now you've fallen into my hands of your own accord, like manna from heaven. I won't hurt you, Nirvah. As long as you don't make me . . ."

The Secretary of State's emotion and cynicism are unsettling. It's true Michel-Ange Lefèvre hasn't been to the house since Daniel's imprisonment. He was someone Daniel spent hours talking with on the patio. A man Daniel respected and loved like a father. I listened to him talk about how, twenty years ago, people like Étienne Charlier and Anthony Lespès campaigned for the first socialist party in Haiti, continuing the work started by Jacques Roumain. Then, men of conviction fought their battles openly against governments and the corruptions of the merchant bourgeoisie. No longer, he lamented. Before, relations between those in power and the communists were not easy; communists were sometimes put in prison, but they were a force that was difficult to muzzle at the time. Lefèvre told us about newspaper articles published in *La Nation*, true masterpieces. On occasion he recited a few lines by Anthony Lespès. Daniel drank in his words. But why, I once asked him, had he founded his own party and not fought with the left that wanted to be heir to the first communist circle in Haiti, that of Roumain and his cohorts? "Because I was advocating for an opening, a dialogue, with those in power, instead of encouraging the tendency toward secrecy and *marronage* that our politicians on the Haitian left can't do away with," he said to me. Now I understand what opening he was talking about. What makes a man change so much? After the arrest I burnt *Masters of the Dew, Das Kapital, Les clefs de la lumière, General Sun, My Brother*, and a whole pile of other books and magazines Daniel kept on the secret shelves of his library. So there is no hope; the roots of the dictatorship are burrowing into Haiti's soil more deeply every day. I'm having trouble assessing my situation. This man's desire is blindingly intense. With me he'll finally realize his deepest fantasy, dominating and possessing a light-skinned woman. He will fuck the bourgeoisie, overturn all the barriers of contempt and exclusion with his penis and his power. Would he like it if Daniel never came back to me? What sort of life can I lead with my husband once this nightmare is over?

"And what about Daniel, Your Ex . . . Raoul? Is he still master of his house? Have you already executed him? If so, why would I agree to accord you my favors? Because of the sheer terror of your vengeance if I refuse?"

The Secretary of State falls prey to a keen irritation. His gaze is fixed on me, hard and exasperated. I wait for an outburst of anger. I notice that any mention of Daniel leads to a state of nervousness he can't control. He stands and observes me; I stay seated and do not lower my eyes under the weight of his gaze. The Secretary of State takes his wallet out of his pants pocket. He searches a bit and removes a folded piece of paper, a note, which he hands to me. I don't understand; I take the note and unfold it; my hands tremble a little. I have to look closely to decipher a few words written in pencil on a dirty sheet of notebook paper. It's Daniel; I recognize his writing, the cast of his words. Daniel, who's suffering, who's alive. I guess at the words more than I read them, my heart is beating too fast, *"darling . . . thinking of you . . . our children . . . doing everything to get out soon . . . my weakened health . . . hope to see you again . . . stay strong . . ."* Finally, a breath of air; finally, water to slake my thirst! I'd like to laugh and cry at once. I'd like to be alone to savor this moment. The Secretary of State is standing before me scratching his throat. For a moment I forget his presence and even his existence. I hear a metallic sound and lift my head. My face is level with his pelvis. His belt is unbuckled and he's having a hard time undoing the buttons of his distended fly. I look at his face; his eyes are fixed, he's salivating abundantly, the corners of his mouth are wet. His pants and underpants fall to his feet like a sentence. There's no doubt about what he wants from me. With the Secretary of State it will be a question of give and take. Daniel's life in exchange for the pleasure of my body. His impatient desire is already seeking a way into my mouth. His panting reaches me, blending with Chopin's Allegro appassionato. I don't recognize the Secretary of State's hoarse voice when he says, "On your knees . . . Nirvah." There's no way out for me. I slide to my knees. At that moment I think of Solange kneeling before Déméplè in her dream. But I am not dreaming.

He was exhausted that morning, emptied of all his substance, his legs like jelly and his head filled with large spots of light. He was happier than he'd ever been in his life. When he went home in the early morning hours, he didn't go back to his bedroom; he preferred the atmosphere in his study, where he could see day break from a corner of the window. His bed, his rest, his body temperature, his most intimate secrets, his tears no longer belonged to this place. They were on Rue des Cigales with Nirvah Leroy. He and his wife had had separate bedrooms for several years now. Today he would gladly have separate homes or lives. The twitches of his penis, spent yet stubborn with desire, kept the images of his night vivid in his mind. Suddenly he loved her. She had revived his strength, his youth. He burned with the memory of her lips wet with his semen when he came in her mouth, when he died and was reborn in her mouth. He could still feel the texture of her skin, damp from love, under his hands. He heard the cries he'd finally released from her at the end of the night, after much caressing. He'd waited for the moment Nirvah's broken body no longer resisted and yielded in spite of herself to the sting of pleasure. A flash went through his head when he thought of Nirvah's feet. He had to protect her feet. She would no longer ruin them walking in the dusty streets of Port-au-Prince, doing her shopping by minibus taxi where her feet might be stepped on. He was going to get her a new car, one of those little

Japanese models that had just arrived in the country. All the bourgeois ladies were raving about them. A Contessa. A display case for her beauty. The revolution had taken her vehicle; it would give her another on the ministry's dime. It was only fair.

Yet from time to time an alarm went off in his ears. He tried to ignore it, chase it away. Wasn't he Raoul Vincent, omnipotent Secretary of State in Duvalier's all-powerful government? A man in whom the leader of the nation had every confidence? Who had the power of life and death over every citizen of the country? This woman was his by right, since he wanted her. He deserved her, for all the times he hadn't been a man. He would deal with the rest. No obstacle had ever stopped him before when it came to guaranteeing the security of the country and its leader. When he had had to assure the stability of those in power, he had no scruples or qualms or doubts. In his eyes a life had no importance of any kind before the supreme interest of the state. Why should things change now? It was a question of his mental and physical stability. The time had come to think of himself. Since he'd met Nirvah Leroy he understood that a life, one life, could make all the difference. One life was in the midst of taking away his strength, his distrust, his cynicism. This life had just given him a taste of happiness. Raoul Vincent knew that life did not give you gifts like these without demanding a high price, the price of blood. Daniel Leroy's blood. The blood of men he had yet to assassinate to retain his power, to inspire fear, sustain the dictatorship. To keep Nirvah. His blood, perhaps. Nirvah's blood. No! He would never let anyone hurt her or touch a hair on her head. If a man looked at her twice he would strangle him with his own hands. He wanted life for Nirvah and all that was beautiful, to make her even more beautiful. He wanted her happy. She would end up forgetting about Daniel Leroy. He would give her flowers, perfume, music, fruit. Books, too—she said she enjoyed reading. He would find a way to make himself indispensable, to give her confidence and protection. She was an intelligent, determined woman who was not afraid of taking what she needed to live. A survivor, that's what she was. The sort of woman he liked, who didn't have time to worry about existence. A woman who didn't lie to herself, who wasn't afraid to look life in the eye. The sort of a woman a man needed so that he would never become weak, who could rouse the inexhaustible resources within him. Time was on his side, his ally and his accomplice. He would assure the well-being of her children. He would make it so that all her needs, from the greatest to the most insignificant, were satisfied. He would have to find money, a lot more money, to supply what she required. He would work it out. He had never accorded much importance to the accumulation of money; he was content to live well and to manage the funds at his disposal in the best interests of his government. He lived in the Bas Peu de Choses neighborhood, in the same family home, which he had fortified, unlike some of his colleagues who had had princely estates built in the heights of Port-au-Prince. Of course his wife loved money and asked him for more and more, more and more often. He had to dip into the ministry's funds just to satisfy her, to have some peace. Now things were going to change. He was going to be paid for the services he rendered based on their fair value. Like almost everyone else. In the end what use was all this power without money? If he fell from grace tomorrow what would he live on? What would become of

Nirvah? He was going to ask for kickbacks, commissions for facilitating the procurement of contracts; he would sell his favors; his protection would now come at a price; he would invent bogus projects to obtain funds. He was part of the old guard. He would work it out.

Washing myself. Washing myself at length and profoundly, getting rid of the filth not only on my skin but also in my soul. Letting clear, fresh water flow over the powerlessness and rage of my hands. Cleansing my memory of the gestures, smells, and sounds of the night that won't leave me. Washing myself of this pleasure wrested by force from my body. A need that's becoming an obsession. I can no longer stand breathing in my skin. Solange . . . Yes, I have to see Solange. Against all my convictions, against all rationality, the need is rising in my soul to be touched by this woman, to let her pour water over my skin, to regain some serenity.

I soon realized Déméplè was visiting Solange that morning. A red silk scarf was wrapped around her head, she wore a peasant-blue smock with multicolored trim around the sleeves and hem, and her honey-colored eyes did not smile on seeing me arrive. She went about her vague business, smoking one cigarette after another. From time to time she took a swig from a bottle of homemade rum that was sitting on the ground. It also seemed as if her movements were slower than usual, as if she were executing them under the dictates of a voice perceptible to her alone. She gave orders to little Ginette and sharply scolded the child when she didn't follow her instructions to the letter. Krémòl, her brother, threw grain in the poultry yard. I spent a moment observing them, not knowing how to tell Solange the reason for my visit. Then she calmly turned around to face me and asked me point blank:

"Did you come for the bath, Neighbor? It's a good day, you know . . . The . . . the person is with me."

Is Solange spying on me? Does she have a way of knowing what's happening inside my house? Can she read my mind? Is she picking up the scent on my skin of the man who forced himself into me all night? Does she have a way of seeing a predator's teeth marks on my body? I want to go back home. All my determination is dissolving under the sense of being surrounded on all sides by inquisitive eyes. I no longer control my life, another feeling that is slowly turning into panic. No words come out of my mouth.

"Don't be afraid. I won't hurt you. But you have to want it yourself. Do you want the bath?" Solange is edgy. Déméplè is impatient, she told me so herself.

"Yes . . ." I finally answer.

"All right . . . then wait for me here; I'll go heat up the water."

I'm sitting on a low chair in a small room with a dirt floor, a *badji*. I don't believe in the virtues of the bath I'm about to take. I feel completely pathetic, waiting for the gestures of a woman who can neither read nor write, who prepares potions and spells for *macoutes*. Solange lives off the credulity of distraught men and women. And yet here I am, passive, waiting for her. Am I punishing myself? Have I lost all self-respect? The same feelings that terrified me when I went to confession as a child are coming back to me now. Holy images decorate the walls of Solange's *badji*, virgins with black skin and others with white skin. Candles burn in all four corners of the room. A large basin next to me releases a deep perfume, a mixture of basil, lemongrass, orange blossom, mint, and other plants Solange picked in the courtyard, one after the other, a lit candle in her hand. Solange completes her preparations by pouring the contents of a flask, which she takes from a shelf laden with bottles and votive statuettes, into the bathwater.

"The rum is for Déméplè," she says gravely. "He'll drink it in your body. Undress, Neighbor," she adds. "Take everything off."

I comply and sit back down on the small chair, its straw pricking my bottom. Solange takes a metal goblet, dips it in the basin, and pours the liquid slowly over my head. The water flows over my body and disappears into the dirt floor beneath my feet. The scent of the leaves, the candlelight, the smell of rum, the images of black and white virgins. Solange's hand sliding over my hair, my face, my neck; the leaves she applies to my shoulders, my breasts, my stomach. Between my thighs. Solange and her song that accompanies the water over my skin, cupful after cupful. Suddenly a strange thing happens. It's no longer Solange touching me: it's Déméplè; it's Dantòr, the black virgin; Fréda, the white virgin; it's the good Lord and all the saints and all the angels. Deliverance. Like a baby finally heading toward the light after so much suffering. Tears flowed from me. A flood of tears. A sudden tide that surprised me but that I neither could nor wanted to hold back. The water from my eyes mixed with the spicy, leaf-scented water, an offering to sorrow. Increasingly violent sobs shook me completely. A climax of the soul, which for a few seconds freed the shadows that had gathered around my head. I cried for the first time since Daniel's disappearance.

I burned the pages one by one. I even burned the blank pages and the gray canvas cover that stretched over them. As if to erase his absence. Deflect his disappearance. For a few minutes, while the sheets of paper twisted in the teeth of flame, life was as it had been before: bland, predictable, marvelous. A series of days punctuated by the cock's crow early in the morning, picking fruit in my garden, preparing lunch, caring for Marie and Nicolas, and conversations with Daniel, both of us like two planets orbiting the same sun without ever touching. This little notebook never existed; I did not read these words that tried to explain to someone else, someone other than me, the reasons for the unthinkable. Words that swept through my life like a storm, leaving behind constant bad weather. I look through the trees; the weather is actually nice; the light opens its arms to me. I slip into its vastness, far away from here. Since Daniel's absence I've lived in two dimensions at once. Shadow and light. Going from one to the other is very unsettling. A physical jolt that I am learning to control, a shudder, a sudden breathlessness. The leaves of the mahogany tree touched by the breeze trace lines of luminous motion on the ground. Constant motion, like a river's. The smoke irritated my eyes a little. Just like when Daniel smoked his cigars in the house. He finally agreed to only smoke outside. I miss the children. They must be having fun in Paillant. I would like that. I would like for no shadows to be hovering over their enthusiasm for life.

Daniel's story stops here. His whole story is in this mound of ashes at the bottom of a tin pot. I fall into the dimension where it's dark. The light disappears; you'd swear someone turned off a switch. Daniel's funeral. I've just performed the rites for Daniel's funeral. His body has disintegrated; even his bones have yielded to flames. These ashes make me a widow. I am a widow and hated. Arlette was right: I brought nothing but sorrow to her brother's life. And for that I should atone. Cover my face with these ashes like widows in India and immolate myself on the same pyre as Daniel. It would be so good to be done with it, to not feel anything anymore, to not be afraid anymore, to leave the world with its problems, its troubles. I am not Indian, and this river of light flowing over my skin is not the Ganges. Everything I see at this moment calls me to hold on for Marie and Nicolas, to live.

"Marie! Marie, come see! There's a machine in my room that's cooling the air!"

Nicolas searches out his sister to show her his discovery. Marie allows herself to be dragged along, delighted and perplexed at once. My children have returned from Paillant bronzed, their eyes still filled with calm open spaces, the chirping of crickets, and night fog in the pine forest. They seem bigger after only ten weeks away. They were amazed to see Rue des Cigales in its new asphalt dress. When they crossed the threshold, in spite of my joy at seeing them again, I felt an incredible fatigue. They were coming back to the same waiting, the same faceless fear. A few days before they were to leave my mother's I made sure to tell them in a letter that Daniel had still not come home, to lessen the disappointment on returning. They're the ones I feel I'm deceiving, betraying, more than Daniel. Daniel would be able to understand the inexorable detours of my life in his absence, but what can I say to these innocents, how can I protect them if not through lies? At the table Marie asked the question I was expecting, for which I had an answer.

"Where did all these things come from, Mom?"

"Uh . . . you mean . . . the air conditioners and the generator?"

"And the little car, too. It's new, isn't it?"

Marie is waiting for my answer, her eyes wide, the corner of her mouth slightly crimped.

"Yes . . . it's new. Beautiful, isn't it? A friend of the family gave us these things . . . someone who knows your father. He thinks the cool air will soothe us. He also got the public authorities to give us a new car . . . to replace the one that was . . ."

Marie looks at me without seeing me, as if my answer were written on the wall behind me. I sense the alarm going through her soul, her uneasiness, even if she might not be able to define the feelings inside her. I feel them for her. What can the eyes of an almost fifteen-year-old girl understand about the sudden affluence around her? Do we need it? Who is going to manage this new comfort? Why does everything seem to be going well when her father isn't here? I can't answer her questions; I can't tell Marie that sometimes life presents us with trials that seem beyond our strength. That I am living through a trial almost beyond my strength, but that I will do all I can so that she and Nicolas do not see their innocence eaten away by senseless bitterness. I'd like to take Marie in my arms, go back to her infancy, give her the milk from my breasts, nourish her with my words and the warmth of my skin. Like before, when there were no doubts, when we thought life would unfold like a long, tranquil river, free of illness, free of violence, and free of *macoute* dictatorship. I should speak to Marie; I don't want to let difficulty create distance between us just as she is slowly becoming a young woman. I should tell her that life sometimes makes a father vanish, makes him seem dead in the space of a day even though he's still breathing; that a piece of the sun can break away and suddenly the days are dark, and a Secretary of State can emerge from the shadows and change the face of the clock.

"That man must be rich," Nicolas announces.

"Is it a man?" Marie asks. Even though I said the benefactor was a man.

"Yes . . . he's a Secretary of State in the government . . . he came here once . . . you saw him . . . he was waiting for me in the living room."

"Oh! That man . . . I remember him, he has eyes like a toad . . ." Nicolas opens his eyes very wide.

"What's a secretary of state, Mom?"

"An important person who takes care of the affairs of the country."

"You said he knows Daddy?"

"Yes . . . he actually gave me some news about him, because he saw him in person in . . . in . . ."

"In prison!" Nicolas says, cutting to the chase.

Nicolas's innocent cynicism makes me wince, and yet I appreciate his candor, which protects him like armor. Very delicate armor. I would like so much for life's thorns never to scratch you, my son, but how would you know the smell of blood if you were never hurt? My son speaks of prison as he would a passing inconvenience. Surely prison is a place you go for a while when you're bored of your house and your family, that's all. Prison is a punishment like kneeling in a corner or being deprived of dessert.

"Will he let us visit Daddy in prison?"

Marie is already doing the math in her head; she's doing the calculus. A man who is very important and is being friendly to us must have the power to satisfy that wish, even though she has never expressed any desire to visit her father in prison. Marie understands much more than I think.

"I hope so, honey . . . one of these days . . . but it's difficult for families to visit political prisoners . . ."

"Did you know that man before?"

"No, Marie, but he and your father knew each other . . ."

"Does that mean they're friends?"

Friends . . . Hmmm . . . Marie, Marie . . . words have lost their meaning today; they're nothing but empty sounds. You will have to relearn them, and each one will hurt you to the depths of your being. It will be up to you to recreate them, with your strength and your love for life.

"They are . . . sort of . . . yes," I say to my daughter, avoiding her gaze.

"What's a political prisoner?" Nicolas is tearing into a ripe mango, the juice dripping down to his elbows.

"Someone you put in prison because he doesn't agree with the way . . . the . . . leaders are running the country. I already told you, my angel. Watch out, Nicolas, you're making a mess! And I don't want you to repeat any of this outside. Our family business concerns no one but us. Never forget that. Do you understand me, Nicolas?"

Nicolas nods his head yes.

"Will he come back . . . the Secretary of State?"

"Most likely, Marie . . . to give us news about Dad. He promised . . ."

And then summer was over. Marie and Nicolas returned from Paillant just before Cyclone Flora hit, a hurricane the force of which I never thought possible. Port-au-Prince, ravaged, writhed for hours like a woman in labor but gave birth only to cadavers and desolation.

Every time I thought of Daniel in prison, in that chaos of wind and rain, listening to the wild clamor of nature, frozen and alone, I had to keep myself from banging my head against the wall. Flora went away. Christmas passed; New Year's, too. Carnival arrived with raucous refrains demanding lifelong power for the sovereign. People were just waiting for that, for their leader to be nominated for life, eternity even, since he called himself immortal, God's representative on earth. What the people want, God wants. All the rest comes naturally. For the past few months a sudden insanity has blown though the country. Kidnappings, imprisonments, deportations, executions. Every day, every night. In the greatest secrecy, in the greatest silence. No one is safe, even those in the inner circle. From time to time the revolution devours one of its own, sowing trouble and confusion from within. Then the others must prove their allegiance through even more cruelty. They vie with each other to see who can be more zealous and bloodthirsty; they betray their friends.

Diatribes on the radio set the tone. Newspaper columns spoke only of the next landslide, supreme victory. While the government's henchmen swept away the undesirable elements, propaganda stirred the minds of the partisans.

The Secretary of State was right: François Duvalier was named president for life in a referendum whose ballots offered only one choice, a single option: yes, like a long battle cry. A three-day free-for-all marked the victory of the revolution.

Daniel Leroy was kidnapped by *tontons macoutes* because he wrote articles denouncing violations of human rights; assaults on the constitution; the rape and pillaging of women, children, people's property. He was imprisoned at Fort-Dimanche, where men die every day of privation, torture, illness, and despair. This pain, this lack, this sorrow have become ingredients mixed with my blood. They inhabit me; I can't get rid of them; they take my right to live, to sleep peacefully, to laugh, to see an end to my disarray. I feel a cold despair that has transformed the cells of my body. The image of my life has become muddled; I'm waiting for it to become clear again, when Daniel is freed. The dictatorship devours healthy life like a cancer; it seems immortal, eternal; it gets stronger, bolder every day; it gets drunk off its own power. Every man here is a leader, and society is caught in the web of a network of leaders at every level, monitoring their citizens' every breath.

I am Daniel Leroy's wife and the mistress of a *macoute* Secretary of State. Not so long ago if someone had told me that a woman of my acquaintance, in my situation, had accepted such a compromise, I probably would have called her cowardly, mercenary, and lots of other things besides. It's true that I'm a coward; I could have fought, refused, cried out. But I would have been alone, completely alone. Alone in the face of fear. I could have disappeared, been tortured or raped like that journalist a few years ago at the very beginning of the dictatorship, the mother of five children. Daniel spoke of her in his journal. She was taken from her house by hooded men before her children's eyes, beaten and raped, then left for dead in the empty fields of Delmas, a wasteland inhabited by thorn acacias, where victims' remains are thrown. She owes her life to a miracle. I'm not as brave as that woman. Her bravery was of no use to her either. But she and I have had to face fear with different weapons. Now fear sleeps in my bed, I fuck it, I give it pleasure, I profit from its generosity. By submitting to the Secretary of State I am keeping Daniel alive. As for the rest, tomorrow, I don't know. I'm certainly not the only one in this situation, but I don't care about other people. I find no relief or satisfaction in knowing that other people are in my situation. This is about me. I'm the one who goes crazy on certain days. I'm the one who has to close my eyes, my pores, my ears to the condemnation of public opinion. I'm the one who opens my legs and my mouth for the Secretary of State's pleasure, a pleasure that is becoming more demanding and voracious with the passing days and weeks. In the freezing darkness of my room the Secretary of State smothers me with his appetite; he devours me. This situation is a divine aphrodisiac for him that he can administer at whim. But my sex is like earthenware; it retains no trace of infamy; each time I wash it, it's like new.

Ziky . . . is that you? Is it really you, Ziky? Come here! . . . I felt your presence . . . there you are . . . I'm not dreaming. You always slip in with the breeze scented by the orange blossom tree. Where have you been? It's been such a long time . . . I've missed our little night games, you know. Were you afraid of coming to my house, like everyone else? You can visit anytime you like, Ziky, only I can see you. You have nothing to fear; at the slightest noise, you can hide in my head. No . . . I'm not sleeping. I don't sleep much anymore. So many things have happened. Come here . . . lie down next to me, I want to feel you close to me. Are you cold? Yes . . . it's true . . . the air is cooler in my room now. Long story. I don't understand anything anymore, Ziky. People are afraid of coming over, and we're afraid of staying home. Things move around the house like shadows, drafts, rustlings. Eyes follow me everywhere I go. There's a sort of menace in the sound of voices in the street, a car tire exploding, the gate squeaking when it's opened or closed, each little nothing now seems to contain a surge of something, a horribleness. Daniel is everywhere and nowhere. Sometimes I think he's in his study, that I can smell the cigar he smokes every night on the veranda. Mom isn't talking to me much; maybe she's afraid I won't understand what's happening. Yva told me about life in prison. That day I didn't sleep at all. I turned fifteen the day before yesterday; it's been three years since my first period. I'm not a kid anymore, Ziky. This is the first time I've wanted to cry on my birthday.

I didn't want a cake. Mom bought one anyway, as if a cake could make things the way they were before. I had to blow out the candles, but I wanted to cry out my anger and the need to understand. I wanted her to tell me about Daniel, prison, fear. I want to know if he's really suffering, if he's thinking of us. Is Daniel going to die? Will he come back to us? I'd like her to tell me what that Secretary of State is really doing over here. Why is the benefactor taking Daniel's place? I don't want another father; he'll never be Daniel. Mom thinks he's a big shot. Is he going to let us visit Daniel in prison? I have the right to know. But she just tells me things that don't interest me, stories for little girls, as if everything were fine. I want the truth that she whispers to the grownups. The rest of the time she juggles ideas in her head that make her eyes look vacant. Come here, slide under the covers next to me.

I've missed you, my friend. I thought you abandoned me, too. My heart hurts. My heart is as hard as a stone in my chest. Why? Because Daniel went away. He's in prison, Ziky. And the girls at school were avoiding me, as if I smelled bad. Not all the girls, but a lot of them looked at me that way, in a way that made me want to sink into the ground. Mom had a good idea, for Nicolas and me to change schools. There are girls and boys in my new high school. With the boys there's a better feeling, and they teach me things. Daniel didn't do anything; he didn't steal, he didn't kill anyone. Why are they keeping him in prison all this time? You don't know how to answer that, Ziky. I don't hold it against you. I don't cross Rue des Cigales on foot anymore. I'm ashamed, I can tell you that. Why am I ashamed? I don't really know . . . I don't have a father anymore; there's a man sleeping in my mother's bed. One night Daniel didn't come home, and ever since then I haven't been the same. That's the whole story. And a lot of nights have gone by since that night. I'm waiting. But with each passing day I lose a little more confidence, I think maybe Daniel won't come back, and I hate everyone. Except Nicolas and you. I'm mad at my teachers who feel sorry for me; they make me want to cry. I'm mad at my friend Alice because her parents won't let her come visit me. I'm mad at my mother. She's like a phantom, she has no substance; she walks around the house like she's looking for something, but she never finds it. She talks to me as if everything were fine, as if nothing's happened. She's wearing makeup these days. But nothing is fine, Ziky! I'd like to go someplace far away. But I can't. So I live in my own world, in my own way. I don't want to hear any more lies. "Daniel will be back . . . Everything will be fine . . . Be patient, Marie. You have to pray for your father, Marie."

It's funny, Ziky, I feel like a castaway on an island. Even when I'm surrounded by people I'm alone and no one sees it. I don't let anyone come onto my island. When I'm there I understand everything going on around me more. From there I see the lies better. I learn them and I say them in turn. I say everything is going well for me, whereas that's false. I say I'm going to school, but a lot of times I skip class. I'm not afraid of anything anymore. It's like I'm filled with all this freedom: I have the right to think the way I want, to live the way I want; on my island nothing is forbidden. Since Daniel isn't here anymore, everything's allowed. I'm only afraid of myself because I can't just do anything and everything, walk around in the street alone, let myself be touched by boys I don't know, drink Mom's rum at night before I go to bed. Everything is empty and everything is full at the same time. Maybe you'll understand me, Ziky. Maybe you'll tell me why I feel the way I feel. I accept money from the Secretary of State without Mom knowing; I'm only telling you this. He gives me a lot of money. So you can have fun with your friends, he says. But don't tell your mother, he says, with a strange look.

I know it's wrong, but I take it anyway. It's my little secret, like the secrets Mom doesn't tell me. He's taken Daniel's place. He gives us everything—money, food, furniture, the car. My ex-girlfriends salivate with envy whenever they see me go by in Mom's little car. I've made new friends. The Secretary of State lied to us. We're never going to see Daniel in prison. He doesn't like Daniel. I take money from him and I smile at him. The Secretary of State is horrible. He scares me, but I don't let him see that. I tell him lies. He touches my mother's body. When he touches her, he looks at me. At first a kind of anger boiled up in me, and I looked away. Or else I felt my blood coursing more quickly through my veins; my body was hot and cold all over. But I don't feel anything now; I hold his gaze when he plants his hand on her ass. If it pleases her to be touched by him, it's all the same to me. But she shouldn't act like a martyr afterward. Those are lies, Ziky. Once I looked through the keyhole. They make love all the time. As soon as they come into the house they go straight to the bedroom. He's always in a hurry to come and go. I know what they're doing. Nicolas asked me once why they locked themselves in the bedroom; I told him they were praying for Daniel. My little brother believes everything you tell him. I have to protect him. Since Daniel left, he wets the bed. I haven't told our cousins; they would laugh at him.

We have a new car—I told you that, right? Daddy's car disappeared the same day he did. Mom sometimes takes us for rides on certain afternoons. Once I saw her cry as she drove down the street. I like to go to the seaside in the evening. There's the smell of the sea that spreads through the car. And there's also Daniel, he's there. He used to take us to the Fair at the Cité de l'Exposition a lot. And he asked us riddles. And my mother laughed and put her arm around his shoulders. I like looking at all the lights at the seaside. I lean my head against the car window and look at the street lamps and the lights going by, which turn into a single ribbon of light moving away, away, that could go up to the sky and take me with it. They make me dizzy. And I also feel the ocean and all its quiet blue. I imagine my little island lost somewhere in that vast moving expanse.

Nicolas and I would sometimes spend the night with Mom when we were scared. We don't do that anymore. He sleeps with her now, Ziky. When I can't sleep, I drink rum; I replaced the bottle I already drank up. Mom didn't notice. She told us not to worry, that the Secretary of State would protect us. He's very powerful; he always carries a gun. She told us that if he left the house, the *macoutes* might lock us up in prison. I don't want to go to prison, Ziky. I would rather die. But you're here tonight, and I want so much to live. Come here; put your hand there, between my thighs, like you did before. Touch the place where I shake. Your hand is burning me, like cold fire. Don't stay away so long. I'll look for you in every moonbeam. Yes . . . Ziky . . . keep going . . . don't stop . . .

Raoul spends time at my house. The whole town knows it. I've lost most of my old friends because of it and have made new friends because of it. New friends who enjoy the comfort of my home, the hospitality of my table, who sometimes ask, in the hollow of my ear, if I could say a word in their favor, to get rid of a persecutor or forcibly eject a recalcitrant tenant; for a lover, a son, or a father in prison. Daniel's arrest has placed our family in a particular social group. We're not partisans of Duvalierism — far from it. Instead we're its victims, but through one of those outlandish twists of fate, we're surviving thanks to the support of a baron in the regime. This same dictatorship that shattered my home provides me with protection and recourse against the systematic reprisals that relatives of opponents are often subject to, and the arbitrary night raids that terrorize citizens. Port-au-Prince is a town with two faces, a treacherous city. It's beautiful, mutinous, dazzling with its colorful clusters of bougainvillea and bay trees, serene after unexpected showers in the middle of the day, offering its balconies and rocking chairs in the soft light of a languorous afternoon. It also devours human prey; it's a predatory town that bellows every night from its center within the National Palace to announce curfew, hour of every terror.

I've joined the club of *macoute* mistresses, those who enjoy obvious privileges but also know the precariousness of their position in this Haiti where power constantly plays a terrifying game of musical chairs. After a rough patch I've stopped feeling ashamed, avoiding people's glances, torturing myself, condemning myself. Between poverty and comfort I've finally made my choice. To each his own. Raoul is the quintessential, archetypical lover, his power and fortune measured in his mistress's well-being. I couldn't ask for more, given my situation. A *mulâtresse* in need quickly withers, and before long she has to sell herself at a discount. There's no turning back. I can't do anything about the moral bankruptcy, but I want to avoid financial bankruptcy. I've discovered my penchant for defiance, provocation even. I'm coming to terms with myself. I'm no longer little Nirvah Goody Two-shoes who lived quietly in Daniel Leroy's shadow. Now I leave behind a trail of heady perfume and sass. The women who condemn me must certainly fantasize about my sex life with Raoul-the-Beast. And certain men, I'm sure, in spite of their professed disgust and condemnation, would pay dearly to taste the woman favored by one of the most powerful men in the country. I didn't choose the circumstances I find myself in. I'd even say that, in a way, Daniel is responsible for what's happening to us. He exalted in his defense of just causes, but did he think about our vulnerability? Did he take full measure of this government that does not recoil in the face of any obstacle? Aren't the kids and I victims of Daniel's presumptuousness, his recklessness? I love him too much to hold a grudge. Stronger wills than ours have decided the shape of our lives. We've been separated with astonishing violence, without a good-bye. I've had to face it and summon my instinct for survival.

Daniel's relatives are divided into two camps over me, too: those who have crossed out my existence and others who refrain from judging out of friendship or self-interest. You never know, it's always good to have access to authority, a matter of survival. Thank God Arlette no longer sets foot on

Rue des Cigales. That's the only good thing that's happened to me in a long time. She's telling everyone I'm sleeping with a *macoute* in Daniel's bed. Easy. First of all, Raoul got a new bed and bedroom furniture at my request, and second, she never lifted a finger to help get her brother out of jail. Her lover, the major, appears to have gone into exile. The hardest words for me were from my brother, Roger. He didn't judge me — he even said he understood my circumstances — but he would no longer come to my house as long as the Secretary of State was paying my bills. I go visit him myself from time to time, and I bring Marie and Nicolas. The circumstances of my life should not separate me from my one close relative.

The Secretary of State came into our home like rain through an open window. How could I make him stay out? We are doing better financially. Even better than when Daniel was head of the family. The Secretary of State sees to all our needs; he leaves an envelope on my dressing table on the first Monday of every month, always cash. I appreciate his discretion. The bank mortgage is honored every month, the children's school fees are paid regularly. My jewelry box has gotten heavier over the past few weeks. And on top of that he never misses an opportunity to give us little presents, signs of affection, treats and trinkets to make our days sweeter. In the midst of our sorrow there's no need to suffer all sorts of privations and humiliations. And to those who think we should starve to death on top of it, too bad.

Daniel will be released in a year or two, maybe more. According to Raoul. He still doesn't like talking to me about Daniel. I have to extract every piece of information by force or persuasion. If he could magically erase Daniel's memory from my mind, he would be the happiest man in the world. But does he sometimes feel the weight of remorse? What does he feel seeing my children grow up without their father? How can he enter this house and take advantage of the family of a man who is unlearning how to be a man every day? Nirvah... Nirvah, can a person like Raoul, a torturer, a cynic devoted to a bloody cause, have feelings like pity, compassion, guilt? You know very well that he can't. If you want to forget his true nature to retain a shred of sanity, go ahead, do it. But don't ever let yourself believe Raoul has become good just because he's good to you. He has no qualms concerning your husband. Daniel could die in jail; the Secretary of State wouldn't do a thing to prevent it. He bought you; you're his most precious object, and he will destroy any obstacle between him and his own well-being. To this day I've never visited Daniel at Fort-Dimanche. This favor has been denied him, and Raoul told me he could not overrule the decision. He agreed to deliver a letter from me, once; this was at the beginning. Would he have run the risk of putting me in Daniel's presence? Certainly not. In the grip of emotion who knows what confession I would have made to my husband? Would he have run the risk of making me feel keen remorse by placing a wreck of a man before my eyes? I don't think so. I have no contact at all; I just have his word as confirmation that my husband is still alive. Even the rumor mill seems to have forgotten about Daniel's existence. Raoul has promised to have a telephone installed at our house.

Some days I wake with the certainty that Daniel is dead, that Raoul has wrapped me up in a large web of lies all these months to keep his pleasure going, to callously take advantage of me. On those days the old Nirvah awakens, the one who wouldn't trust a man in power, the one who wouldn't be able to accept an obvious compromise. I know Raoul is playing with me. But all of a sudden my mind finds reasons to justify my passiveness and tolerance. It's nice living in

Port-au-Prince. Rue des Cigales has become lovely, laden with flowers, free of dust. Music, the sun, the sea, and love are within reach of every heart. Raoul sometimes takes me out to eat in chic restaurants, at Dan Allen or Vert Galant, and the staff always reserves a special table for him. It feels good to dance in the gardens at the Beau Rivage hotel. I love Issa El Saieh's orchestra; the rumba is a dream. Raoul dances well and when he holds me in his arms his body is seized by trembling that glides under my skin. Why upset the daily routine? Why deprive my thirst for existence these precious drops of life? Why annoy Raoul? And what if he's telling the truth? There are so many political prisoners who have been moldering for years in the jail of the dictatorship. What if Raoul got tired of my jeremiads and left me? He wants me strong, able to rise to the challenges of my life. So many times I almost asked if Daniel was still alive. So many times I wanted to cry out my doubts, tell him I don't trust him, that he makes me sick. I held myself back each time. Deep down inside, I'm afraid that one day, at some point, he'll say yes. Yes he's dead, your Daniel; a bullet in the back of the neck. They threw him into a hole in the ground, a mass grave in an empty field behind Fort-Dimanche. With only young goats to keep him company, to bleat out a few prayers for him. He's dead, leaving you with two kids to raise — your beautiful Marie with her womanly body to feed and keep from the lust of predators, your exceptionally gifted son for whom you could not afford tuition at a decent school — and your sadness, which has gotten lost in digressions of pleasure and buried by people's opinions. You are being buried, too. I'm taking off, my dear. I've had it up to here with your guilt and sniveling.

What will I do then? I lie in wait in a state of calm uncertainty that I don't care to disturb. I prefer not to know, not now. As long as Daniel stays out of our relationship, I will get what I want from Raoul. And we will stay alive.

I have discreetly removed all reminders of Daniel from the bedroom. I finally realized that, for this government, forgetting is a way of getting rid of opponents. Sometimes their total disappearance elicits protests or newspaper articles abroad. They're kept in prison for as long as possible to break their wings, to turn them into zombies so that they abandon any intention of a repeat offense after their release. Raoul assured me that he had two dissidents released last month, friends of his, arrested almost four years ago. But he has to be careful, too; while enjoying complete power, he makes sure not to come across as a renegade. Enemies, the envious, rivals who resent his omnipotence are just waiting for him to slip up. He moves in a world woven with intrigue, fraught with low blows. Things are not easy for anyone, partisans or enemies. Informing has become a national sport. What's more, the madman in power appears to obey occult impulses and mere whim, and is capable of eliminating his most faithful servant overnight. Still, Raoul is sure Daniel is being treated relatively well. He told me that he was hospitalized twice because he went on a hunger strike. That thought is unbearable to me.

The children are not as difficult anymore. Marie is a beautiful young woman of sixteen and has inherited my mother's buxom figure and Daniel's dark complexion. With her long cinnamon hair, she always looks like she's just come in from the sun. I can't believe how much she's changed in two years. She likes going out; she needs to forget. Our house has become a gathering place for a small group of girls and boys, Marie's friends. The offspring of Duvalierist families, for the most part. At our house, we have TV, AC, magazines, the latest records by the Beatles, Johnny Hallyday, Dick Rivers — music the kids love. Marie almost never talks about her father. But I know she hasn't forgotten him. She's awaiting his return, like me.

I would like so much to be closer to her, to understand the movements of her heart, her hopes, her doubts. Sometimes we exchange a glance, and in it there's a flutter of anxiety. Too many unspoken things are building up between us. The words I'd like to say to her are shards of glass that cut my tongue. Can we ever go back to our life from before, get along again as before? Will this wound ever heal?

Nicolas has grown up, unbeknownst to me. I don't know him well, but the love between us doesn't require comprehension. It's a sort of silent, instinctive love that has nothing to do with the sorrows of everyday life. He's still shy around strangers. He's still as affectionate as ever, and his hugs surprise me at the most unexpected moments. He has fewer friends than his sister. I feared my children's judgment for a long time, but their love for me transcends life's cruelty. We've never spoken openly about Raoul or about his presence in our house. When I should've done it, I thought they were still too young to understand; at least that's what I told myself to justify my cowardice. Now that they're bigger it wouldn't be much use. We can't undo what's done; we can't go back to the past. My son draws. It's wild how talented he is. It just happened — one day he started drawing and he hasn't stopped. Raoul pays for his classes; he's already getting attention from experts. Daniel would be proud of him. Raoul is a sort of uncle to Marie and Nicolas. I've discovered another man in him. He's not the uncouth person he appears to be. His overall knowledge is very broad; he's traveled a lot. He hates vulgarity. I love those leisurely moments after making love, when he tells me about his trips, his life experiences. Then I can forget who he is today. Reading is still his favorite pastime, though he doesn't have much time to read. He's also an amateur Hellenist, fascinated by everything having to do with Ancient Greece. He recently gave me a gorgeous illustrated edition of *The Iliad* and *The Odyssey* in three volumes. Marie doesn't like him, she disdains him; she hides it well, but she can't fool me. Raoul promised her a trip to New York this summer if she did well in school. He has a soft spot for Nicolas and spoils him a lot. He's always asking me to watch who the children hang out with. I haven't forgotten what Solange once told me about Raoul's secret garden. But I can't believe the man I know would be attracted to men, much less children. He never seems to get enough of my body, even after all this time. His desire for me is clear the minute he sets foot in the house. Raoul doesn't get in the way of our life; he knows how to stay discreet, and yet he's omnipresent in our home, taking care of everything, anticipating our needs. Sometimes, at dusk, he takes us for a ride to the Bicentennial. I love those long rides along Boulevard Harry Truman, from La Saline to Carrefour. The scent of the sea intoxicates me and takes me away. There is the beautiful, languorous ballet of the palm trees and all the lights in old Port-au-Prince and at the seaside. The casino opens its doors every evening, restaurants start bustling: Africana, and Sunset Chalet, where we go to have ice cream sodas. The hotels get a regular flood of tourists who come to enjoy the sun and beaches of Haiti. I remember the inauguration of the Cité de l'Exposition fairgrounds. I must've been eighteen; it was when Estimé was in office. Daniel and I had just gotten married. We were madly in love. Raoul visits us two or three times a week; those nights he sleeps with me. My bed is cold when he isn't there. I'm starting to believe it's all for the best, and at those moments I recall the infinite sweetness of the days.

Men are devouring me with their eyes, especially the old ones, the ones Daniel's age. They look at me everywhere I go, and their glances make me feel more alive. They make me feel warm under my skin. I'd like the entire world to adore me the way Daniel adored me. I'd like to be a movie star with tons of delirious fans at my feet. I read in *Nous Deux* that BB shot her first film at my age and was already successful. Why not me? But nothing happens around here. If I lived someplace else, Paris or New York maybe . . . Girls my age pale in comparison to me. My friends at school call me a mix of angel and devil. It's true that I'm beautiful; I look like Mom, but that's where any resemblance ends. In other words, there are nothing but misunderstandings between us.

I've been sleeping with Raoul since I turned fifteen. It happened one day when I stayed in bed because of a cold. Raoul happened to come by the house; Mom went shopping in her little car. He came into my room to chat, asked how it was going at school, and left. Thirty seconds later he came back into the room, eyes wild, hands on fire. He jumped on me like an animal. I struggled, wordlessly, without complaining. He was panting like a bull. Saliva ran down his chin. He slapped me twice; my head buzzed like a hive, it was the first time I tasted blood in my mouth. He was right about me, I ended up giving in; my strength gave out. He hurt me, and I bled. Afterward, I was lying there, incapable of moving. With his white handkerchief he wiped the blood and slime flowing from between my legs and put it in his pocket. Then he excused himself; he seemed even more terrified than I was. Everything happened so fast—a brutal, unexpected assault, a flash of pain, then nothing.

For several days I thought the pain and shame could be read on my face, that everyone could see it and condemn me. Condemn me of what? It's funny, but I felt I was guilty of something. Raoul Vincent hurt me, and I was upset at myself. I seemed to deserve what had happened to me. Like I deserved to have a father in prison. Otherwise why all this rotten luck in my life? A current that only I knew about swept me away. I had to hold onto something, resist the current. I held onto Raoul. I didn't go to my mother; she didn't notice anything, didn't see it. And I was mad at her for not understanding the cry for help in my eyes. Mom found a balance she negotiated with herself; she decided to believe that life was not so bad, that she could live without too much worry in the cool shade of her house on Rue des Cigales. She applied the same principle to the *macoute* peace. As long as you didn't make those men angry by going on strike or handing out tracts, the chances of injury were small. Daniel did not accept that principle. I heard him talk about the disappearance of schoolchildren and students, but I had my share of sadness; I lived in the most secret recesses of my flesh. The days pass with their small pleasures; at night, there are gunshots; we don't make waves. Waiting for Raoul filled her life during the fake wait for Daniel. Why tell her the Secretary of State raped me? I don't want to see my mother's undoing; she was already hiding her defeat so poorly in my eyes. There would be too much confusion in the atmosphere. She was living two lives, one where she waited for Daniel and the other where she enjoyed being the mistress of the Secretary of State. I found myself at the intersection of those two lives, a neutral place where we ignored our feelings, talked about dresses, outings, grades, Sunday mass, and coming home early on curfew days. I knew the outlines of my existence very well and had to struggle every day to keep them from closing in on me and crushing me. And time passed. I started to ask myself if I'd really been raped. Had I imagined that scene, had I really heard the panting that took what was left of my innocence? My innocence . . . it seems like I lost it light-years ago. Ziky doesn't come through my window like the scent of orange blossom anymore. The little friend I imagined as a child seems so remote and ridiculous to me now. I was in a sort of fog for a long time, constantly asking myself questions about myself. Asking myself how I felt, if I was supposed to go on living, how the sun could continue to rise every morning and then set at night after what had happened to me. But there you go. It was over. The days went by, and the damned sun followed its path from dusk to dawn. I was no longer the same, and I didn't die. Was that what it meant to be a woman? The great adult mystery? Pretty disappointing the first time. The second time was less painful; I didn't fight it, and Raoul held me like a child, coddling me like a baby. His presence and smell terrified me, but when I closed my eyes everything was fine; I just listened to the echoes of my body filling my head. A long sigh rose up from my skin, freeing me. And I learned how to like what he was doing to me; after a few encounters my hands anticipated his desires. I was a good student, the kind teachers like. And then I saw that I could control him with my body. In the end, men are not so bad. To think I was so afraid of Mr. Secretary of State. The whole reputation they give him, I don't see why. If I don't show up at one of our appointments, he's sad for days. If I want to get something from him I sulk, and in the end he always gives in. Sometimes Mom asks me not to be so unpleasant with him; what a joke. He's jealous of me and of my friends who come to the house. I organize little parties from time to time; he doesn't like that. I have a boyfriend he hates, he warns me about him; he knows his family, social climbers, he says. I like Anthony a lot; he's handsome, he makes me laugh, and he likes to have fun, like me.

Sometimes I think about Daniel. Thinking about him opens a huge hole in my chest. I refuse to imagine his life. Can it be that we live in the same country? Raoul promised me he would do everything in his power to free him. I don't believe him; he wants to keep us, Mom and me and Nicolas, for himself. We have betrayed Daniel with our bodies, our thoughts, our acts; even the house is forgetting him a little bit more every day.

Raoul Vincent didn't like the boy. He didn't like his troubled eyes, his lovely, expressionless face, his reserve, which could come across as arrogance or disdain. He didn't like his frail puberty, his long, skinny limbs, his corn-straw hair. Nicolas was not a real young man in the making. With Marie he knew what to expect from the start. That little flame of defiance in her eyes said so much about her deep nature. A girl spoiled by her father, whom Nirvah could no longer connect with when things got hard. Marie's rebellion found a complex outlet in her mother, who symbolized all the injustice in the world. It had been easy for Raoul to play on that emotion to achieve his goals with the teenager. Marie was part angel, part devil; a young rebel; a survivor who showed up and meant business. She resembled him in a way. She inspired him with her boldness, reignited his taste for conquest. Since conquering Marie, he'd been on top of the world. Nicolas remained an enigma, though. His revolt remained internal. Asthmatic and fragile, he seemed not to want to leave the land of childhood, despite being thirteen. Maybe this was his way of escaping reality. Withdrawn, he lived in a secret universe. The boy watched Raoul live with his mother intimately; he observed him from a distance, speaking to him rarely or through an intermediary, but no real exchange had taken place between them since Raoul began coming to the house on Rue des Cigales. What disturbed Raoul most was not knowing what the boy really thought of him. The Secretary of State reacted much better when faced with an enemy; he understood hatred and how to exploit it. But indifference upset and annoyed him. For Nirvah he'd made an effort to take an interest in Nicolas. He'd given him a bike, which the nonathletic boy never used, and a wristwatch, the latest model, which the child never wore. Nicolas only cared if someone showed an interest in his sketches, his drawings, his only passion. His talent as a draftsman was asserting itself more and more. Raoul Vincent paid for lessons with a noted and rather eccentric painter and provided all the necessary art supplies. He did it for Nirvah — Nicolas was her soft spot. She loved this boy with a limitless love, while demanding that he meet excessively high scholastic standards. She stifled him, prevented him from becoming a man, a real man, the Secretary of State thought. Raoul Vincent was sure he no longer desired men. Anyway, Nicolas, this frail thirteen-year-old with teenage acne, was not one yet. Still, the boy oddly reminded him of the adolescent he had been, at a loss in the face of life. Their stories had few similarities, but they did share an adolescence taken over by cruelty and the uncertainty of days. Almost unwillingly, the Secretary of State had written off that time in his early youth when men had introduced him to the pleasures of the flesh. His uncle, hoping to help his father, introduced him to a respected figure in Port-au-Prince society. He was asked to sponsor the boy, who was bright in school but whose future was hobbled by poverty. The man agreed; Raoul Vincent started attending a private parochial school in the capital and successfully passed his final exams. He paid for his benefactor's largesse with his body; he was brought to a private club for homosexuals. Among them there were brutes and perverts. But those men could no longer recall their exploits with the young pubescent, now an all-powerful Secretary of State — their lips had been sealed forever in death. Those who remembered made sure to avoid prosecution by Duvalier's strongman, choosing amnesia in order to survive. It's true that he was loved by men and, until his early twenties, carnal pleasures came only from ambiguous exchanges with bodies similar to his own. By force of sheer will, sustained by his great ambition, he succeeded in surmounting that penchant, repressing those impulses, which did not suit his future plans and a strongman's virile image. The spirited, resourceful young lawyer who saw the revolution of 1946 as a golden opportunity to make his way in the world and position himself in politics, discovered a voracious taste for women, though it surprised him to learn that he couldn't come without violence. Yes, Raoul Vincent no longer desired men; he no longer indulged in this practice, the shameful memory of which he hid like a stigma. And precisely because Nicolas was not yet a man, the heat that traveled to his extremities and the tremors that traveled to his groin when his glance intersected with the boy's could not stem from this ancient need, which he had mastered so long ago. He attributed his reaction to vaguely paternal feelings mixed with curiosity about a bourgeois boy who knew nothing of life—the real life of the average Haitian, born with the odds stacked against him. His myopic eyes behind thick glasses made him seem slightly pathetic. That's all it could be, nothing else.

It started one evening when Nicolas asked if he would help with the translation of a Greek text, his homework for the following day. This request took Raoul by surprise. Why him? Why now? The child truly seemed to be struggling; the request had been hard for him to make. Raoul sought out Nirvah with his eyes, and she smiled at him, encouraging him to respond. Nirvah often blamed herself for Nicolas's coolness toward Raoul. Her son's gesture perhaps meant that he was growing up, letting go of his repressed resentment toward the man who, for reasons that were unclear, was taking the place of his father. The child's gesture soothed her conscience a bit. Nicolas so needed a father, a role model; if Raoul wanted to give him a little attention, he could play that role, even temporarily, Nirvah thought. Raoul liked Greek. When he studied humanities, he read Latin and Greek texts in the original; he took smug pleasure in immersing himself in the history of ancient Greece, its gods and myths, its heroes and philosophers, with whom he identified.

In the end the Secretary of State agreed to the boy's request. They shut themselves up in a small room adjacent to the living room, so as to work far away from the noises of the house. Against a backdrop of vague sensations, Raoul revisited his first notions of the language that had brought philosophy, art and architecture, music, medicine, mathematics, and astronomy to western civilization. He remembered the quotation by André Chénier, the epigraph of the first chapter of his Greek textbook in high school: *Un langage sonore aux douceurs souveraines, le plus beau qui soit né sur des lèvres humaines.*[4] Raoul explained the elements of grammar to Nicolas. He clarified patiently and in simple terms the use of the real, the unreal, the eventual, the potential, and the iterative in Greek syntax.

Without knowing it, the kid brought him back to a time of terrors and wonders, discoveries and sorrows. Nicolas was an extremely intelligent boy hobbled by his fearful nature. He just had to be put at ease for the best to be brought out of him. Raoul Vincent understood this and was very careful not to antagonize him. Nevertheless, Nicolas was nervous during

4. A sonorous language with sovereign tones,
   the loveliest one human lips have intoned.

the entire lesson and tried to keep himself as far away from Raoul as possible. They spent almost two hours together.

Erômenos ... The Secretary of State could not get that word out of his head as he watched Nicolas produce a clean copy of his work, bent over his notebook. Time seemed to leap backward. Everything came back to him—his adolescence, his dreams, his troubles, the stifled ambiguity, the swallowed revolt. He saw himself in Nicolas's innocence, and old feelings brought him under with new force. The little desk lamp threw golden light on the boy's chestnut hair, highlighting his thick lashes. Raoul was moved by his bitten nails, his habit of biting his lower lip to concentrate. The same heat radiated to his limbs, the same tingling sensation was felt in his groin. He devoured the child with his eyes. His throat was dry. *Erômenos*, the beloved. The clarity of it appeared with burning urgency. He would make Nicolas his beloved, as in the noble tradition of the Greek aristocracy. He would be his *erastês*, his mentor, his lover. He would teach him about life, politics, pleasure; instill in him a taste for beauty, quality. A man was needed to bring the man out of this child, to pull him from the *gynaeceum* that his home had become, and from the two women who overprotected him. For several centuries, from Crete to Sparta, from Athens to the islands of the Aegean sea, from Anatolia to the shores of Sicily, from the south of France and Spain to northern Africa, the practice of intergenerational love was the quintessential pedagogical medium for elite boys ages twelve to eighteen. Raoul Vincent reviewed the images engraved on amphora, cups, and antique bas-reliefs showing beautiful young men lying beside their mentors, who were in charge of their education on every level until the boys were no longer pubescent. An *erômenos* accompanied his *erastês* to gymnasiums, symposiums, special festivals, and banquets. The adolescent wore a tunic that went to midthigh, under which he was naked. He would bring Nicolas out of his shell, give him the confidence he was lacking. Raoul Vincent was afraid for a moment. Doubt, like a heavy cloud, passed through the sky of his anticipated happiness. Had he been taken over again by the demon of homosexuality, with a child no less? Was he submitting to those drives that both repelled and fascinated him in his early years? Did he have a subconscious need to make this innocent boy undergo the same treatment he had? No . . . All that was long ago. Abject pleasures, promiscuity, lust, violence, that was in the past. Any spirit of revenge was in the past. Was this pederasty then? Perhaps . . . but in the noblest sense of the term. It was an intergenerational exchange in the great rite of passage toward eloquence, physical strength, and knowledge. Sexual penetration between an *erastês* and his *erômenos* was quite rare. On the other hand, they indulged in stroking and erotic rituals that led to ecstasy in a much more refined manner. The Greeks had raised this tradition to the rank of a civic virtue and had set up a detailed codification of the question. Plato, Socrates, and many other philosophers of classical Greece left pages of commentary on the practice and its usefulness in society. Even their gods engaged in it. Zeus kidnapped Ganymede and made him his companion in pleasure. Achilles and Patroclus were lovers. Heracles took his nephew Iolaus as an *erômenos*, a young traveling companion who helped him sever the nine heads of the Hydra one after another. Raoul now felt a great tenderness toward the teenager. He only wanted the best for him. But he had to begin by winning him over, putting him at ease, subtly awakening in him an awareness of his blood, arousing the curiosity of his sex. No doubt nature was already starting to manifest itself in his body, by way of wet dreams and early morning erections. Raoul was already thinking of ways to spend time with him in the private context of their new relationship. Raoul promised to grant Nicolas one hour, twice a week, for two or three weeks, to go over the basic elements and general rules of Greek, get him caught up with the class. At the end of these sessions Raoul was sure he could get Nicolas to relax, arouse him sufficiently, and meet with him outside the house. Don't be afraid of anything, my little one. I will teach you about friendship, real friendship, the kind that unites men for life. I will be able to free you from fear. I will bring you to the edges of rapture, and you will do the same for me. You will be my beloved. And I will be your lover.

Maggy inserts the last bite of dessert into her mouth and furrows her brows. She takes a swig of cola, wipes her mouth with her napkin, burps, sighs, and leans back to rock in the rocking chair. The bracelets on her wrists clatter. Now she's going to talk to me; the light is right.

"They're saying strange things in town, Nirvah . . . about your family . . ."

"Maggy, my dear . . . I've become immune to gossip. You know, otherwise, I'd be dead. But I agree with you, I live a strange life."

I was sort of expecting these words. Since she got here, her face told me she was harboring dark thoughts. How I'd love not to hear them! My detachment does not convince her; something is really bothering her. It's Sunday afternoon. Maggy has had lunch with me, as she does almost every Sunday. We've sprinkled some rum liqueur over our sweet-potato pudding, which Yva has made to perfection. A gentle languor makes my eyelids heavy, my joints sluggish. The house is quiet. Marie is at a picnic with friends at Mer Frappée, and Nicolas is spending the day with his cousins at his uncle Roger's. Raoul rarely visits us on Sunday. Why come disturb the tranquility of my afternoon with idle gossip? But Maggy will not shut up; there comes a time when certain words have to be said.

"You know me, Nirvah . . . Even though my beauty shop is a hotbed of gossip, I always take these stories with a grain of salt, a certain skepticism. It's not even fun anymore to see these ladies smear each other with their toxic shit. But this time . . .

I think you should be careful. It's about your children."

Alarm. I sit up on my chaise longue.

"Who's talking about my children?" My voice is suddenly high-pitched.

"Hmmm . . . They're saying that . . . Raoul . . . is abusing Marie and maybe even Nicolas . . . in your house. It was like a bomb, Nirvah. I swear! I had to stop working for a few minutes and drink a little cold water to pull myself together. Your children are my children. Nicolas is my godson. We have to . . ."

"Stop . . . Maggy, stop. Am I understanding this? They're saying Raoul is sleeping with Marie and Nicolas? Here?"

"Yes, that's what they're saying . . . At least that's what I heard two clients say to each other very clearly as they got their manicures."

I burst out laughing. I have to laugh to expel the violent emotions squeezing my throat like the hands of an assassin trying to strangle me. Maggy looks at me, troubled; she smiles in turn, confused; she was not at all expecting my reaction. Finally, I stop.

"I'm glad you told me about it, Maggy. Do you see how far Haitian perversity can go? Deep down, that's what they'd like. They'd like to see me destroyed; they'd like to know I was shattered. I resisted the blows of fate, and they can't forgive me for it. I have to bite the dust. That's why they're attacking my children, what I have that is most precious to me. My God!"

"Well, in any case, be careful, Nirvah. Raoul is not a saint. Because of the circumstances, you're obliged to . . . see him . . . but we know his reputation. Have you noticed anything suspicious about his relationships with them?"

"No, Maggy . . . Nothing. Nothing at all. Raoul is fairly strict with Marie, he worries about the people she sees. I even asked him once, jokingly, if he wasn't a little jealous of my daughter. She doesn't like him; she makes him feel unwelcome in the house. Raoul tries to win her acceptance by giving her all sorts of little presents. It's not an easy situation to deal with. You'd never believe it, Maggy, but even Nicolas is a little more accepting of him now. Raoul spent three weeks helping him catch up with his Greek. Since then, their interactions in the house have been much more relaxed. Nicolas is becoming more open to his surroundings; it probably has to do with adolescence. He's growing up so fast! It was about time there was a little less tension in the house. Did I tell you Raoul is also paying for Nicolas's drawing lessons twice a week?"

"Oh, yeah?" Maggy says, perplexed. "Who's giving him lessons?"

"Oh . . . a painter, a sort of very talented eccentric; he doesn't live far from here. Nicolas can walk to his studio, it takes him about twenty minutes."

"Hmmm . . . well . . . I hope you're right not to worry, Nirvah . . . I've heard of several cases of fathers or stepfathers who have abused young children in their own homes."

"But, Maggy, where, when, how?" I shout. "I'm always here whenever he comes over!"

Maggy looks at me with empty eyes, at a loss for an argument. But she soon starts up again: "Who knows what schemes can be hatched in a mind that's . . . perverse? You leave the house from time to time, after all. You . . . like to pray in church and on Friday afternoons you spend at least two hours at the beauty parlor . . . You go shopping on a regular basis. I know that, Raoul knows that. Maybe he lures them to other places. I admit it's crazy, but . . ."

"No, Maggy. Raoul is busy. He doesn't have time to run after children."

"So maybe you should let him know about these rumors, just to see his reaction."

"So you think . . . this horrible thing could be possible?"

"I don't know, honey. But anything is possible in this world of ours. I hope with all my heart this is just the idle gossip of vicious women. But . . . only you can protect your children."

I breathe in deeply to ward off my tears. My friend is relieved to have gotten these words off her chest. She had to warn me; now her conscience is clear, she's leaning back in her rocking chair, but I can tell she's still tense.

Once past the shock of the news, for a moment I have no reaction, my mind empty, disoriented. Like a key, Maggy's words open a box buried within me. My pleasure with Raoul. My sweet shame. The pleasure he infused me with night after night in the cool bedroom, possessing my body front and back, often assaulting me. The unexpected dimensions of pleasure I found in submission to this man. Including his ugliness, which thrills me in a way that is obscene. Even the scent of him intoxicates me, before he even touches me. Raoul taught me how to be a woman, to seek satisfaction in my flesh, to reclaim it to the point of leaping into the unknown. He says things to me that make me go pale with shame, words that consume my body. I didn't know such intense pleasure was possible; I didn't believe in it. I was content with the little shivers of joy that my teenage loves brought me. Until Raoul's arrival in my life, I knew no erotic pleasures aside from those I learned by marrying Daniel around seventeen. I give Raoul everything. I agreed to tarnish my reputation, lose close friends, look like a renegade in the eyes of society. Why does he need to destroy my children's innocence on top of it all?

I remember Solange and her crazy offer to protect Marie and Nicolas with spells to make their bodies inaccessible. It was at the very beginning of Raoul's presence in my life. I visited Solange, and out of the blue she offered to work on the children, to protect them from *lusts*, she said. She hadn't mentioned any names, but I knew she was thinking of the Secretary of State. Another sinkhole under my feet. I could not have subjected my children to that sort of treatment. Because I don't believe in it and also because I felt capable of defending them myself. Even though I go to Solange's courtyard, I don't want to get caught up in the trap of her beliefs, in spite of their appeal. I have to keep a level head. Daniel would never forgive me. Solange knows the human soul well — every day she observes its impulses, yearnings, wanderings, and perversities. She predicted an inherent danger in Raoul's proximity to our lives. And what if she was right? Now that Maggy has told me what people are saying about us, I'm like marble. I have to keep calm; these stories are just lies, fabricated nonsense, malicious gossip, a bunch of crap, nothing else. Anyway, how could anyone know what's going on in my house? That information could only come from Raoul himself. Raoul? Abusing my children and talking about it in town? There's also the staff at home. Maybe Tinès, Auguste's replacement? He was hired by Raoul to take care of the generator, among other things. Now I could see that above all Raoul wanted eyes and ears in my home, to know about comings and goings, visitors. I pretended I knew nothing. What else could you expect from this Secretary of State in the Ministry of Defense and Public Safety, the head of the government's secret police? Tinès is mild-mannered, he does his work, the house is clean, but he has darting eyes. Any leak would have to come from him. Yva is devoted to me, I'm sure of it. Did the children themselves confide . . . What am I talking about? There's no way I'll entertain the vicious comments of bitter people in my head. Marie and Nicolas are fine. Raoul respects my children.

I didn't feel the wave of nausea come on. My stomach was wrenched by a brutal spasm, and my mouth suddenly filled with bile, telling me disaster was imminent. I ran to the bathroom, my hand pressed to my lips, but I couldn't hold back my lunch, which rose in violent surges and spread all over the tiled floor.

The Secretary of State had prepared everything, planned it all out. He had no trouble convincing his friend the painter, Wilhelm Saint-Amand, to allow him an hour with Nicolas during the drawing lessons. Saint-Amand, who owed the Secretary of State several favors, did not have to be coerced. The two men understood each other with half a word, a single look. A room in the house had been completely rearranged in preparation for these educational encounters. The room, situated at the heart of the old wooden house, was protected from the intensity of the sun; it stayed pleasantly cool all day long and was bathed in soft light. The leaves of the mango and mahogany trees, which made their way in through the windows, rustled gently with every breeze. Engravings of images from Greek antiquity adorned the walls, now repainted mint green. They portrayed beautiful boys with curly hair attending sporting events in the nude or going to festivals, eating and drinking and lying beside bearded men who were obviously older. The Secretary of State took great pains to find these images and enlarge them.

At the Secretary of State's first, supposedly accidental visit to the drawing teacher's house, Nicolas tensed up, despite Raoul's preparations during their sessions on Greek grammar and composition. Nicolas was torn between two forces of equal weight. The force of the shadows into which his life had slipped since his father's absence. Shadows in which his body, his mind, his impulses had gotten caught. His only lifeline in this troubled world was his mother. But then for a while came the force of optimism in Raoul Vincent's glittering words, in the confidence this man had in him, in the immense world he opened up for him, far from the pettiness and fear of everyday life. A force of redemption scarcely impeded by his doubts and troubles. Nicolas, like his mother, like Marie, was living through a time of shadow and light, unaware that the salutary light fell from a dark star.

With tact and skill, Raoul convinced the boy to join him in the bedroom for the first time and spend a moment talking there, like father and son. He spoke of his work, his heavy responsibilities; he recounted the history of Haiti: the true history, not the one reproduced in pamphlets trafficked by false historians. Nicolas drank in the Secretary of State's words, overwhelmed by the interest this very important man — now his friend — was taking in him. Raoul had already predicted a career for him in medicine or law, and — why not? — a future in government. The current one would be there for decades. With each encounter the child's suspicions diminished a bit. Each encounter was a small victory for the Secretary of State, a stroke, an ambiguous word whispered in an ear, a confidence wrested from the child about his teenage fantasies. For fun Raoul sometimes asked him to describe the scenes depicted in the engravings decorating the room's walls; his heart beating, he took pleasure in the halting words that came out of the beloved and very desired mouth.

The man felt, in his blood and in his flesh, that today would be the right day. He thought the boy was ready to move to a decisive stage in his apprenticeship, to cross the threshold of a new dawn. Everything about the day — the light, the air, even the song of the vendors in the street below — told him the cosmic configuration of the moment was favorable.

From a vase on an antique cabinet set against a wall at the back of the room, white lilies, symbols of purity, released an intoxicating perfume. Next to the flowers three white candles burned in a bronze candelabrum. The Secretary of State had used patience; he had taken great pains to restrain the hunger of his hands, to control the eagerness of his lips, the impulses of his body, in order to put the boy at ease and win his trust and friendship. Above all he didn't want to rush him. He made him swear to keep their special friendship a secret. The women would certainly not understand. The Secretary of State was dancing on a wire and felt the vertigo and euphoria of an aerialist. He also felt he was the very soul of a juggler, keeping several plates in the air, switching things around to satisfy his fantasies. The beautiful edifice of his dreams could topple in an instant. Because of a simple lapse he could lose everything—Nirvah, Marie, Nicolas, the house on Rue des Cigales. His life. Playing this game, the Secretary of State burned with anticipation and the electricity of withheld pleasure. Each conquest he made in the Leroy family made him more powerful, more daring, more appealing. And this little game transported him; it made him love Marie more ardently; it kept him awake at night, even when he slept in Nirvah's bed. The thought of the boy sleeping peacefully in his room, a few steps away, within reach of his feverish hands, made him reel.

The Secretary of State undressed and with great tenderness helped Nicolas take off his clothes. He carefully pulled back the exquisitely delicate, off-white, crochet bedspread. Sitting at the edge of the bed, he had the boy straddle his thighs, facing him. On the nightstand there was a bottle of red wine, a silver cup, a flask of sweet almond oil, and a bright-white handkerchief. Raoul was going to fulfill the promise made to the boy so many times, which he had led him to anticipate.

In the great tradition of the sons of noble Greek families, his mentor, with his paternal hands, would today acquaint him with sublime ecstasy. His forehead damp, his breath short, the Secretary of State filled the goblet with wine, brought it to the child's lips, and made him take a sip, and then another. He never took his eyes off Nicolas. He swallowed the rest of the wine and then slowly rubbed the palm of his right hand with a little sweet almond oil. The man swallowed several times in a row; saliva kept flooding his mouth.

The seconds flew by lightly, like the wings of a butterfly drunk on light. When in a long, astonished shudder the boy reached the heights of pleasure for the first time, Raoul Vincent, wild with joy, rushed to collect the precious nectar in his immaculate white handkerchief.

Almost two weeks with no news from Raoul. No news from Daniel. I'm worried. The Secretary of State has been taking frequent trips to the countryside for the past few weeks. The last time we saw each other he told me a guerilla movement had been located in the southwest. A big manhunt had been launched. I hope he doesn't get sick traveling over potholed roads and living in precarious conditions, in discomfort and heat. Yet one more attempt to overthrow the dictatorship that will end in blood and harden the repression everywhere in the country. The farmers receive supplies of machetes. Riled up by armed men who come from Port-au-Prince, they go off in search of people they do not know, who perhaps wish them well but whom they fear. They will kill them because they have no other alternative—kill or be accused of complicity. They're even more afraid of the cruelty of the men in power than of the weapons of the invaders. Even if *macoutes* steal their land, the deeds to their property, their workers, their wives, they defend a cause that is fatal to them but elicits a perverted patriotism in their heads. They're defending the territory . . . the fatherland. What is it with these young invaders chasing martyrdom? They're like Daniel, with a thirst for justice but a profound naïveté in the face of human perversion. They're most often betrayed by their own brothers in arms or strung along by the American secret service. Raoul is in a position to know. The Americans are playing a cynical little game, claiming to support the government of the dictatorship in its hunt for communists and at the same time luring young men to camps in Florida who will then be butchered in our hillsides by cannibal machetes. I wonder which fate would have been better for Daniel: to rot in prison or be hunted down by *macoutes* in the hills? A slow death or a quick death? Knowing him, he surely would have preferred to fall with his weapon in hand. My God, you didn't even give him a choice in his suffering!

Since Maggy told me about the rumors concerning Raoul's alleged activities with my children, I haven't seen her again. I look at Marie differently. Is it possible she's submitting to this man's outrageous behavior and not talking to me about it? What is in those big, innocent eyes that I can't read? Is it possible Nicolas is being profoundly hurt, body and soul, and I know nothing about it? Certainly not! I would have sensed it in their fractured laughter; my heart would have heard the wails of their ruined childhood. How could I have failed so pitifully in the duty to protect my offspring? I'll confront Raoul. That's the only way to deal with the doubt Maggy has planted in my head. I'm not mad at Maggy, but I truly don't need this poison in my life. I'm becoming obsessed and ill. What am I going to do? What words am I supposed to use to ask if he's been abusing my children under my own roof? Raoul, are you forcing Marie and Nicolas into perverse and degrading relations? Raoul, are you traumatizing my children? Raoul, are you cheating on me with my children? Hmmm . . . My God! Could it be I've come to this? What will his reaction be? He's violent at times, and in such an unpredictable way. Like that time more than a year ago, when I mentioned the demolished newspaper's premises now inhabited by squatters. Raoul shrugged his shoulders as if to say that all that was part of the natural course of things, that the squatted premises would serve as an example to everyone, communist or not, who contested the government's legitimacy. That day I couldn't hold back; with words I couldn't control, I spat out my disgust and repulsion to his face. I reeled from the massive slap he gave me, and then Raoul left the house in the middle of the night. I didn't see him again for a week. I was afraid he wouldn't come back. Life would no longer be livable without this contentious presence in our lives. How could I face my financial obligations without Raoul? I didn't have a penny to my name. How could I confront the hardness of the days and the meanness of other people without his fearsome presence, like a guard dog at my front door? How would I get through the nights in my freezing bedroom without his heavy desire and the obscure joys he brought me?

Jocelyn drove through the west entrance, paved with round stones and framed by terra-cotta bricks, and parked at the end of the drive in front of the bay windows of the offices. Two bodyguards quickly got out of the car, and one of them opened the back door. As he started to extract himself from the vehicle, Raoul Vincent felt a counterweight push him back inside. This feeling disturbed him in the extreme. It had just undone all the assurance he had gathered from his brief stay in Chardonnières, his village in the south of the country, during which he'd offered a large sacrificial ceremony to his family's spirits and to Sogbo in particular. A black bull, a young goat, a few black pigs, and a surplus of fowl had been slaughtered in three days, and the drums almost never stopped beating. With this formality fulfilled, the lucky bath received, and the spells recited by his uncle, the voodoo priest, Raoul Vincent left, taking with him the solid illusion of invincibility. Not for long, alas. He'd just seen that. The enemy was lying in wait. Potent antagonistic forces were trying to block his path. But he would prevail. It took a lot more than that to rattle him. God knows he wanted to live, live a long time. He thought of Nirvah, Marie, and Nicolas. His true family. His recent occupations kept him far from that little world, which had become indispensable to his well-being. But he knew that many years of happiness lay ahead. The Secretary of State was devising a plan, the mere thought of which filled him with joy. He would become Nirvah Leroy's legitimate husband.

To achieve this, only two obstacles had to be overcome. First, legally separating from his current wife—weren't they already separated in fact? With his contacts in the legal world and his political power, it would be done in no time. As for Daniel Leroy, he would either die in prison, or the Secretary of State would take it upon himself to end his suffering. In either case Nirvah would be better off, he knew that. It was too beautiful a dream . . . but not an impossible one. Nirvah was the woman he needed, the most beautiful *mulâtresse* in the country, her two gorgeous children an added bonus. Why not? Even François Duvalier harbored the secret dream of marrying his two daughters off to mulattos, or even white men. Otherwise, why all the fuss around Mohamed Fayed, that Arab businessman who got the red-carpet treatment for weeks in the capital? That so-called millionaire came out of nowhere, traipsing back and forth to the palace, traveling with a military escort. Marie-Denise Duvalier was already crazy about him, and Mama Simone treated her future son-in-law like royalty. François Duvalier offered him the keys to the city, Haitian nationality, and control over the country's customs. With the utmost discretion, Secretary of State Vincent inquired among diplomatic sources for information on the presidential family's new guest; nothing had been sorted out at that point. In fact, it was the first time he'd seen the chief of state act so breezily. But no one dared try to reason with him.

Raoul Vincent had not been to the National Palace in two weeks. By naming him chief of the special commission in charge of reprisals against *kamoken*, the president had personally asked him to make a bloody example of the city of Jérémie after the takeover attempt by Young Haiti's bourgeois rebels. He'd recommended making an impression on the entire county, creating an event no one would forget in a hundred years. Raoul Vincent had orchestrated the brutal execution of several families with a link to the rebels. After it was over, Duvalier's vengeful horde left Grand'Anse drained of blood. The mulatto dissidence had been nipped in the bud.

When he was not on a mission in the country's interior the Secretary of State came to the National Palace every day, for matters of the greatest importance relating to the country's security. He met religiously with the chief of state, most often alone, to report on the citizens' state of mind and to reveal all he knew about the plots being hatched to overthrow his government. Even when the president's health was visibly failing, he insisted on evaluating the forces himself and, as if on a giant chessboard, moved human pieces through this Haiti of which he wished to be absolute master. The doctor-president was obsessed with increasing the number of *macoutes*. This paramilitary corps was his thing, his creation, which he had fashioned with the love and patience of a goldsmith. And he had no qualms calling on a detachment of American marines for a while to give his guinea fowls military training and instill a code of fidelity in them. Still, he'd had to go to great lengths to expel a marine colonel from the country who'd lost all sense of measure and thought himself above authority. With his men and women in their coarse, blue uniforms, Duvalier feared nothing. They wore the rough fabric of Papa Zaka and symbolized the earthly force of that peasant god. Duvalier used the dark side of his own beliefs against the people to keep them in a state of dread and obedience. Voodoo priests and priestesses became precious auxiliaries of power, often called upon to consult at the National Palace alongside mayors, police chiefs, and leaders from rural areas. The familial voodoo worship with its secular, all-inclusive rituals was now just an exercise in witchcraft, cultivating wariness and betrayal.

The corps of *macoutes* grew day by day. He preferred it to the army and military, a nasty bunch partial to plots and coups d'état. Duvalier knew he was invincible as long the influence of these men and women — devoted to him body and soul, ready to spill their blood for him unflinchingly — was spread throughout the land. Even if he had to spend time resolving conflicts of all sorts that kept the biggest *macoute* leaders in a kind of violent rivalry, checked only by the supreme leader's authority. When Duvalier had to settle a dispute to calm his turbulent children, he felt he possessed the wisdom and power of King Solomon. After Papa Doc, the Secretary of State was the one person who could claim a certain authority over *macoute* leaders in the nine geographical regions of the country. He shared with the president a preoccupation with their very existence.

On either side of the driveway there were vast, manicured lawns, bordered by the trimmed boxwood hedges the Secretary of State saw every day. In the undergrowth next to the enclosing wall he heard the chilling screech of the president's guinea fowls. The chief of state saw these birds — vulture-like, with hideous faces, full of cunning, nerves, and vigor — as the living symbols of Duvalierist power. Fond of mythology, like the Abyssinians and Byzantines millennia before him, Duvalier may have believed in the eternal virtues of the mysterious black bird, the *oiseau nègre* described by Jean-Marie Lamblard in his book of the same name. Two palace employees had the exclusive task of assuring the health and well-being of these cold-blooded icons.

On the left the driveway curved, running alongside the palace's main façade; on the right it led toward the large gardens in the back, a good part of which was being turned into quarters for the presidential guards. The construction site was thick with heat and noise. The president had to be surrounded by weapons. The Forty-Eighth Company of the Haitian armed forces occupied the entire west wing of the first floor, which had been transformed to accommodate it. The president wanted reports of the activities of the special military intelligence corps at his disposal day and night. *Macoutes* also carried weapons and had access to almost every office in the building. That day the Secretary of State found the same controlled effervescence that characterized the palace's daily life, but its thick, high walls gave him a strange impression, one that first-time visitors often felt upon entering. They marveled at the building's beauty and majesty while they sensed an invisible but ubiquitous danger. After being proclaimed president of Haiti, Papa Doc waited three months before moving into this overwhelming residence with his family. He needed all that time to purge the hallways of the spirits his predecessors had summoned and to usher in his own.

Taking advantage of his mission in the Grande'Anse region, the Secretary of State had taken his mysterious trip to Chardonnières. Yet he felt the weight of the presidential dwelling on his shoulders, the columns and three imposing domes, the weight of all the beauty of that building, every hallway concealing silent threats. He made sure to place his left foot over the threshold of the administrative antechamber first, and entered the building, vigilant.

"A little hen died in my courtyard yesterday. For no apparent reason. She was pecking around happily with the other animals when all of a sudden she started spinning around, once, twice, three times, and — bam! — she fell backward and dropped dead. I said 'for no apparent reason,' but there's always a deeper reason for these things, Neighbor. A dog knows why he starts barking in the middle of the night . . . and if leaves could talk they would tell us why they shudder sometimes even when there's no breeze. Animals and trees can pick up vibrations that escape us. Hmmm . . . do you know what that means, Neighbor, a chicken dying in my courtyard, just like that, out of the blue?"

Of course I have no idea. And I don't care. Besides, I'm not going to turn a poor animal dying of fever or indigestion into a major event. Why do I come to see Solange when her inevitable questions annoy me so much? Why do I feel the need to speak to her when I don't believe what she believes? What is it that makes me feel calmer after visiting her? Now I'm becoming like her, asking myself useless questions I can't answer. An avalanche of questions has been torturing me for a while now. As soon as my hands are not busy with household tasks, as soon as I find myself alone, they invade my silence — insistent, shameless, petty, mundane — and throw my soul into turmoil. Solange is the one who fills my silences best. When the children aren't there, when no one is visiting, the atmosphere in the house oppresses me to the point of physical illness. I want to flee, flee myself. I come to share my secret torments with Solange. She turns them into questions, illuminations; she gives them meaning and depth; she paints them the color of forgetting. Solange knows how to put the silences on hold for a while. But today I get the sense I won't find respite from my discomfort—on the contrary. Solange's first question confirms my apprehensions. I should not have come to see her.

"I don't know, Solange. Your hen died of old age . . . or else she choked swallowing a pebble. What do I know?"

There is a lot of empathy in Solange's eyes. She lights the last cigarette from a pack and crumples the pack into a ball in her hand. The crinkling of cellophane. The smell of the first blue puff of tobacco around my head. Daniel and the days before. For a second, I travel very far away from here.

"There's a reason I keep all these birds here and feed them, Neighbor. I never touch them. I only slaughter the animals I buy at market. These animals that you see here are like lightning rods. When death, disaster, bad luck, or evil spirits visit a place, they're on the lookout at first, retreating to the corners of a home, waiting for a moment to penetrate the private lives of living Christians. But even when their mission is to affect human beings, they do not resist the impulse to swoop down on the little lives moving around them, any blood that's pulsing. Animals are often their first victims. No . . . this animal died to warn us . . . that trouble is lurking around us . . . that it will strike around us. Such a thing would never happen to one of my guinea fowl, they're too leery. This little hen liked to slip under your fence . . . explore your garden. When she fell, she was coming back from your house. I saw her. Krémòl saw her, too. Didn't you, Krémòl?"

Solange's brother nods, smiling vaguely.

"So she was sacrificed for us? She had a bad encounter in my courtyard? Oh, Solange, please! Save your tall tales for your clients. Hasn't death been stalking us since the day we left our mothers' wombs?"

"Are you scared, Neighbor? You prefer not to believe me to keep your fear at bay?"

"I might be scared, the way everyone gets scared. But I will not see the wing of death in a lizard changing colors or a chicken passing away."

"And yet these are real signs, Neighbor. There are steps we can take to ward off bad luck or misfortune when they threaten us. Do you have any news from . . . your husband?"

Why is Solange talking to me about Daniel right now? Does she know something about his situation? With all the *macoutes* who come to her house she must have reliable information about a lot of things. No sign of Raoul for two weeks. That's it. Daniel has died in prison. And Raoul doesn't have the courage to come to my house. Maybe he's afraid I'll read it in his eyes, smell it on his skin, in his pants — the scent of my husband's death. Or else maybe he's afraid I know he's abusing my children? Basically he can't stand deceiving us anymore. He's grown tired of this sadistic game. As I feared, he left without saying good-bye, without giving me the time to spit out my hatred at him. Yes, his absence condemns him. It's as if he signed off on these infamous acts himself. What will I do?

"No . . . no news. And you? Have you found something out? Don't hide anything from me, Solange . . . I want . . . I should know."

"I know you're strong enough to take bad news . . . But I don't know anything . . . all I know is what that dead animal told me yesterday, and I believe in it firmly. Be vigilant.

There's a dark cloud over your house. You're free to do nothing about it . . . I saved you a basket of ripe guavas. This year the tree had a wild harvest, as if it would never stop dropping fruit. Ginette will bring them to your cook. I can't stand that girl, Neighbor. When we cross paths on the street she acts like she's seen the devil in the flesh. One day I'll really scare her, she'll find out who Solange is . . . Ha, ha, ha! The guavas are succulent. You can make jam and jelly with them. They're beautiful, plump, and scented, like you, Neighbor. Ha, ha, ha!"

I needed to hear that laugh. Solange's laugh is the connection between the shuddering leaves, the shadow of death, and the scent of ripe guava.

When I went back home the Secretary of State's car was parked in front of my gate. Jocelyn, smoky-eyed, and two bodyguards were chatting calmly on the street.

Right away I could see that Raoul was not well. His skin looked sallow; he was breathing heavily. The air conditioner in the bedroom was emitting glacial air. He'd come back to my house; that's where he'd sought the relief that his bones, his flesh, and his spirit needed. He smelled raw, sticky, like the scent of blood. All the blood that had been spilled on his orders. The blood was stifling him, burning him up, and all the air conditioners in the world could not help him. He waited for me, lying in bed, pillows propped against the wall to support his torso. When I entered the room, his eyes lit up. His leather briefcase was where he always left it, on the chest of drawers at the entrance of the room. His pants and jacket were carefully folded and placed over the back of the chair next to the bed, as usual. The handgun in its holster lay on the nightstand, within reach. With a nod of his head he called to me. My legs shook; I was approaching a wounded lion. I sat on the edge of the bed, facing him.

What to say to this man who had come to place his spent weapons and tormented mind at my feet? I stumbled, entangled in the mangrove of my feelings. My tongue was as heavy as lead in my mouth. Where had my rage gone? Where were all the questions I'd ruminated over for days? When would I get the explanations I needed to calm my fears and defuse my silences? Even in this state of weakness Raoul scared me. A wounded lion loses none of his dangerousness. I would be better off waiting, finding a more favorable moment to address the question of the children, to erase this obsession in my head. No. Nirvah, you must speak now. Hurl out your rage now. Confront him now, while he's tired and demoralized. You can't put off this confrontation any longer. Who knows, he may leave again for days or weeks. I listened to the Secretary of State speak, his cold hand caressing my knee. He told me about the past three weeks, traveling over terrible roads, patrolling rural sections of the southwest to mobilize the partisans, galvanize the troops, and stir up excitement. Day after day, in the hillsides, over fields, soldiers chased invaders. Despite their ferocious resistance, they kept falling. Farmers and *macoutes* fell, too. While the rebels were being hunted down, the threatened government was already taking revenge on their families. In Jérémie the parents of *kamoken* paid for the offenses of their offspring with their lives. The Secretary of State described the horror, the screaming, the color of the blood spilled in the moonlight, the cries of the innocent. Under his closed lids he saw the summary executions again, the soldiers in pursuit, the grisly killing. Gradually, as he told his story, he seemed calmer; life returned to his limbs; the hand caressing my knee became more specific. My head was spinning. I couldn't listen to this lugubrious account any longer. He had transferred his burden to me, like poison slipping slowly under my skin, toxic. I had my share of sorrows, too, which were sufficient. Why did I have to relieve this man of the weight of the crimes he'd chosen to commit? And what about the first crime, the one that connected us, Daniel's arbitrary imprisonment, Daniel's slow death? Why didn't he ever talk to me about it? There's noise in the house. I hear Marie laughing, talking on the phone. So she was here, then, alone in the house, with Raoul? Did they see each other? Did they speak to each other? What is she doing home at this hour, anyway? She should be in school. Has this happened before, meeting by chance in the house? Maggy, could you be right? Raoul has no right to even look at Marie in my absence! A red veil of adrenaline liberates me.

"Raoul . . ."

The Secretary of State does not hear me. He keeps his eyelids closed. His face calm, he continues to caress my knee. I abruptly get up from the bed, which continues to sway for a moment. I raise my voice, I tremble, I shout. Raoul looks at me, surprised at my behavior.

"Raoul, I want to know now if Daniel is dead. I understand this little game amuses you, but it can't go on much longer. I can't stand it. I want to know! I can't handle this morbid uncertainty. I can't lie to myself any longer. You will also tell me if . . . if these rumors going around about you and my children are true. Raoul, tell me now if you're abusing my children, Daniel's children. Daniel is no longer here to protect them . . ."

I can't say another word. I have to lean against the dresser not to fall over, I'm shaking inside. Powerless tears fall from my eyes. I shake more and more from anger. I'm angry that I'm so scared. He says nothing. Roused from his torpor he looks straight ahead, as if searching for his words. He wasn't expecting this outburst from me, the first in all this time. Say something to me, Raoul. Break this silence. Break me out of the silence I'm sinking into. The silence that can no longer provide me with an alibi, that refuses to be my accomplice any longer. My silence is full of shadows; it's killing Solange's chickens. Have the courage to be what you are: a brute, a cynic, a savage beast. Give me the courage to look myself in the face, to recognize my deviation. It's not too late for me to start again, to accept my defeat and save the lives of my children. You, before whom so many have trembled, have the courage to tell me the truth I'm waiting for, even if it destroys

me. Are you afraid I'll get back up again, that I'll get rid of you and go on living? No woman dares leave Secretary of State Raoul Vincent? I know that macho story. Since you started calling the shots in Haiti, no woman has ever turned her back on you. Will I dare? It's a risk worth taking, don't you think? But you wouldn't take it. You're not a good gambler; you only believe in force.

I will get back up. I'm a strong woman — you know that, Solange knows it. I have seven lives. My sex is made of earthenware. I could start another life. Tell me you scorned me from the start, that you gave me pleasure as the price of your contempt and revenge. Then we'll call it quits today. Thanks for the good times. You've had your revenge. It will leave a profound disgust with myself in my mouth and between my thighs. I'll wash my hollows with soap and water and leaves of wild mint. My sex is made of earthenware. Free me, Raoul.

Raoul finally gets up. He looks at me and smiles. A smile as cold as ice, as stinging as a slap, my face is hot. He takes his pants from the back of the chair and slowly puts them on.

"Women are all whores, Nirvah. I've always known that, and unfortunately you are no exception to the rule. Whores . . . whatever their social class, their fortune or their poverty, the color of their skin, their age, their profession. My wife is a whore and my two daughters just want to get married to a bank account. Your pretty Marie is a lovely little whore. I've had sex with whores my whole life. I admit you were one of the most gratifying, honestly. But I made the mistake of thinking you were a whore who accepted herself and could profit from the circumstances life had given her, instead of just enduring them. A whore who knows the price to pay for saving her skin. But no . . . you think you can win on all fronts. Pleasure, affluence, safety, and a clear conscience. Life is not made that way, Nirvah. Oh, no! Everything has its price. You're like my wife . . . a grasping, greedy pleasure-seeker but so hypocritical. In her disguise as a churchgoer equipped with a rosary, she has only one interest in life: money and all the pleasure it affords her. She doesn't care about me, my worries, my mistresses, or the enemies who threaten me, as long as money flows into her hands in torrents."

Raoul's words lash me. He speaks in a measured, contemptuous tone. But his words have an unexpected effect on me. Spurred by his contempt, my fear vanishes. The masks fall. I have nothing to lose. I have to make him tell me the truth I'm waiting for.

"Now that you've made your disgust clear to me, will you answer my questions, Raoul?"

My calmness surprises me. The Secretary of State goes to put on his jacket. He replies, lifting one arm to slip into a sleeve.

"You're wrong, Nirvah . . . I feel no aversion toward you, just a little disappointment, perhaps. I desire you as much as ever, and I'll come back to take you in this very bed, as many times as I want to. And you'll want to, too, you're made that way, you just don't know it . . . After this conversation, we'll be better lovers, believe me. Are you really worried about your husband's fate? Maybe you are . . . I still have my reservations about that. But I know you're a very intelligent woman. Whether Daniel Leroy is dead or alive, what does that change about your situation? He never should have gotten himself thrown into the death trap they call Fort-Dimanche. There, one story ends and another begins. Another story of survival. You understand it. I give you everything—protection, pleasure, money. In return I

ask for neither gratitude nor deference, just a little decency. You only got my protection and my money because I saw a woman in you who knew the price of her skin, the price of her sex, and made me pay. So don't come crying to me now because some gossip got back to you."

"This isn't about gossip, Raoul. It's about Marie and Nicolas . . . Tell me . . ."

Raoul lets out a cry of rage, his face becomes distorted, his eyes seem to want to explode out of their sockets. He grabs me by the arm and drags me brutally into the bathroom, in front of the big mirror above the sink. He stands behind me, glued against me, holding my neck and arm, and makes me look in the mirror. He whispers in the hollow of my ear.

"I don't like men, but I've known some in my life. I prostituted myself with men to rise from the muck, from anonymity, to pay for school, because I had ambition. They had fun with me, passing me from one ass, one pair of balls to the next. But today they fear me . . . I had some of them eliminated with great pleasure, you've no idea. Your son . . . your son doesn't interest me. He looks too much like his father, a shitty little mulatto. He doesn't get me hard. That's it for Nicolas."

Raoul is red with anger. He squeezes my arm, and the pain is unbearable. His eyes in the mirror are draining me of life.

"You're hurting me, Raoul. Let go of my arm! . . . Let me go, I said! Ow!"

"I won't let you go. You'll listen to me, Nirvah, since you want answers. Let's talk about Marie, shall we? You ask if I fucked her? If I did things to her that you wanted done to you alone? Are you jealous sometimes? It's time to read into your soul, my love. You can't stand the idea of a rival under your own roof, of your own blood? Why not? With the two of you, you're more certain to keep me. Mother and daughter, daughter and mother . . . a rare, erotic trap . . . a pleasure reserved for the gods. I'm a satisfied mortal. Marie is as sweet and as warm as you are, maybe a little more daring. She surprised me. Today, girls aren't shy, you know. So, do you believe me, Nirvah? Am I lying to you, or am I telling you the truth? Ask Marie, if you dare. How could you not have seen something so massive happening here, before your eyes? Or is there nothing to see? Can you imagine Marie open, swooning, dancing on my lap? Do I force her, do I have to brutalize her, or does she want it, too? Does she ask for it again, like you? Surely the greenhorns she brings around here can't satisfy the passion she inherits from you. What will you decide? To believe me or not? What's your truth? Did you pretend to see nothing? Are you trying to emotionally blackmail me? I won't tell you anything. I won't play those little games. Look, Marie didn't come to you either. What's your truth, Nirvah? Are you a real whore, the kind I like?"

Raoul says these last words yelling. I'm deafened. I'm suffocating. My ear is wet with the saliva he spat out in the intensity of his rage. I should not have provoked him and accused him. He's a master of the art of confusion. Maybe he doesn't even know what the word *truth* means anymore. I can't organize my thoughts. I try to free myself from his grip, but he's holding me in the same position, pinned to the sink. His hands are now wandering feverishly over my body. He's trembling behind me. I feel weak in the knees. His hard cock is stuck to my ass like a magnet. The excitement has me in spasms. I don't want to give in to him, but I can't say no to my body. Raoul finally releases me. I turn toward him, hold out my arms, thinking he's going to embrace me, that we're going to fall onto the bathroom's tiled floor and take each other with the rage that is hurting us so much. But he moves away, looking at his watch. Without a glance, he leaves me, takes his gun and leather briefcase from the bedroom, and goes.

At the meeting of the secretaries of state that afternoon, the reigning tension was higher than usual. Sitting around a conference table, government officials awaited the president's arrival with febrile restraint. The chief of state often began these meetings an hour late, sometimes more. There was his diabetes to deal with, solicitors to receive, quarrels or power struggles to resolve between *macoute* leaders, a backlog of important mail to be sorted through with his private secretary, and rivalries within his family that required his personal intervention. He had to keep up with his hobbies, profit from loyalties, clamp down on troublemakers. He spoke a lot on the phone, a tool he was particularly fond of. While they waited the secretaries of state discussed recent events, extracting last-minute information from one another to improve their presentations, passing along false information to hasten the downfall of colleagues on the verge of disgrace. The end of 1964 proved difficult. The country was having a hard time recovering from the ravages of Cyclones Flora, in October 1963, and Cleo, the following August. Famine and drought had devastated the Northeast.

Obvious hostilities existed between certain members of government, tensions and even hatreds fostered by the supreme leader himself to control this little world of which he was rather suspicious. Some secretaries of state stayed in their jobs for less than a month, while others seemed eternal, going from one ministry to another, dancing a permanent waltz of intrigue and influence until they were dizzy.

Secretary of State Raoul Vincent loathed the conference room as much as the conferences. He found the room boring. The inlaid parquet cedar floor, the upright chairs upholstered in green velvet, the high ceiling with its moldings and enormous crystal chandelier — all that Louis-something style struck him as off-putting and incongruous. The brocade curtains embroidered with the republic's coat of arms adorning the windows were in especially bad taste. Often in the middle of a meeting his mind would leap over the terrace, run lightly across the lawn, linger for a moment in the entanglement of vines hanging from the garden pergola on the eastern façade, skirt the replica of the Venus de Milo, cross the Champs-de-Mars toward Chemin des Dalles, snake through the passageways of the city's hills, and find the warm body of his own Venus on Rue des Cigales. He preferred his informal meetings with the president in his private office, under the gaze of Pope Paul VI, Lyndon B. Johnson, and Martin Luther King enclosed in their frames, the only witnesses to their conversations. The courtiers and sycophants had to leave the office when he arrived, with the exception at times of the very private secretary. The latter did not appear to like him much, but she respected him, knowing how important he was to the president. She also knew the Secretary of State was aware of her relationship with Gérard Daumec, a young speechwriter with poetic verve, who was always loping around the palace halls and whom the president loved like a son. A snake, a dangerous schemer to keep an eye on, Raoul thought. To greet the Secretary of State Duvalier wore his burgundy bathrobe and a cap on his head, an outfit he never changed out of except to greet diplomats and attend official meetings. His submachine gun was always within reach, on a corner of his desk, to protect against sudden rampages by once-loyal servants.

The sole point of discussion on the council's agenda was the release of a number of political prisoners. To foster his new relationship with his American neighbors, the chief of state thought it a favorable time to make a grand gesture, granting presidential pardon to a few imprisoned government opponents. He also needed money. It was certainly a decision he made reluctantly. After President Kennedy's assassination, the new U.S. government openly supported Papa Doc's anticommunist politics. Lobbyists of a new stripe assured communication between the National Palace and the back rooms of American politics, where the big decisions were made. Because beyond political motives, the conciliatory American attitude aimed to ensure that no market, however small, would have competition. The Haitian government's anti-Americanism was just a smokescreen; economic cooperation started up again timidly, insufficiently. The U.S. Department of State exerted pressure on the Haitian government to show proof of a modicum of democratic activity. Assaults had to be warded off from groups that denounced human rights violations in Latin America and the Caribbean and condemned American policies in Haiti.

Every secretary of state kept a list tucked away in his brief-case — the names of political prisoners he wished to submit to the president, along with the reasons for the soundness of his recommendations. Some had been waiting for this opportunity for months. Friends, relatives, intermediaries requested intervention at the top for clemency or simply for confirmation of a prisoner's existence. This morning's exercise required particular tact from every man around the table, since each had to try to satisfy his goals without giving the impression of expecting too much.

Secretary of State Raoul Vincent found himself seated across from Maxime Douville, a colleague from Finance and Economic Affairs and his rival par excellence. The two men looked at each other furtively. Douville lost members of his family in the Jérémie Vespers. He had a second cousin among the thirteen invaders from Young Haiti whose entire family was exterminated, seven members in all. He bore no anger toward François Duvalier, the *macoutes*, or the military. All his hatred was directed at the man seated across the table, the principal enforcer of the dictatorship's dirty work. This man who today was the lover of Nirvah Leroy, one of the most beautiful *mulâtresses* in the country. A woman who fueled the fantasies of every man worthy of the name. The prison gate had barely closed on Daniel Leroy before this coarse and detestable person took over his house and his wife. Those *nègres* were all the same. Their humanity was only legitimated by the presence of a light-skinned woman in their bed. But it got worse. People claimed he was even sleeping with Leroy's daughter. Enough was enough! Raoul Vincent would pay for that dearly. Douville had begun to set up a very tight system of financial control of Raoul Vincent's ministry. He knew the sums diverted by the latter down to the centime and the ploys used to justify large expenditures. Douville knew that the irregularities — which went far beyond suitable limits — started when the Secretary of State began to enjoy Nirvah Leroy's favors. This joke had gone on for far too long. Even if Vincent took refuge under the chief of state's wing, Douville would figure out how to dislodge him. Before long, this shameless man's head would roll; it was Vincent or himself, he swore it on his mother's ashes.

The chief of state finally entered the conference room in a black suit, white shirt, gray tie, and round tortoiseshell glasses; scrawny and somber, he was flanked by his bodyguard, a burly man with a small submachine gun in one hand, who would spend the entire meeting on his feet behind the president. All the secretaries of state stood for the chief's arrival against a background of scraping chairs. The president greeted the men around the table with a vague hand gesture and sat. Raoul Vincent was to his right. Without any preface the president addressed the man to his left and asked him to communicate the names of his candidates for release. He took notes, nodded his head, smiled, murmured a few words from time to time, and passed on to the next. Secretary of State Raoul Vincent would be the last person to give his opinion on the secretaries of states' choices, thanks to his position as head of Public Safety.

Douville had done his homework, issuing promises and veiled threats to anyone he needed to. The mere prospect of a tour through their fiefdoms by inspectors from the Ministry of Finance and Economic Affairs was enough to persuade most of the government men to yield to their colleague. Others, in rare cases, supported Daniel Leroy's release out of a principle of solidarity. So the only name on every list was Daniel Leroy. They were all aware of Secretary of State Vincent's relationship with the dissident communist's wife. Some hated him even more for it; others conceded him a certain admiration. All the men present were aware of the feelings held by the government's two most powerful secretaries of state. That's why they didn't discourage Douville from pushing for Leroy's candidacy. Vincent hadn't asked them for anything. They also knew Vincent would use all his weight to keep Leroy in jail and hold onto his wife. But in the face of this unexpected united front he would have to backpedal and go along with the overwhelming majority—if Vincent had a shred of intelligence, which they were certain he did. The chief of state also knew about Vincent and Nirvah Leroy. If Raoul Vincent went against the choices of all the secretaries of state he would be putting himself in a tight spot; his motives would be too obvious. The chief of state's sense of modesty was well known; he would certainly not be able to defend such a flagrant sex scandal, even as he carried on a passionate affair he believed was secret with his private secretary in the National Palace.

They went around the table. Every time Daniel Leroy's name came up, Maxime Douville internally rejoiced and checked Raoul Vincent's reaction. His face was expressionless. He's strong, Douville thought to himself, but he'll have to give in. Secretary of State Vincent would be the last to profess his views.

The bastards! They let themselves be swayed by Douville. They want to bury me. That's it . . . it's the beginning of the end. A year ago a thing like this would not have been possible. Philibert is letting me down, too; he owes me everything, even his place at this table as secretary of state of Public Works. Arsène . . . Vérélus . . . Badio . . . Bastards! Sons of bitches! My power is being put to the test today, in front of the president. They want to teach me a lesson. Logically, I should ask for Daniel Leroy's pardon. They want me to disappear from Nirvah's life. A way to avenge the mulattos who died in Jérémie. Douville hates my guts; that's nothing new. But Daniel Leroy leaving prison is out of the question. I'm not ready to give him back his freedom. Nirvah can't handle that situation yet. Things have to be done gradually, when the time is right. I knew I would have to fight for this woman. That every moment spent with her would be paid for in anxiety as well as the purest joy. They don't know that without that woman I go wild, that today's proposal puts them all in grave danger. A cornered animal can only

kill. I need Nirvah, and it's not this bunch of phonies around the
table who are going to steal her from me. I should have shortened
Leroy's days in prison while there was still time. I hesitated too
long. I got weak. Today it's too late. Everything that happens
to him now will bear my signature. This woman has shaken my
center of gravity. I can't stand being without her.

"So, Secretary of State Vincent?" François Duvalier said
in his nasal voice. "Could you enlighten us as to your point
of view concerning citizen Daniel Leroy's liberation . . . ?"

There was a silence. Secretary of State Vincent's voice
was detached but firm. He felt superior to his colleagues in
his confidence and composure. He spoke of Daniel Leroy
unemotionally, as of a man he didn't know.

"Hmmm . . . Thank you, Your Excellency . . . hmmm . . .
contrary to the opinion of my colleagues . . . I vote in favor
of keeping Professor Daniel Leroy in prison. My opinion is
motivated by the fact of the influence, I would even say *aura*, of
citizen Leroy on the youth of this country, schoolchildren and
students he sends to slaughter without a second thought . . .
We also know that citizen Leroy will provoke a coup d'état,
the scope of which we cannot yet measure." The Secretary of
State paused and quickly scanned the table. He stopped for a
second on Maxime Douville, who looked away, discomfited.
"Moreover," he went on, "this influence extends to the union
sector, whose leading figures have maintained regular relations with him, relations that have been documented and that
in the short and long term endanger our nascent industry, the
security of lives, the goods of our country, and the longevity
of the Duvalierist revolution. My colleague the secretary of
state of Social Affairs can attest to this . . ." Raoul Vincent
took a document from his leather briefcase. "Your Excellency,
I have the surveillance report . . ."

"No, Anthony, don't touch me . . ."

"Come on, baby, relax. Your little Tony is asking you. You've been here for over an hour, Marie. Do I have to beg you?"

"It's no use, Tony . . . I don't want you to touch me."

"But, baby . . . Look at the state you've put me in . . . you can't leave me like this, baby . . ."

"Hands off, Tony. Once again . . . This morning I can't; it's as simple as that."

Tony pouts. God, he can be so cute when he wants me! All the girls are jealous of me. Tony's got it all—he's handsome, tall, well built, funny, and when he smiles he makes me wet. I skipped class this morning to meet him in his room. Tony graduated two years ago now. He's waiting to go study law in France, but since his family has had a few run-ins with the government, his name still has not been *passed down* from the National Palace to the Immigration Office. This morning, unlike other times, I remain cold to his advances. My body isn't reacting.

"Not today, Tony . . . I don't feel well . . . I'm not quite myself."

"Hmmm . . . Babyyyyy . . . just for a minute . . . I want you so bad . . . You don't have to do anything . . . Just relax, okay?"

Instead of being flattering, Anthony's persistence is extremely annoying. I've never been able to resist his advances until this morning. He always ends up getting the better of me.

Even though he doesn't satisfy me, I like giving him pleasure. At the moment my skin, my mouth, don't feel like giving in. Tony is rubbing his fly against my thigh, and this brings my annoyance to its height. I'm not a bitch in heat, after all. Can't he understand that I don't want to make love right now? I push him away more forcefully than I mean to.

"What's wrong with you, Marie?" Tony shouts, irritated. "You want to make me work for it? That excites you, to be begged?"

"No . . . that's just it, you're not exciting me . . . I just want you to leave me alone this time, Anthony."

"Shit! Then why did you come to my room?" he says angrily.

"To be with you for a while . . . to talk to you. Is that so hard to understand? Do I have to spread my legs every time we see each other?"

Tony is surprised by my question. He seems to be thinking about it. His anger lessens a bit. He changes tactics.

"I . . . I'm not saying that . . . I like your company, too, but the other times you always seemed in as much of a hurry as me . . . the two of us are good together . . . we're a great couple . . . You don't love me anymore, is that it?"

"Of course, I love you . . . idiot."

"So come on . . . just for a second. You'll see . . . I won't take long."

Of course you won't take long, Tony. You never do. Guys are all the same. A direct flight to the panties, a few thrusts, and — bam — it's over! And I pretend to like it. I re-create the passion in front of my girlfriends. I make up hours of torrid pleasure, and they drool with envy. Tony has never asked me if he satisfied me in bed, not once. And I don't say anything to him about my frustrations. He thinks he's giving me a privilege that so many other girls dream of getting from him. The honor of making him come. Whereas with Raoul, I often beg for mercy. He's old, ugly, knock-kneed, and yet he knows how to get me to ecstasy. He doesn't let me go until I've come at least once. I'm a real woman with him. Who would believe it? Not Tony; he'd laugh in my face if I told him. He doesn't know anything about my little secret.

Satisfied, Tony lies on his back and smokes a cigarette. A silent nausea rises to my throat; I'm suffocating so close to that burning tobacco. I go to wash myself off in the bathroom, to get Anthony's semen, the acrid odor of which is making me queasy, off my private parts. What's happening to me? Something's going on inside my body. I've never felt this way before. In the morning I have no energy, even after a night of sleep. I can't eat anything until noon. I don't want what's happening to me. I don't want to be pregnant. I've been waiting for my period for two weeks now. What will I do? The more time that passes, the deeper in shit I'll be. No way am I talking to Mom. No way am I getting her involved in my business. In fact, I came here so that Tony would help me. He has to get me out of this jam.

"Tony . . . I have to talk to you about something . . ."

"What, baby?"

"Well . . . I've been waiting for my period for two weeks . . ."

Tony, still on the wings of his orgasm, doesn't understand me. He caresses my back and replies distractedly.

"Hmmm . . . what, your period?"

"Can you put out that cigarette, please? You're making me sick!" The high pitch of my voice startles him. He looks at me, upset.

"What's the matter, baby? You have a problem? You've been like a bomb ready to explode since you got here. I didn't give you enough? Let me recover for a minute, and we can fix that. Relax."

"But I just told you what's the matter, Anthony! All you think about is fucking! A late period . . . that's my problem. I think I'm pregnant, Tony . . ."

The message finally gets through. He props himself up on an elbow and looks at me.

"Are you serious?"

"I . . . I don't know. I just feel funny all the time. And my period hasn't come."

"Hmmm . . . What are you going to do?"

That was my mistake. I should never have spoken to him about it. What was I thinking? *What are you going to do?* he said. He doesn't care.

"I don't know . . . I think I'll have to see a doctor . . . to be sure. I'd like you to come with me."

"Me? What for? This is a girl thing . . . Ask Caroline or Julie . . . your best friends . . . I don't know." There is a trace of panic in his voice.

"But I'd rather you come with me, Tony, to help me sort it out. You don't think this is something the Holy Spirit made happen, do you?"

Tony scratches his head, his jaw tightens. He gets up and paces around the room. He does some intense reflecting.

"And if your worries are confirmed, what do you plan to do?"

Tony again puts my anxiety in the singular. I don't know what made me tell him. There was never any question in my head about having a kid at sixteen, especially in my family's situation. My mother married my father at seventeen, but that was another time, another story. I just wanted to believe, even for a minute, that Tony loved me . . . to provoke his tenderness in a way. Once he gets over his panic, maybe he'll have other feelings. I hear myself say to Tony:

"That depends on you . . . on us. We could get rid of it . . . or else keep it."

"No way are we keeping it!" Anthony's response is a slap, like a sail in the wind. Wind that carries me far away from this room, where I offered him my body during the golden hours of playing hooky. "I have no intention of burdening myself with a child, when I'm not even sure I'm the father . . . My parents would never let me . . . They warned me about you . . . My folks knew what they were talking about."

Oh, those words that shouldn't be said, that mark you like a branding iron. I already know the words that will follow. I face Tony to deliver a final challenge, so that the wound he opened in my side won't kill me.

"Ten minutes ago, not even, you shot your sperm inside of me. Whether you believe it or not, that's how you make babies, Anthony Placide. The least you could do is accept your responsibility."

"But it takes two to shoot you full of sperm, Marie, my dear." His sharp response comes out like snake venom. I'd like to rip the smile off his face with my teeth.

"What? What did you say?" I act brash so that Anthony will stop talking. I'm suddenly cold. But he doesn't stop.

"Don't play shocked and innocent; you know very well what I'm talking about, Marie. You're getting your kicks with that *macoute* secretary of state, the so-called family friend. They say he's your mother's lover, too. What a family you make! In your situation you're not in a position to be making demands, much less giving lectures. All you had to do was make sure you didn't get pregnant. It's up to that secretary of state to take care of you; he's filthy rich."

Anthony is right. He's a coward and an idiot, but he's right. I was just good enough for his pleasure, and I was wrong not to want to believe that. As long as I was Marie the pretty little light-skinned girl, Marie with the generous hands, he showed me off like a nice catch, a choice cut. He enjoyed my readiness to oblige, my openheartedness, my body, which he was never able to satisfy. He might have bragged to his friends about sharing a girlfriend with a secretary of state. But I knew all this would happen. Raoul won't let me down. I get my bag and go, telling him with vicious calmness:

"You're just a loser, Tony. A wimp. And you're worthless in bed. You knew about my relationship with the Secretary of State, and you went along with it. It just bothers you now that I need your help, now that I'm asking you to be a man. Yeah, I'll go find him. It's true he's a *macoute* secretary of state, but at least he's a real man."

They came in two jeeps the color of night. The gate's chain was blown to pieces under machine-gun fire, a terrifying noise that hung for long seconds in the foliage of Rue des Cigales. I wasn't completely awake yet, and they were already in the house. They lined us up against the wall of the hallway to the bedrooms: the kids, Tinès, Yva, and me. For half an hour they've been searching, or rather pillaging, all the rooms. They speak loudly, racing around, slamming doors brutally. One guy is pacing with wild eyes, weapon in hand, and I'm waiting for him to start shooting in every direction any second now. They won't find anything. After Daniel's arrest, I burned all his books, magazines, notebooks, even his correspondence. I didn't give them the chance to persecute me on the pretext of subversive literature. But this raid has nothing to do with Daniel. Accounts are being settled with the mistress of the chief of the secret police. The message to the Secretary of State is clear: he no longer inspires fear. Nicolas is shaking, Marie is pallid, Yva is clutching her stomach to keep from spilling her guts. The courtyard boy doesn't flinch; was he expecting their arrival? Raoul trusts him; I don't. There are seven of them, all in civilian clothes, two of them standing guard in the courtyard. Their leader is highly ranked in the military. He must be Daniel's age; I've seen him around. He avoids my gaze. I can't say whether the six other men are *macoute* or military. As far as I'm concerned it doesn't make any difference; they all get along to do their dirty work. The tides have turned. This surprise search at eleven o'clock at night says a lot about Raoul's situation. I would never have thought it possible. His power is disintegrating a little more each day. I sensed it a while ago in his poor sleeping habits, the nervous movements of his hands, his tormented silences. The other day he spoke to me in rather vague terms about the tensions between him and certain colleagues in the government. But there's a lot more going on, I'm sure of that now. The tragic disappearance of the secretary of state of Public Works is the talk of the town. He was burnt alive the night before last in his car in Mariani on Route Nationale 2. He was found in the company of a body that could not be identified. His mistress, according to scandalmongers. Payback from a jealous wife or political vendetta, again according to scandalmongers. The investigation is open; we'll probably never know the results, but these deaths reek of assassination, base crime. Raoul, what do you know about this crime? Will I ever hear a word of truth from your lips? Raoul, tell me you didn't set fire to Philibert, even though you resented him so much. Is a man's life just a dried leaf that falls from a tree and is trampled underfoot? A cobweb swept away by a broom? A nut crushed by a kid with a rock?

The tides have turned. I've got to get out of here. My gut is telling me so. The men's hurried steps through the house have sounded an alarm in my head. My mind is racing at a terrible speed. A sort of urgency has taken over, making me feverish. An urgency to live, to save my life and the lives of my children. Daniel will not make it out of prison alive. I know this now. And if he ever gets out, the gulf between us will be impossible to bridge. Raoul's head may roll before long. The battle against him has begun; only the chief of state has supported him, but he'll have to reject him soon to maintain the equilibrium among his accomplices. I can't wait until then. In the space of a few hours, my life has been turned upside down yet again. What do these men want? There are no weapons here; there is no money. To provoke Raoul? To give him a scare? What about my jewelry? The strongbox is in the dresser drawer under lock and key. A minute ago they shattered something in the bedroom with a crowbar. How do I leave the country with the children when we're on the immigration services blacklist? That liberating authorization from the palace will never come. I don't have to say anything to Raoul. I shouldn't let him know what's happening inside me. He'll find a way to escape the chasm that's opening beneath his feet. It's up to me to escape mine. The border, maybe. I heard that if they're handsomely paid, the guardsmen on both sides let fugitives pass. But where do I get the money? Raoul gives me enough to live comfortably, that's all. And for how much longer? I'll need a lot more than that to pay for my passage.

The search seems to have ended. They obviously haven't found anything since they weren't searching for anything. At most, my jewelry. Raoul would not be crazy enough to leave weapons or compromising items here. The men's attention is focused more on us now. They walk back and forth in front of us, their glances as heavy as their breath. Their superior is in the living room, I hear him talking on the phone. The man with the gun approaches Marie and plants himself in front of her. He gives off the strong smell of sweat and trampled papaya leaves. His face is emotionless. His eyes do not leave Marie's as he moves the gun over her neck, her chest, and down to her abdomen. Three other henchmen watch him do it, snickering. They pay no attention to me or the other inhabitants of the house; we don't exist. The barrel of the gun is now between Marie's thighs, being moved back and forth roughly over her vulva. My heartbeat is strangling me. Yva can't stop sobbing, she's holding Nicolas by the shoulder with one hand and her stomach with the other. A cry of horror escapes my lips as I rush toward my daughter. The man looks at me, and I stop short. Death is dancing in his eyes. He sticks his face close to Marie's and licks her cheek. A violent sob makes Marie shake; her features are fixed in a grimace of horror. Marie, my baby, close your eyes, you're just dreaming . . . it's nothing but a bad dream; a little cold water on your face will soon wash it away. The other henchmen voyeurs have simultaneously pulled their guns from their holsters and stand close to us, encircling us. I get the sense this situation is quickly turning tragic. *Soldiers, to your posts!* The order cracks like a whip and makes us all jump. The man in front of Marie turns around slowly, looks at the chief a few yards away, stares him up and down, glaring, and detaches himself from my daughter. With a nod of his head, the military man orders the men to leave the house. Marie faints.

"A cup of coffee? Some fruit juice?"

Dorothy and Lola, two regulars at Maggy's beauty shop, have come over to see the diamond and sapphire jewelry I'm selling. Raoul's first present. A testament to a time when my life got away from me. This jewelry is all that has survived last night's search. It wasn't in my safe. The last time I wore it I was too tired to put it back, so I slipped it into a pocket of my dress, which I then hung in the closet. I have to find the money to leave. I'll sell off anything that'll bring fast cash — the car, the gold-plated silverware, the three television sets, the freezer, the new record player. The generator. I'll even sell the house if I find a buyer. Maggy immediately sent me these two potential customers; her sense of urgency is comforting. I greet the women, but my head is elsewhere. Marie has been sick since this morning; she's burning with a sudden fever. No doubt the shock of last night. Raoul called me late this morning without mentioning anything at all. As usual, he was laconic and emotionless. I'm sure he knows about last night. I told him about Marie's condition. Is he afraid the phone is being tapped? He's worried about Marie most of all. He didn't say whether he was coming to see us this evening; Raoul doesn't generally announce his visits.

"Uh . . . coffee, thanks," Lola says.

"If I drink a drop of coffee after lunch, I'll be up all night," Dorothy says, looking at the face of the small marvel that is her watch. "Two thirty . . . I'm very sensitive to caffeine . . . hmmm . . . what sort of fruit juice do you have?"

"Cherry juice . . . from the cherries in my garden . . ."

"Oh, no! Definitely not! Poison for my acidity. I'll have a glass of water then."

God! Give me patience . . . the next few hours are going to be difficult. It's true that my nerves are frayed, but this Dorothy . . . I feel sorry for the man who has to spend all his money supporting her.

She clucks when she speaks. She clucks and casts furtive glances. She's come to see what the home of Raoul Vincent's mistress looks like. She bothers me so much. The news of the raid has gotten around town. Several friends phoned to see if we were all right. Roger came to see me in the end; I asked him to take Nicolas to his house for the next few days. No word yet from Daniel's family. Arlette must be jubilant. According to the rumors, Marie and I were raped and hundreds of thousands of dollars seized. If I had all those dollars I wouldn't be here anymore, that's for sure. I broke a sweat this morning, trying to give the house a semblance of order, which was also a way of forgetting the past few hours. On the veranda everything looks pretty normal.

Dorothy won't stop jabbering. She's thrilled to be here. She's rubbing up against something huge, which she's never done before. Spending the afternoon at Raoul Vincent's mistress's house, this hotbed of perversion? Her friends will never believe it. It'll leave them gasping for days. Where did Maggy find this eel-like creature with her long, thin neck? I saw her eyes flash as she looked at the jewelry. True treasures. I don't have time to bemoan their loss. Dorothy is the eldest daughter of a rich businessman in the black middle class whose lucrative contracts with the government are his bread and butter.

Logwood, essential oils, cement, bridges and highways—he's got a hand in everything. He's become wealthy in less than five years. He has entrée in every circle: military, *macoute*, bourgeois, religious. A master opportunist. Where is Raoul? Why am I worried about him? The news about Marie really shook him; I felt it even in his silence. I hope this goose buys the jewelry. If Marie's fever doesn't subside in an hour I'll have Dr. Xavier come by. As soon as these ladies leave I'll call Roger to ask him to keep Nicolas at his place from now on. Maggy offered to spend the night with me. I don't think I run the risk of two consecutive raids, but you never know. Her presence will reassure me and help me with Marie.

"How's Marie?" Maggy asks. My friend senses what's going on inside me; she understands the panic setting in, growing in my soul and gut with every passing hour.

"I gave her some tablets for the fever . . ."

"Hmmm," she says. We speak in low voices because of the other two.

"So do you like it, Dorothy? Wasn't I right to say you'd see real treasures? I can see you in this necklace; your neck was made for beautiful jewelry. Blue is your favorite color, isn't it?" Maggy takes on the very serious tone of an auctioneer, and Dorothy regards her with attention and a rigid smile.

"Well, yes . . . A beautiful set . . . but I already have so much jewelry . . . Daddy won't like it . . ."

"You know how to soften him up, I'm sure," Maggy encourages. "Here, put on the necklace. Try the earrings, too."

Dorothy doesn't hesitate. The coldness of the jewels against her skin gives her a chill that surprises her; her nipples harden, and her hands flutter.

"It's true that he asked me to attend a party being thrown next week by a diplomat posted here . . . one of the most influential ambassadors . . . I love being invited to diplomats' homes . . . You meet so many foreigners," Dorothy clucks.

"Oh, yeah?" says Lola, who hasn't said much until now. "What's wrong with the locals?"

"Uh . . . nothing . . . except they often lack refinement." Dorothy's tone is somewhat dismissive.

"Hmmm . . . Maybe you hang out with the wrong people. I happen to know Haitians who are well educated and very cultured." Apparently Lola did not appreciate Dorothy's remark.

"Maybe you're right, Lola, but you have to admit those compatriots are in the minority! Otherwise, everywhere I go, there are *macoutes* who think they can pick me up . . . Vulgar people . . ."

"And yet . . . your father gets along well with them . . . when it's a matter of business . . ." Lola is the daughter of a Duvalierist who is asserting herself, and Dorothy is a party girl who doesn't know when to shut up.

"Yes . . . you could say that . . . I wonder how he's able to stand them. I attended a ball recently, and to make Daddy happy I danced with a young volunteer in the militia . . . He'd drunk quite a bit and took the liberty of inviting me to spend the night with him . . . What nerve! Me, sleep with a *macoute*, and a dark one on top of it? I leave that to the whores!" Dorothy's anger makes the jewelry flash against her skin even more.

"Oh!" Lola and Maggy exclaim at once, both looking at me. Dorothy realizes her gaffe — or was it a gaffe?

I'm not so much offended as annoyed by this long-necked girl.

"To act like a whore you have to be a real woman, with a real pussy between your legs . . . and you have to know how to use it . . . You hold onto a man with pleasure . . . all the money in the world won't keep a man by your side if he's unsatisfied . . . *macoute* or not."

"Well, I didn't mean to upset you, Nirvah."

"I'm not upset, Dorothy. Are you?"

"No . . ."

"Then everything's fine . . ."

"You already have an occasion!" Maggy interjects to change the subject. "This cocktail party has come at a great time. As elegant as you are, you'll find the perfect dress to wear with this jewelry. You'll be ravishing."

"Darling . . . it's as if you knew! I had a long dress made for the occasion . . . with a V-shaped neckline . . . Just yesterday I went to a fitting . . . Mrs. Simon has magical hands . . . Do you know her? She makes dresses for the president's daughters, too . . ."

Dorothy looks at me out of the corner of her eye. She wants me to understand that she is an important woman who knows people, who frequents the cream of Port-au-Prince society. Do I need this right now? A woman who needs to get laid shooting her mouth off? If it weren't for Maggy . . . I leave these women for a moment to see to Marie. The fever hasn't subsided. I get nervous.

"How much are you asking for the set?" Lola says. Finally a question of interest to me, but I don't know what to propose.

"Hmmm . . . Five thousand dollars!" Maggy answers quickly. She beat me to it, sensing my discomfort. It's true that we didn't agree on a price beforehand. What a pathetic businesswoman I am.

"Five thousand dollars!" Dorothy exclaims. "That's . . . a lot."

"It's worth three times as much!" Maggy says with conviction. "Earrings, a necklace, a bracelet, and a ring. Five gorgeous pieces. A real bargain, which I'm sorry I have to forego myself. But if you make an offer, Nirvah may consider it . . ."

"Two thousand!" Dorothy says, tightening her jaw.

Damn her! She's offering me nothing . . . she must think I'm desperate. Yva appears on the veranda, looking worried. I wave her over, and she leans in and whispers in my ear:

"Miss Marie is talking nonsense . . . you have to come . . ."

"Three thousand dollars!" Lola cries.

"Three thousand? Sold!" I reply as I rush away. "Take the money from your friend for me . . . See these ladies out and join me once you're done," I shout to Maggy.

As I leave, I catch a glimpse of Dorothy's spiteful pout as she grapples with the necklace's fastener, arms raised.

Raoul Vincent wondered how many suns would rise before he got the axe. He wanted to hold on for a few more days, long enough to get some money together. Money for himself, before requesting political asylum for his family at the Venezuelan embassy, and money for Nirvah, so she could pay for her escape with her children. He was dancing on a tightrope, racing here and there, staying at the ministry no more than an hour at a time, eluding enemies who might appear at any moment in unexpected form. When he saw Nirvah this evening he would tell her the time had come to leave everything behind. He would ask her to stay with someone not directly related to her while she prepared to leave. His collaborators and moles knew nothing about the raid on Nirvah Leroy; the order had come from authorities outside their jurisdiction. The enemy struck in the shadows and in the greatest secrecy. Raoul Vincent was no longer in control of much at the ministry, since he no longer controlled the money. With Machiavellian precision, Douville had gradually shut off the taps supplying secret accounts at the Ministry of Defense and Public Safety. New arrangements had taken away the Secretary of State's limitless, uncontrolled manipulation of great sums. He would not last long without funds to distribute, which he used to buy the loyalty of *macoutes* and people of all sorts working on his behalf. He did have a quarter of a million dollars on deposit in a short-term account in an American bank, but he couldn't cash it yet. The few thousand dollars he presently had at his disposal would not get them very far. Between satisfying the appetites of his wife and daughters and his obligations to Nirvah and Marie's whims, he was practically destitute. He could always ask for a sizeable loan from the Syrian he knew at the seaside, but he wanted to save that option for later; news traveled too fast. He had to find something else. François Duvalier would not let him go; it was unthinkable. He, who had given his life, sold his soul, for the revolution. But he also knew what toxic slander his enemies were feeding the president about him. Duvalier wouldn't touch him, but he would allow his accomplices to take him down. During a recent meeting at the palace, when the topic of secret funds drying up at the ministry was broached, Papa Doc, pokerfaced, simply said not to worry, that he had every confidence in the secretary of state of Finance and Economic Affairs to improve this no doubt temporary situation. A harmless sentence with the whiff of a verdict. Above all he had to keep his cool, stay alert, and not panic. He did not wish to be skinned alive by this hunting party. The president's attitude toward him had been changing for a while. He phoned him less often, shortened their appointments and noticeably reduced their frequency. Certain security reports no longer reached him, and staff members in his department at the ministry wore the expressions of castaways. Soon a day would come when the gate to the National Palace would be closed to him. Last year a secretary of state in the government who had fallen from grace went through that unsettling experience. He got back into his car, listened to his survival instincts, and went straight to an embassy for asylum. He, Raoul Vincent, would not suffer that final affront.

Nirvah. Those brutes dared touch her, enter her home, his home. The home of his woman and her children. He imagined those filthy pigs searching the house for secrets as though through mud, a house warm and sweet with the scent of the three people dearest to his heart. He who had launched so many vicious raids against the enemies of the revolution could not stand the idea of brutal boots soiling the home that had become his. He chased from his mind the heavy cloud of suffering that he had inflicted at will and that now tried to envelop him. Those stories belonged to another world, justified by motives he never had reason to question. He was not going to start now; otherwise, he'd lose his mind. He had failed at his task. Nirvah tried to stay calm on the phone, but her voice was trembling. He didn't know how to repair the damage just done to a woman he loved so much, to the two children whose lives he was responsible for. Impotence like burning bile rose in his throat. The machine he had created, whose workings and cogs he'd dreamt up, was turning against him to crush him. You couldn't fight that power; you could only try to save your skin.

Marie . . . They had touched Marie's skin, the worst offense. A humiliating challenge he could not take up; time was cruelly lacking. Oh, he would be ecstatic to eliminate Douville! He would make him bleed and watch him go lifeless without ever touching him. As for his accomplices, he'd let them die of thirst. One of his spies reported seeing Dorothy Desormeaux visit Nirvah the day after the search. What did that little tart want? Didn't Nirvah know that horrible woman's father was in league with Douville to bring him down? André Desormeaux, the opportunist, now felt comfortable enough with the First Lady to actively covet his job.

Simone Duvalier only believed her eyes. With Douville's help, Desormeaux, since being named head of government supplies about five months ago, was making the president's wife richer every day. Each week he would slip her a note on which the new balances of her various local and international bank accounts were written. She would give him anything he wanted. Like Salomé, she would offer him Vincent's head on a plate as long as he continued doing the dance of gold. But he wouldn't be the only one to go. Others would leave with him. Philibert had already experienced this. Two other members of the government would also meet a tragic end before long. Raoul Vincent hoped with all his heart the gods would grant his wishes.

He couldn't bear the idea of Marie suffering. This sudden fever worried him in the extreme; emotion alone couldn't justify a breakdown like this. Marie . . . his angel, his little darling. As the days had gone by he'd discovered in her Nirvah's femininity and intensity but with a spark of insolence and rebellion that stirred him deeply. A child-woman learning of her powers. When he took her at fifteen, she was still a virgin physically but not mentally. He did not premeditate the rape, and retained a vague taste of it. He had been afraid this act would close the doors to him forever at the house on Rue des Cigales. But she kept quiet and to his great surprise sought him out. As if to make herself suffer. She used him to inoculate herself against the evil he represented in her eyes. An unsettling initiation. She learned the gestures of love quickly, discovering the pleasures of the body with curiosity, but to her they were only gestures — unlike Nirvah, who knew how to love with her soul and was often frightened by it. Marie wanted the good things in life and wanted them now; struck by her hard life at a tender age, she went from adolescence to adulthood in a blink. Her mother hadn't found the words to retain her innocence. Marie spit on innocence. She learned about betrayal and trust, doubt and lies, loyalty and hypocrisy; she learned how to find these things in other people and exploit them when necessary. She learned very quickly that the world around her gave nothing away, that she would have to get ahead with the means at her disposal: her angelic smile and her cynicism. And how hungry she was to live! A consuming hunger fed by pleasure, sensation, and challenges accepted. She gave an eye for an eye, letdown for letdown, pleasure for pleasure. She was playing chess with the pieces of her life and soon acquired the finesse and high strategy of this art. All with disarming candor. Of course, Marie did not love him. How could she love a man like him, ugly and unfit? She hung out with the gilded youth, kids her own age with flat stomachs and empty heads. But with him she experienced the vertigo of power, because he placed his life, blood, and whatever was left of his fortune at her feet. By spending money freely on her friends, she kept up the illusion of deciding the course of things. She wanted to be loved at all costs, without being able to love herself. Once, she admitted to him that he was the only person who could make her come. The emotion he felt at that moment was worth every lost paradise. Marie was intoxicated by this unnatural complicity, by their silent exchanges in front of other members of the household, by the illusion of possessing him, which he readily conceded. She hid behind a mask of false maturity to escape her fears. She devoted a violent hatred and desperate love to her mother. Nirvah was unaware of the essence of the soul of this child living under her roof. And Marie saw her mother as a fossilized woman lost in time and lost in feelings that were long gone. When a few days earlier Marie had asked him for money for an abortion, Raoul had gotten the sense, for the first time in his life, of being complicit in an odious crime. What if he were the father? The tiny breath of the pure fruit in Marie's stomach symbolized the beauty he had often dreamt of for himself, the innocence he had never known. He begged her to keep the baby, but she didn't want to. Maybe she was right. This little being would surely upset the fragile balance between Nirvah, Marie, Nicolas, and himself.

And Nicolas? Nicolas . . . the son he'd never had but had begun to love like his own flesh and blood. Nicolas, whom he had yet to make a man. From a string of days with the boy he'd woven a connection of exquisite subtlety. With Nicolas he was living a dream of purity and respect. A strange friendship. When he touched the young hairless body, his feelings electrified him to his fingertips. Oh, how he trembled that first time when the adolescent allowed him to bring him to Olympian heights. With Nicolas he wanted to go slowly, savor the awakening of his senses, move gradually through the stages toward amazement. There were so many sensations waiting for them, so many pleasures to explore. He had so many things to teach him about the greatness and smallness of men from antiquity to the present. He would teach him suspicion, which he had had to develop and call on as much as his survival instincts. Suspicion, his best weapon in a brutal environment. Nicolas was a good student, fond of tales of travel, curious to know what the world was like beyond the horizon line of his island. He was becoming more imaginative. His drawing was ridding itself of its childlike quality, his lines were becoming bolder, freer. Raoul could imagine his terror and utter confusion when those brutes vandalized his house, shattering the frail foundations of the security he had begun to construct. How was one supposed to get back to the equilibrium of before, reinstate the happy course of days? Raoul felt the taste of blood rise to his mouth.

"How's Marie?"

"Not well . . . Dr. Xavier is with her . . . I'm waiting for him to finish his exam . . . Thanks for coming."

Roger revised his decision not to set foot in my house as long as Raoul Vincent was seeing me here. Today, with my family in danger, he's rushed over. Despite his worried face, his presence reassures me. Roger is a ray of light amid the shadows that surround me. I realize how much I've missed our conversations. I feel like I'm returning from a faraway place and on the threshold of a journey at once. Everything around me is terribly present and intense but periodically dissolves in a haze. I am myself and several women at once. Sounds come to me from elsewhere; the cooing of pigeons in the trees, the laughter of children on Rue des Cigales: another Nirvah hears them and is moved to tears. I am with Roger and at the same time in the room with Dr. Xavier, holding Marie's hand. My stomach is a tight knot. Roger has burned through two cigarettes since his arrival a short time ago. He hesitates before asking me again:

"Nirvah . . . how is she . . . really?"

"Her fever won't let up . . . She was delirious earlier . . . She looks around from time to time and doesn't seem to recognize anyone . . ."

"But . . . it's so sudden," Roger says, unsettled. "Is she coming down with something? Malaria or dengue fever?"

"Maybe we'll know soon . . . this illness has come at a bad time, Roger . . ."

"Hmmm . . . I know . . ."

Roger understands my situation. With Raoul in trouble, my life is automatically endangered. I've become a target for everyone who resents him. I weaken him. What's more, I'm the wife of a political prisoner; everything happening to me is in line with that status. Dr. Xavier seems to be taking a lot of time with Marie. When the doctor asked me to leave the room to examine her, I was afraid. As if Marie didn't belong to me, no longer belonged to me. Suddenly there was a strange and hostile world between my daughter and me that erased the nine months she spent growing in my stomach, the long hours sitting by her cradle, the little joys of childhood. How I need to love her, to undo the damage she's undergone. Roger has been waiting to ask me something since he got here. A horrible question that cuts me.

"Nirvah . . . was Marie raped?"

"No, thank God. But she has . . . she has . . ."

I panic. Finding the words to reply to my brother is beyond my strength. It's the first time since yesterday that I've had to describe my revolt and sorrow in words. To say them is to relive that reality, which I reject with all my soul. To say them is to express the anger seething in my head that I must control in order to face my situation. I risk falling to pieces saying the words expected of me. What should I tell Roger? What exactly happened in this house last night? No words come to my mind or lips. For a few seconds, fragments of images go through my head, like shards of a mirror in the sun, disordered, sharp-edged and blinding. The scent of those men that won't leave the house. The calmness of the house shattered by the arrival of those men. The vivid fear within these walls. Dr.

Xavier's look when he came into our house. I have to chase the fear away. Nothing happened. The gun being run over Marie's skin by that man is a figment of my imagination, and I can't speak to Roger about it. Marie's whole body did not shake, and a trickle of saliva did not run from the corner of her mouth down her neck. My son did not pee in his pajamas, and he is not refusing to take a shower. Time stopped for him last night with the first burst of machine-gun fire in the night. Soon Raoul will tell me everything is fine. Marie is not afraid, Raoul will protect us, he's powerful. And even Uncle Roger is here, see, he's come back to us.

"Nirvah? Are you okay?"

"Yes . . . I'm okay. No, she wasn't raped . . . but she was very scared."

I can sense Roger's relief. But surely he is not familiar with all the faces of rape. Roger, they rape us every time they make us shit our pants, every time they burst through our gates with gunfire, every time their fetid breath runs over our faces and breasts, every time our tears make them laugh.

"I think you should leave the country, Nirvah. The Secretary of State . . . is in deep trouble. I sense a fall from grace. The rumors are really spreading. You're too vulnerable right now. Myrna agrees. Your life and your children's . . ."

"No need to explain; you're absolutely right. I've thought about nothing else, Roger . . . I've begun to make arrangements. Marie's condition has delayed my plans. I'm worried about her . . ."

I won't leave without Marie. I don't want any more separations in this family. Daniel is no longer with us, but wherever he is, he's counting on me to take care of his children. All three of us will stay together. I will be their father and their mother. We just need to be somewhere else, start over somewhere else.

"Your passports?"

"They've been held in a safe-deposit box . . . at the bank . . .
since Daniel's arrest."

"Hmmm . . . that's what I thought. In any case, you can't
travel by the normal routes. Unless you ask for political asylum, all you have left is the border. Personally, I'd take that
chance. Stays at the embassies can be very long . . . The government can take months to deliver safe-conducts."

"Yes . . . I think so, too. I want to get out of here as soon
as possible. Do you have any contacts?"

"I could try to find some . . . and, as far as you're concerned, is he . . . ?" Roger is thinking of Raoul, wondering
if the Secretary of State is taking care of me. I don't tell my
brother that I haven't seen him in several days. That since the
events of last night, we've only spoken once on the phone,
that maybe I'll see him tonight.

"Yes, he's making plans . . . I'll know tonight . . . or tomorrow . . . But you should try to find a network, too . . . do you
know what it costs?"

"No . . . but you need a lot of cash. Haitian and Dominican
soldiers rake it in with this system. They have the same appetite. You have to grease palms along the way. The hardest part
is getting a four-wheel drive and making it to the border; the
road's bad. You should have about ten thousand dollars for
each of you. But that's just a random guess."

"Okay. I'll try to find it . . ."

"Hmmm . . . I think it would also be a good idea to move
in the meantime . . . not to my house . . . it would be too logical to find you there . . . maybe you could ask Maggy or Dr.
Xavier . . ."

"Yes . . . I'll see . . ."

Only Raoul can get me this money. I should let him know

I'm leaving. I hope he understands. But where is he? A door creaks, the one to Marie's bedroom. I rush over to the doctor, scrutinize his face, put a hand on his arm.

"Doctor . . . how is she? Can I see her now?"

"Not now . . . in a minute . . . we have to talk first, Nirvah . . ."

Those were not the words I was expecting. I am chilled. I join Roger on the veranda with the doctor. I sense Dr. Xavier's concern. He's weighing his words as he speaks to me, I can see he's trying to spare me.

"So . . . Marie is suffering from a very advanced infection. She has to be hospitalized right away for urgent care."

I don't understand. Marie fainted when that creature approached her. Otherwise, she was doing fine until last night. All this emotion has made her sick, that's all . . . Have I understood the doctor's explanation? I get the sense that words are liquefying in my head.

"What's she suffering from, doctor?" Roger asks in my place.

"I'll ask that she be seen by a specialist in the emergency room, but I'm almost positive Marie's infection is the result of a botched abortion . . . the work of a charlatan . . . three or four days ago . . . she certainly hid her fever and pain from you, Nirvah . . . she's been in agony for at least two days. She must have a scraping immediately. The bacteria have to be kept away from the other organs at all costs. We can't waste any time. Every second counts."

Raoul Vincent does not believe in providence. He believes in chance and the intelligence that reigns over chance. His swift rise to one of the top posts in the government was due to his flair, his perseverance, and his innate cruelty, which made him climb onto the bandwagon of the randomness underway. Another page of his life will soon be turned, and he doesn't regret a thing. François Duvalier's lack of gratitude does not surprise him in the least; it's inherent in his deepest being and has kept him in power up until now. Soul-searching sounds the death knell for dictators. It's likely he would have acted the same way in the president's place. The Secretary of State has not slept in days; he's putting together his escape plan. So long as his body holds out. An epileptic seizure at this point would weaken him considerably, just when he needs all his faculties. He has to figure everything out: the maintenance of the house while he's gone, the liquidation of their three vehicles, the destruction of compromising files at home and at the office. Succession won't be easy for André Desormeaux. All this must be done without attracting anyone's attention. Even his wife doesn't know about his plans. He'd rather wait until the last minute and tell her to pack a suitcase for herself and their daughters until further notice. Otherwise she might panic, talk too much, and cause a lot of trouble. Recently, he noticed his wife's worried looks and hushed whispers on his arrival, but she didn't dare ask him what was the matter. The gossip mill must have clued her in on his bad luck. So far he hasn't ruled out the possibility of abandoning his family. If the situation gets complicated, he'll have to save his own skin; they'll find a way to join him later. The parcel wrapped in plain brown paper sits on the desk before him. A small, harmless-looking package. He's counted the bills down to the last one—big, new, somewhat stiff bills with sharp edges that smell of ink from the printer's. Five hundred thousand American dollars. The key to every border. Providence did not make all this money fall from the sky like manna. Providence goes by the name of Maxime Douville, André Desormeaux, and a few others in league against him.

When he arrived at the ministry late in the morning, flanked by his driver and two of his bodyguards, about twenty people were waiting outside his office to speak to him. Men and women rushed toward him, greeting him with deference. The hallways of the ministry were teeming with the same flood of pilgrims who came to surrender at the feet of sacred power. Raoul Vincent inhaled the familiar scent of this place, which had become his second home. A sweet smell of faded flowers mixed with paper and dust. He heard the clicking typewriters behind the thin partitions that separated the offices. He knew these little details would be as hard to get out of his system as the arrogance maintained by his own sense of power. The Secretary of State did not want to see anyone and cancelled a meeting with a few department heads who had come from Jean-Rabel to report on a bloody land dispute that had already caused the deaths of several farmers. For the moment he had other fish to fry. But his secretary insisted he receive three men who claimed to be on an urgent mission for the secretary of state of Social Affairs. He had them sent into his office.

Raoul Vincent was surprised to recognize his friend, Hénock Duracin, godfather of his older daughter, accompanied by two light-skinned men he didn't know. He did not expect to see his old friend here at all. They had formed a deep connection in their youth; the same ambition to get out of the ghetto and use their intelligence to serve their country had motivated them in high school and later at law school. But Hénock kept his distance when Raoul joined Duvalierist circles in the midfifties. They only saw each other at birthdays and funerals now. The Secretary of State knew that Duracin disapproved of everything he had become; some of his friend's imprudent remarks had been reported back to him more than once. But he let him live because of the good old days. Duracin was just a small-time lawyer pleading pathetic little cases.

For two days, during an interim, Secretary of State Vincent was overseeing the Ministry of Social Affairs. His colleague, gravely ill, had flown out the night before to receive treatment in Jamaica, where he had family. This was why the visitors wanted to see him. The men with Duracin were emissaries from one of the biggest sugar companies in the Dominican Republic, controlled by American capital. Like last year, they were transporting a large sum of money, the special fee paid directly to the Haitian government for the employment of thousands of workers in Dominican *bateyes*. Every year, Dominican recruiters crossed the border and, with the blessing of local authorities, illegally brought truckloads of Haitians, young and old, into the neighboring republic to cut a season of cane, offering inhuman conditions and miserable pay. It was better than what they had at home. The growing prosperity of the neighboring state depended in large part on the sweat and blood of Haitian workers. It fell to the secretary of state of Social Affairs to take this money and transfer it to its recipient. Raoul Vincent knew of the existence of this hidden transaction of the president's and many others involving migrant workers.

But he had no access to it. He also knew that all of this money would go to the First Lady of the republic. But what role did Hénock Duracin play in this scheme? Duracin, who did his best to seem relaxed, explained that a friend with business ties in the Dominican Republic had come to his house the night before to tell him about these two Dominicans, who, unable to find the secretary of state of Social Affairs, had contacted him. They wanted to meet with the secretary of state's replacement; otherwise, they would leave with all the loot. There was no way they would see anyone else; they had strict instructions. Duracin's friend found out the name of the replacement and, knowing of Duracin's relationship with Vincent, asked him to accompany the emissaries to the ad interim secretary of state. This merchant, who did not want to get involved in the affairs of wheelers and dealers, nevertheless hoped to obtain a substantial commission as payment for his goodwill.

Raoul Vincent observed his visitors carefully. The two foreigners hadn't said a word; they were content to follow the conversation between the Secretary of State and his friend without understanding. They were clearly cold, since the air conditioner in the office was set very high as usual. One of the men held a package wrapped in brown paper on his lap. The Secretary of State sensed a trap. This crazy money that came along like a deliverance had the whiff of a carcass, burnt and ashy. Raoul Vincent didn't care that this package of cash cost the sweat and blood of thousands of his countrymen, outrageously exploited. He didn't care that the government sent the sons of his country to be treated like animals in the country next door. The only thing that interested him was the parcel the man held on his knees like a skull. Why now? Why Duracin? To reassure him? Douville knew he was in a tight spot, desperate. He sent this final temptation by way of a friend, hoping he would make a fateful decision. Douville had found a great solution. If he kept this money and tried to flee, they would be on him like vultures on a corpse in the sun. But his colleague's illness was sudden and brutal, and no one could've predicted it. Douville and his consorts could not have arranged, in so little time, to have this sum delivered by the Dominicans at the very moment he was there to receive it. The Dominicans maintained the greatest secrecy around their arrangements and did not ask for a receipt for the money. Moreover, each secretary of state dealt with specific negotiations for the president that the others were not aware of or from which they were excluded. The ministries functioned as separate compartments. Some sold indigent families' blood and cadavers, which they bought for a pittance, to American universities at steep prices; others allowed the natural resources of the country to be outrageously exploited by way of untaxed commissions. It all happened without leaving any traces. Who knows? Maybe chance was making things right again, offering him a way out of his mess.

No, I can't be that naïve. That you, Duracin, who detests and despises me, are the instigator of this process today is enough to tell me that a dance of shadows is being performed behind your back. Duracin, you're letting yourself be manipulated . . . Unbelievable! What sort of promises did they make to convince you? Have you, too, become a slave to your appetites and all the neuroses you tried in vain to conquer? Do you now believe in their *noiriste* farce, their second-hand indigeneity, which justifies the unjustifiable? Surely you don't. Your will and your soul, my friend, have not resisted temptation. Period. What did they promise you in return — money, power, women? Where did the young, spirited Hénock go, the one who read Anténor Firmin, Louis-Joseph Janvier, Georges

Sylvain, and wanted to stop the randomness, the contempt for laws and liberty corrupting the country? What became of the young crusader eager to bring light to those kept in darkness and obscurity? Could it be you've given up this liberty, that you're selling your intelligence and your spirit? Maybe you think you're doing a useful thing by destroying me? They probably tried to appeal to your patriotic fiber, to convince you of the soundness of eliminating the monster that I am. Do you know, Hénock, that you've started down a path of no return? The dictatorship is a cruel and demanding mistress. She's full of comfort and cozy satisfaction, but she will enchain your soul with no hope of redemption. You will become like me, Hénock, cynical and mean, if they don't crush you first, like the cockroach that you are.

When he agreed to take the money from the Dominican envoys, Raoul Vincent noticed Hénock Duracin's careful sigh of relief. He counted the bills for a good fifteen minutes and verbally confirmed receipt of five hundred thousand dollars. He exchanged handshakes with the Dominicans and ended the meeting, assuring Hénock Duracin that he would suggest the First Lady give him a sizeable reward for his friend's services.

With the visitors gone, the Secretary of State remained seated for several minutes, hypnotized by the package containing the money of his salvation. The decision was clear to him when he thought of Nirvah, of Marie suspended between life and death in a hospital bed, and of Nicolas, even more fragile than the women. His informers kept him posted about Marie's condition. He hadn't seen Nirvah since the raid; he hadn't checked in for four days. Prudence told him to keep his distance. Maybe she thought he had abandoned her. How she must have cursed him. He could imagine her dismay. Who could she count on, if not him? And here he was, not giving her a sign of life. No! He was at this very moment putting his life on the line, balancing on a wire, to save them. The risk

didn't matter; he had to give Nirvah a chance to get out. He had to act fast, outrun his enemies. He would arrange to slip between their fingers. It was only a matter of hours.

Can I resist the tension that inhabits me night and day? For four days, my brain has functioned outside my head. Can you consciously sink into madness? My skull is like a ripe mango that Nicolas is biting into the top of and sucking all of the juice from, pressing gently upward from the bottom. My ideas and thoughts hurt me, orphaned by the rest of my body; some turn into hammers and knock at my temples. But I can't flinch; I have no right. I haven't washed in four days. The smell of rotting vegetables rises from my armpits and crotch. Marie went into the operating room less than an hour after we got to the hospital. The doctors didn't even wait for the results of the blood work. Despite Roger and Maggy's insistence, I've refused to leave the premises. Maggy has been going back and forth between the house and the hospital, bringing underwear and toiletries for Marie; what would I do without her? Sometimes the nurses force me to leave the room; I go sit in the little garden at the end of the lane to get some air for fifteen minutes, then I return to her side. She's improved since this afternoon; her fever broke and she's sweating profusely; I have to change her often. The massive dose of antibiotics along with the surgical intervention saved her from certain death. Though she's very weak, the doctor said her life is no longer in danger. The vise around my head has released its grip slightly. This evening under cover of night I'll go back to the house to bathe, change, and get the things the kids and I will need in case of imminent departure. I want to keep hope alive, find the strength and means to succeed. I'll spend the last night at Dr. Xavier's house; there's no way I can spend the night on Rue des Cigales. Still, the tension of the past four days won't leave me alone. Fragments of sentences swirl in my head like threats . . . septic shock . . . a drop in blood pressure . . . respiratory difficulty . . . inflammation of the spleen. For hours I held Marie's ice-cold hands in mine; for hours I stared at her gray-tinged face; my beautiful Marie.

I step out for a breath of air, the urgency to leave prodding me now that my daughter is out of danger. I'm waking up to another struggle. The lack of news from Raoul for almost five days confirms that our situation is not improving. It's just not normal for him not to show up, even by proxy. I know Roger has made arrangements for our secret departure. Today he learned from a source in town that Raoul has fled, while another source confirmed seeing him enter the ministry under heavy escort the same day. I don't know whom to believe anymore. In any case, he's not getting in touch. He's forgotten about us. And money? Medical costs have pretty much eaten up whatever we got from selling the jewelry; not much is left. I didn't dare tell Roger I'm not in a position to pay for our passage. I'm still hoping against hope Raoul will come through. Otherwise Roger will have to come up with the money. I could also ask Dr. Xavier for a loan against the house; between the two of them, I might be able to make it. My undoing is complete.

There are questions in my eyes, in the back of my throat, in the hollows of my hands, that I've avoided ever since Dr. Xavier announced Marie's condition. Every time they try to enter my field of consciousness, I tiptoe away and escape them. They're currently taking advantage of my somewhat relaxed state to slip over my tongue, fill my mouth, almost stifle me.

Whose baby did Marie abort? But the question doesn't even start there. It begins with shock. Who was Marie making love to? Since when has Marie been interested in men? Why didn't Marie confide in me about this important part of her life? Why didn't she come to me when she got pregnant? What use am I in my daughter's existence? Why was I always afraid to talk to her about her body, her sex, her blood? Because I was using mine in a way that hurt her? But Raoul? Am I really blind, or have I lost all sense of decency? Could Raoul have fathered this child who never saw the light of day? Did I surrender to this man, selling myself along with one of the people dearest to me in the world? That's not what I wanted; I was just trying to protect us from fear and poverty. I look at the sky, at the impassible moon. It's so beautiful you could cry.

"*Nirvah!* . . ."

A muffled voice says my name, but I don't recognize it at first. I look for Raoul; he's standing in the shadow of a large clump of red hibiscus, away from the road where hospital visitors pass from time to time. Lost in my worried thoughts, I didn't see him arrive. He probably has security men around him, even though I can't see them. I really didn't think I would see him again; I thought he might send an emissary. His presence gives off a sort of electricity that is communicated through the air around me, to the leaves of the hibiscus releasing its intoxicating green scent, to the hairs on my forearms standing on end, making me sick. For a few seconds, no words come to my lips. I wasn't expecting him; I despaired of ever seeing him again; I'm relieved he came himself; I wish I had a dagger in my hand so I could stab him in the stomach over and over. He came back, he always comes back the moment I wish he never existed. He came back with his strength and shadows, and the pulse of the world starts up again. Raoul holds out his hand and draws me toward him. I should run from this man; he's hurting my soul and subjugating my blood, even now in this moment of confusion. I am so, so tired. I bury myself in the harbor of his chest and cry silent, bitter tears. The first word he says to me is:

"Marie?"

That name in his mouth sounds like sacrilege. I stiffen and pull away from him. Raoul mistakes my reaction, thinks I'm reluctant to give him bad news. He holds me by the shoulders. Did I feel his hands tremble?

"Is everything okay . . . with Marie?"

"Almost," I reply, searching his eyes in the half-light. "She's gotten over the worst of it. Did you know Marie was pregnant?"

Raoul suppresses a cry; a jolt goes through his body. But my question should not have surprised him. I get the profound sense he has something to do with Marie's condition. A connection, from which I am excluded, holds them in an odious complicity. He'll lie to me one more time. I hate myself for speaking to him, for hoping he'll tell me he didn't touch her. He'll ask me to be strong and not hide behind false problems. And I will believe him.

"Yes . . . I knew. Marie made me swear not to tell you. She didn't want to worry you. She was so upset with herself . . . Marie loves you, even if she doesn't show it. It would have been too painful, Nirvah."

I wasn't expecting this confession at all. Raoul is speaking softly, with tenderness, handling me with kid gloves. Now I'm the one with a knife in my gut. What is he talking about? Marie told Raoul? Why? I'm her mother, for God's sake!

"About ten days ago," Raoul went on, "Marie told me she'd gotten pregnant; it was an accident. She wanted money for an abortion. I did everything I could to convince her to keep the child and to speak to you about it. But she absolutely refused. In the face of her determination, I gave her the money to get rid of it. I didn't want her to go to a stranger. Forgive me, Nirvah; I didn't have the courage to tell you about it . . . I'm so sorry she was in such pain . . . I should have made sure she went to a competent doctor . . . I would kill that charlatan with my own hands if Marie . . ."

"Are you the father of that child?"

I take possession of all my senses again. Fear and anxiety recede from my soul. Raoul can feel it; I am like stone. Will he go all the way and confess everything? I may die in the next second.

"You had to ask, didn't you, Nirvah?" I remain indifferent to this touch of irony. At this moment, I'm rediscovering the lying Raoul. "How many times did I tell you to watch her relationships? She came and went as she pleased; she dressed like a grown woman — more than a woman. To make up for Marie's difficult childhood and her father's mistakes, you gave her too much freedom, and she turned it into license. All those young bucks who came to the house, don't you think one of them might have felt the desire to make a conquest of your daughter? Do you realize how beautiful Marie is? How she might cause a man to obsess about her?"

Raoul's heartfelt outburst opens my eyes once and for all. You are the man who's obsessed with her, Raoul. I know you well enough. No scruples could limit your lust. Today everything is clear. The web of lies is finally tearing. I add nothing; my anger is icy; it concerns only me. It will transport me to the other shores of my life, where Raoul does not exist.

"You really love her?"

My voice is trembling a little. My question isn't one; it's

a statement. Raoul knows I understand, and that tactics of confusion are no longer necessary. This is not the time for endless discussion, death is at our door. He looks at his watch. He takes my wrist and says words I never thought I'd hear come out of his mouth.

"Nirvah, I'm going to request asylum at an embassy in Port-au-Prince. My life is in danger. The president's relatives resent my power. I'm being hunted. I'm going to get out of the city for a while, for a long while. I'm sure you've heard the rumors."

"Yes . . . people are talking about it. I've decided to leave, too. My brother, Roger, has made arrangements for us to get to the border."

"Hmmm . . . very good. But you should leave as soon as possible, tomorrow even. Don't stay at your house, and leave as soon as night falls. As soon as they find out I've taken cover, they'll come after you."

I feel the sharpness of the urgency Raoul is still trying to conceal.

"But . . . Marie is still weak . . . and I can't . . ."

"Marie is weak, but she's young, she'll make it. Otherwise, she'll die in prison. The circumstances don't give you much choice, Nirvah. If you cross the border tomorrow, she could get care in the Dominican Republic. The trip to the border lasts about two or three hours, unfortunately. The road is very bad after the last rains. You'll need a good vehicle. The town of Jimaní is only thirty minutes from the border by car. The main thing is to get to the other side. Here, Nirvah, this is enough to pay for everything you'll need. This money will open roads and buy consciences. Don't skimp on anything. Don't be afraid. Act quickly. Remember that your lives are priceless to me . . ."

Raoul slips a small, black canvas bag that I hadn't noticed off his shoulder and hands it to me. It's pretty heavy. From the feel of it, it seems to contain a lot of cash. I wonder where all this money came from and whose blood it's marked by. But I don't have time for internal debate. I have to save my family. Raoul is leaving; I struggle to make out his words.

"I don't know if we'll see each other again . . . but I'll do everything in my power to find you. Take care of yourself and your children. Give Nicolas a kiss, tell him not to forget my advice. Remind Marie that life can always begin again. Good-bye, Nirvah!"

I don't have time to add a word. Raoul turns and blends into the darkness of the garden.

"Marie . . . Marie?"

"Hmmm . . ."

Marie turns toward me, her face less ashen. This morning she ate, not a lot, but her body is starting to redevelop a taste for salt and light. She's no longer on an IV. A great joy fills me, chasing away my anxiety about the road ahead, for now.

"Marie, honey . . . I'm so happy you're better. Dr. Xavier says you're completely out of the woods. In a few days your strength will be back."

"It's true, I feel better. When can I leave the hospital, Mommy?"

My heart tightens. I have to tell Marie she can't go home again, that this very evening we're leaving everything we know behind us—the walls of our house, the purple bougainvilleas, the bursts of sunlight moving across the leaves of our mahogany trees, the blue silence of the moon, the song of cicadas, and the hope of seeing Daniel again. I have to find a way to explain to her the arbitrary nature of fate. But just for a moment I want to forget everything unrelated to the life flowing through Marie's veins.

"Just now you took a few steps in the room, Marie, and it reminded me of you as a toddler, walking toward your father and me, arms stretched out for balance."

Marie and I have not spoken of the reason for her hospitalization. It didn't matter before, faced with the urgency of saving her. I wonder when we'll have the chance and strength to broach the topic. I'd like to know whose child she was expecting, and at the same time I'm sure this won't help us move forward at all or change anything about our situation. But the question is obsessing me. This interrupted pregnancy should mark the end of a long silence. I stroke Marie's hair and see a slight shudder go through her body, as if contact with my hand repelled her. She couldn't repress that impulse, which reminds me of the depth of the gulf between us. Our skins unlearned each other, our eyes avoided each other, our hearts no longer beat to the rhythm of the same blood. Somewhere along the way, we lost contact. Marie is like a blank wall, an unmarked canvas on an easel. I can't read the signs, can't decode the slightest clue. There are no words we can say that aren't traps or evasions. We read between our lines, read what is left unsaid, while pretending not to see these things. And yet there is so much love in this hospital room. Marie is alive. And so what if she can't stand me or condemns me. One day, perhaps, we'll relearn the gestures that forgive and heal. We will sit and face each other like the deaf, slowly saying with our hands all the words our lips could not convey, to the point of exhaustion.

"Marie . . . Raoul's situation is bad. So is ours. He's fallen from grace. Do you understand what that means?"

Marie nods yes. She is paying close attention.

"I don't want to make things more difficult for you when you've been so sick . . . But Nicolas, you, and I have to leave Haiti in the coming hours. Our chances are good of leaving without a lot of attention, but we don't have much time."

"Where are we going?"

"Hmmm . . . to the Dominican Republic. We have to cross the border tonight in a car. I'll go back to the house soon to get a few things for each of us. We have to travel light."

"Tonight, already!"

The news seems to shake Marie. I wonder if she can handle
it. But she has to. Be strong, Marie.

"Yes . . . Uncle Roger is taking care of everything. This
afternoon we'll leave the hospital and spend some time at Dr.
Xavier's house, to avoid suspicion. Nicolas is there already.
And then when night falls, a car with a driver will come to
get us. Uncle Roger will accompany us to the border where
we'll switch cars."

"And Raoul?"

Why have I never noticed that Marie says Raoul's name
like a woman saying the name of her man? With a touch of
possession, a hint of complicity, as if to assert in the face of the
world that she knows him nakedly, body and soul. My God,
teach me to eliminate these voices speaking the language of
confusion to my soul. Free me from myself.

"He came by last night. He's the one who suggested leaving
tonight . . . He . . . he's asking you to hang in there."

A deep breath inflates Marie's chest. She turns her head
away and stares at the wall for a moment. Then she turns to
face me and asks a question that catches me completely off
guard.

"So we'll never see Daniel again?"

Marie, Marie . . . it hurts you not to see him? Your suffering
is a balm on my heart. I, who thought you'd forgotten him,
that his fate left you indifferent. I have no answer to your
question. I haven't had one since the day Daniel was first
taken away. Hope was the only glue that kept our lives from
falling apart. But hope is often fed by lies. Sometimes hope
prostitutes itself to power. I lied to you, to you and Nicolas,
to protect you; I prostituted myself to power to counter the
misfortune that struck us and to soften our fate.

"I hope with all my heart we'll reunite one day. But our chances of seeing your father again lessen with every passing day, Marie. I've heard nothing; meanwhile, our situation is getting worse. No . . . I don't know if we'll see him again . . . I can't lie to you."

"Mommy . . . I'm sorry about what happened."

Marie sighs.

"But you couldn't do anything about it, Marie. The people who took away your father's freedom . . ."

Marie interrupts me, I can tell I'm annoying her. She's making an effort to say these words that are costing her so much, and I'm not getting her message. The muted cacophony that clouds our exchanges is not ready to dissipate yet. It will take time for us to truly hear each other.

"No, Mommy . . . I'm talking about the abortion . . . the hospital . . . everything."

Marie, at this point, can barely stand my presence at her bedside. She wants to sleep, forget, gather strength for this trip into the unknown. She'll go from a hospital to a foreign country, another separation. We're going to leave, Marie. Tomorrow we'll be far away, and we'll leave these hostile years behind us. We'll learn to forget, forget the land of Haiti, Port-au-Prince, Rue des Cigales, the *macoutes*, and everything that causes pain in our country, which no longer wants us. We'll discover other suns. Don't be sorry, Marie. Life is just beginning, beginning again. We've survived a long night that fell over our lives. Tomorrow a new dawn awaits us.

"Don't be sorry, my love. Try to forget. Anything is possible if we have faith."

"Hmmm . . ."

Marie looks at me, her eyes half-closed. I'm going to sit outside and wait. Maggy will be here soon to go over the final details of my last moments in this country of mine. Every minute of this day, of this wait, has been like something gnawing on my skin. A question is obsessing me. I know that right now it's too soon; it's petty and useless to ask Marie, and yet a perverse curiosity compels me, and I yield to it.

"Marie?"

"Hmmm?"

"Whose . . . baby was this?"

Marie looks at me, astonished. She stares at the ceiling for a moment. Will she tell me the truth? What sort of influence did Raoul have over my daughter? Will she keep her secret to protect me or to absolve this man who betrayed us? Who is this young woman who sprang from my loins? A tear wells up in the corner of her eye. She smiles at me weakly, and answers, closing her eyes.

"Ziky . . . it was Ziky. Let me rest a little, Mommy."

I did not go back to the silent house to get clothes and a few useful items for Nicolas, Marie, and myself in preparation for our long trip. Roger was not waiting for me in the courtyard, testing the battery of his Taunus, which was running poorly. I did not feel the shadows flutter over my hair when I pushed open the gate, those shadows that kill Solange's imprudent chickens. The enormous moon was not balancing on the finest point of the araucaria tree in the garden. My footstep did not waver when I inhaled, to the point of vertigo, the heady scent of ylang-ylang suspended in the silvery air. I did not look for long in my set of keys for the right key to unlock the front door, with the impression that my house had already become foreign, even hostile, to me. There was not a spiderweb blocking the door to my bedroom after only four days of absence. Raoul Vincent's smell did not cling to the four walls of the bedroom as I searched my memory in vain for the scent of Daniel's body. It did not seem as though a hundred years had passed since his being taken away. Leaving again, thirty minutes later, arms full, the box containing Nicolas's drawings did not fall out of my hands as I was shutting the front door. Gathering up the large portfolio, I did not notice, in the riot of color all over the steps, an unusual sketch that stood out from the others. No, I did not hold before my incredulous eyes this drawing in which Raoul, a crown of laurels on his head, touched a naked boy lying by his side. This boy did not bear a strong resemblance to Nicolas. All those things are just the fruit of my tired, sick imagination.

The deep night envelops us. The car's headlights illuminate only the dusty road. Shacks, cattle, fields of corn and sugar cane blend into a great mass of shadow. Only the ever-present smell of wet earth reminds me we're crossing the solitary countryside, where sap is infusing the buds, where rain is glutting ears of corn, and where young goats roam free, grazing on grass by the side of the road. It's the scent of our vacations in Paillant, our childhoods sustained by open air, and long days in July and August when we drank in the sun by the mouthful. I look at Roger's profile; he's tense — my situation, the children's, worries him very much. He must also be thinking of his own children, and Myrna, who won't sleep a wink until her husband is back at the homestead. A hazy mix of feelings resides in me. Guilt and fear predominate. My God, make everything go all right! I ward off anxiety by thinking of us waking up the next morning in Dominican territory — the light, the colors, the unknown faces and words, all these new things to fill our eyes and ears. It's hard to imagine going through an entire day without censoring my words or looking over my shoulder for the specter of a threat. For now, I feel like I'm slipping down a long, bumpy tunnel. This is certainly the first time darkness has reassured me. In the closeness of the car, like a womb, I feel safe from the persecution of a dictatorship chasing me tooth and nail. We've been driving for almost an hour. Roger is sitting in front, next to the driver. Marie, Nicolas, and I take up the back seat. Marie is to my right, leaning against me to support her body, tossed about by the endless jolting of the car going over potholes. She's gritting her teeth and not complaining, but I can tell she's suffering on this uncomfortable trip, her body still so fragile. I'm afraid all this rocking is going to make her hemorrhage. Dr. Xavier gave me enough medicine for two weeks. Nicolas has fallen asleep, tired of asking questions about our destination and waiting for this border, as far away as the end of the night. Only Roger and I exchange a few words from time to time. Nicolas . . . Nicolas . . . my son, my love, what I wouldn't give to have you in my belly again, to shape a new memory for you, other eyes, another skin untouched by malice, a new innocence not lusted after by that animal. What I wouldn't give to give you another sun.

The man at the steering wheel is a colossus by the name of Beauvais, and not very talkative. He's driving a jeep that's in pretty good condition. Roger didn't know him before tonight's crossing, but he came recommended by a trusted friend. As much as one can trust people who say they are our friends. Distrust lives and breathes in the most private parts of our existences; I know about that now. In any case, we can only put ourselves in God's hands, trust in providence. Roger didn't have the time to ensure his contacts' reliability. Beauvais comes from Hinche; he knows the Central Plateau and the border region well: the roads and the roundabout paths, the passages to avoid and the routes that present the least danger. Roger is also familiar with the area; he comes hunting here during the season. The big challenge is getting to the border without passing checkpoints manned by soldiers and *macoutes*. Beauvais is apparently an expert at this sort of marathon. In any case, we've avoided the Croix-des-Bouquets post, taking a long detour outside that little town on roads barely traveled.

The tires of the car have been put to a brutal test and so have our bodies.

I gave Roger enough money to pay for the jeep rental, the gas, and the fees requested by our guide. Roger made no comment as he took the stack of brand-new American bills from my hands. He knew Raoul Vincent had arranged the financial aspect of our expedition. I also gave Roger a substantial amount of money for unforeseen expenses along the way, in case some makeshift honcho decides to threaten us, or a bunch of evildoers on a nocturnal outing ask us to pay a toll. We still have to pay our contacts on the Haitian side of the border, immigration officers by day transformed into clandestine human traffickers by night. The soldiers will get their share, too, for looking the other way. The border closes at six in the evening. Later, when the night thickens, the fugitives' crossing, handsomely paid for, begins. Then they'll bring us to their Dominican accomplices. Each stage requires generous compensation, and yet there is no guarantee our accomplices won't betray us or be betrayed themselves. The black canvas bag is still very heavy — I haven't found a moment to count the bills discreetly, and I don't know what the total is, but it must be a fair amount. Raoul paid very generously for the years he spent subjugating us.

I feel no regret at leaving my country. Nostalgia, melancholy, beloved Haiti — all the pangs of the exiled poets seem ridiculously lyrical right now. I bless the arms of exile. This isn't my choice. I'm among a growing number of men and women leaving behind their share of the island, chased away by the hatred of a regime that tolerates no protest from citizens with the slightest awareness of their rights to live in dignity and respect. Every mile we cover fills me with despair, taking us further away from Daniel, and yet offers me relief, outlining another future for my children. I still don't know if Daniel is alive. Did the famous shadow of death that Solange told me about come from his spirit, freed from his body? In a way I would prefer it if he were dead already, instead of suffering a slow, endless agony in the hell of Fort-Dimanche. Living through Daniel's pain and being totally helpless has depleted me for too long. And what if he were freed? From now on, I refuse to agonize over this fundamental question that I have asked myself for the past few years ad nauseam. A question that I have made the alibi of my undoing. I will lock it away in a box and throw it to the bottom of Lake Azuéi, to the caimans that inhabit those secret waters. I have forgotten the taste of Daniel in my life. If he came back tonight, we would be two strangers, two neighboring countries, like Haiti and the Dominican Republic, crossed by a border of silences and tears. Ultimately, Raoul Vincent got the better of me, of us. He satisfied his impulses and fantasies by taking over our lives. I let it happen — complacency agrees to every compromise, even a fool's bargain. Raoul doesn't bear the weight of this alone. With him I discovered a woman inside me I didn't know. A greedy woman. A blind woman. I took the easiest option: submitting to Raoul Vincent and expecting to return to a life that was already lost with Daniel's disappearance. I didn't believe in the irreversibility of the days. I wanted to have the best of both hells. But I had to fight all my demons, one after the other. I still want days when it feels good to be alive, to taste the blue hour of serenity, without fear. From now on I will know how to look life in the face, how to not turn away. I will look Marie in the eyes and not see the image of my defeat and my remorse. I want to start loving myself again, loving her better, if it's not too late.

Almost two hours on the road. This isn't really a road so much as a hilly trail interrupted from time to time by large, muddy puddles. At times the jeep tilts at extreme angles, and I expect us to tumble out the side at any moment. Our driver is concentrating on making the best choices. He informs Roger of our progress little by little, based on the places we happen to be, as if he recognized them by their smell or by some vibration perceived in total darkness by him alone. I learn that we have just left the vicinity of the town of Ganthier. All these long detours are considerably stretching out the trip. My lower back hurts. Marie is exhausted as well, still leaning against my shoulder, which has stiffened. The next and final stage will be Fonds-Parisien. Then we will begin to follow Lake Azuéi to the border. Over this distance there is no choice but to take the only available road, between the lake and a long stretch of hillside. The most difficult passage.

I scan the darkness until my eyes hurt; I should lean back and rest a bit instead. We haven't encountered a soul since Croix-des-Bouquets. Suddenly Beauvais slows the vehicle down and pulls over to the side of the road. He wants to check the jeep's tires for a flat. I suspected it for a while, but the news makes my heart race. My fears have been confirmed. The right front tire has succumbed. It will have to be replaced quickly. Roger, Beauvais, and I step out; for safety, Marie and Nicolas, still asleep, remain in the car. We've brought two flashlights. The men get to work finding a spare tire, a jack, and a wheel wrench. I stand by the side of the road, filled with the strange sensation of a multitude of hands waiting to snatch me up and carry me into the night. The night is alive, it has flesh, breath, intimate smells, and a million eyes. Roger tries to reassure me. He stands close to me as he shines a light on the side of the jeep where Beauvais is working. The man is already sweating in big drops. From the silence climb the sounds of a mass of tiny lives in the grass.

"We're not very far," Roger says.

"What a trip, Roger! . . . I'm not going to forget this." I stretch. We needed this break after all to stretch our painful limbs.

A sudden beating of wings near our heads. I jump.

"Don't worry," Roger says. "This is an area rich in game . . . There are duck ponds . . . that was probably a marsh bird or a flock of guinea fowl alarmed by our presence . . ."

"My God! I'm scared."

The thought of those birds in the darkness sends shivers under my skin.

"Nirvah?"

"Yes, Roger." Why is Roger saying my name? I'm right beside him; he just has to speak to me. What will he say to me? I'm still afraid of words that take their time in coming.

"Tonight, right before I picked you up at Dr. Xavier's house, a friend came by to tell me that the Secretary of State . . . that Raoul Vincent was arrested . . . in the early evening . . . They intercepted him trying to get asylum at the Venezuelan ambassador's residence in Musseau . . . disguised as a woman. He was carrying a large amount of money, money from the state's coffers, they say. He is being accused of high treason, of ordering the assassination of three government officials — one of whom was already executed — and of embezzling the money of the people. He's been nailed . . . He has no chance of getting out alive."

A small laugh escapes me. The grotesqueness of our situation is nevertheless infinitely sad. Raoul Vincent . . . disguised as a woman! What a pitiable end for His Excellency. I don't know what to feel, but I reassure myself by telling myself that feeling is not an act of will. I assume the emptiness of my being. My heart feels nothing, neither joy nor pain. Not yet hate. Maybe the money Raoul gave me comes from the same source . . . the money of the people. I realize again that I feel nothing from knowing this. I am not in a position to have qualms; I'm in the midst of escaping, trying to save my skin and my children's skin. This questionable money is saving my life, and I'm not going to throw it into the marsh. Good thing I can't see Roger's eyes; I couldn't bear his judgment.

"Hmmm . . . Raoul Vincent had a beginning and an end . . ." I'm not too sure what that sentence means, but I give it to Roger as a reply.

Raoul will learn to watch himself die, day by day, in turn. I hope he leaves no one behind to miss him. I will not miss him.

We set off again. Beauvais worked quickly. I look at my watch — we've been traveling for over three hours. But Malpasse is not far, Beauvais assures us. Soon we'll be driving by the lake. My impatience to get there grows with every passing minute. I can barely stand to be in the car anymore. Is this impatience, or growing anxiety, now that we've almost reached our destination? Marie and Nicolas are still asleep. I'll wake them up so they'll be alert when it comes time to walk.

The air is somewhat cooler near the lake. We still have fifteen minutes to go until our meeting place, according to Roger. Reeds roll past to our left, at the edge of the great, brackish pond we've been driving along for the past ten minutes. I've never seen Lake Azuéi in the daylight; in fact, I've never seen a lake in my life. They say its waters are blue. A hybrid water, self-contained, that is part of the earth and the sea. I guess at the slight movements that ripple its surface. I leave a part of myself in this dark water, my share of shadow and forgetting. The children, who've just woken up, are trying to reposition themselves in the tight space of the jeep, which they abandoned long enough to have a dream. Bizarrely, a veil of dust comes to meet the jeep's headlights. I feel the pull of Roger's alarm. This dust isn't being raised by the breeze, which is too gentle — it's coming from tires rolling toward us, from the other direction. I don't see their lights, though. The air in the car is suddenly thinner. Just as I lean forward to ask Roger what's going on, Beauvais slams hard on the brakes, the tires skid desperately on the road's pebbles as he barely avoids the obstacle looming up in our headlights and lets out a violent *Fuck!* The sudden stop of the vehicle jolts our spines. At the same time, a burst of machine-gun fire moves the depths of the lake. Two jeeps, the color of night, emerge from the dust and block the narrow road.

In Haiti today, the evils of Duvalierism can be discussed openly, and in *Savage Seasons* (first published in 2010) Kettly Mars takes full advantage of the fact. Where her predecessors had to deal with the subject most obliquely in order to avoid not only censorship but also sometimes deadly reprisals, Mars operates under no such constraint. She is free to use real names and places, and in many cases she does, although the Haitian bourgeois family at the center of the plot is fictional. Targeted by one of the regime's most powerful enforcers and preyed upon in every way, including sexually, the members of the family learn their utter helplessness. There is no effective means of resistance, and there is no way out.

Daniel Leroy, the husband and father of the victimized family, is a political prisoner in Fort-Dimanche prison, and so remains offstage throughout. The wife and mother, Nirvah Leroy, is a strikingly beautiful mixed-race woman who becomes the target of Duvalier's (fictional) Secretary of State, Raoul Vincent. Nirvah wants nothing to do with him. Watching her struggle and eventually succumb is like a watching a mouse in a tank with a snake. Mars's tremendous skills as a writer bring forth this horrifying process with a lyrical precision as disturbing as it is beautiful.

From the start, the Secretary of State has a perfect sense of his omnipotence in this situation. "He had entered the house with a sort of profane fervor. An exalted sense of total power that stayed with him for the length of his visit. He controlled the situation perfectly. He had penetrated the private life of the dissident known as Daniel Leroy, and the fate of his wife, children, domestics, and cat all depended on his appetites."

At first Nirvah hopes to manipulate his interest to keep her husband safe or perhaps even to secure his release, though she suspects from the start how illusory this hope is: "I'm starting to understand the meaning and depth of the word *power* in my country. Power in the service of urges, instincts, and lust."

Having no choice, Nirvah yields to her suitor soon enough, accepting his gifts, which range from jewelry to air conditioners to the paving of the dusty street outside her home. With the support of Solange, the voodoo priestess who lives next door, she tries to convince herself that "Women's *foufounes* are like earthenware . . . Once washed, they become new again. We keep no trace, no mark, on our bodies." But as months, then years go by, she begins to take a reluctant pleasure in her unwilling couplings with the Secretary of State — "this pleasure wrested by force from my body." Despite mounting evidence and the gossip surrounding her, she will not let herself realize that the Secretary of State has extended his sexual predation not only to her now-adolescent daughter but also to her even younger son.

Her situation is a microcosm of the capital when struck by a cyclone: "Port-au-Prince, ravaged, writhed for hours like a woman in labor but gave birth only to cadavers and desolation. . . . Port-au-Prince is a town with two faces, a treacherous city. It's beautiful, mutinous, dazzling with its colorful clusters of bougainvillea and bay trees, serene after unexpected showers in the middle of the day, offering its balconies and rocking chairs in the soft light of a languorous afternoon. It also devours human prey."

Enmeshed in her own complicity, Nirvah can imagine no escape from "the club of *macoute* mistresses." Her absent husband grows ever more distant — voiceless except for a journal he left in the house, which Nirvah, for her children's safety and her own, finally burns. The family's security, such as it is, now depends entirely on the favor of "a baron in the regime." But Duvalierism creates a mechanism of state-run terror so fearsomely efficient that it devours its executioners as well as its victims in the end, and there is no way out for anyone.

In the throes of her inner conflict, Nirvah reflects on guinea fowl, a common bird in Haiti and a symbol of the regime: "I find these short-legged birds repulsively ugly. The *macoutes* wear this terrible animal as a logo on their uniforms. Like them, they are shady and elusive. They say that in colonial times wild guinea fowl represented slaves running away, the *marrons*. But what master are we fleeing a century and a half later? When will our nation stop running away?"

Kettly Mars's historical sense is deep, and she knows how to ask the right questions. The Haitian state today is much weaker than in Duvalier's time and still seems to have little to offer Haitian citizens. Since the late 1990s, in some quarters there has been a strange nostalgia for Duvalierism: brutally unjust, viciously oppressive, yet immensely stable. As *Savage Seasons* makes painfully clear, that situation is nothing to go back to, but it remains unclear where the nation will go instead. The freedom won at such high cost in the Haitian Revolution, now more than two centuries ago, must still be recoverable — but how? Reflecting on the present as well as the past, *Savage Seasons* asks that question of the future.

Madison Smartt Bell

TRANSLATOR'S ACKNOWLEDGMENTS

My sincere thanks to Kettly Mars, French Voices, and the Lannan Foundation writing residency in Marfa, Texas, where part of this translation was prepared. Thanks also to Kristen Elias Rowley and Sabrina Stellrecht for their careful editing of this work.

—*JH*

Other works by Kettly Mars

NOVELS

L'Heure hybride, Vents d'ailleurs, France, 2005;
Prix Senghor, 2006

Kasalé, Vents d'ailleurs, France, 2007

Fado, Mercure de France, France, 2008

Le prince noir de Lillian Russell
(coauthor Leslie Péan), Mercure de France,
France, 2011

Aux frontières de la soif, Mercure de France,
France, 2013

SHORT STORIES

Un Parfum d'encens, Imprimeur II, Haiti, 1999

Mirage-Hôtel, Éditions Caraïbe, Haiti, 2002

Lightning Source UK Ltd.
Milton Keynes UK
UKHW011849180122
397356UK00002B/675

9 780803 271487